~

An

Uncertain

Path

Sandra Carly Cody~

Also by Sandra Carey Cody

An

Uncertain

Path

A Peace Morrow Novel

Sandra Carey Cody

ISBN-13: 978-1974276325
ISBN-10: 1974276325

For Pete

My husband, my best friend, my rock.

AN

UNCERTAIN

PATH

SATURDAY

One

The album lay heavy in Peace Morrow's lap, daunting in both size and content. It was an impressive volume, covered in burgundy-colored leather, with page after page of thick, coarse-textured paper, each page filled with pictures. So many pictures.

She stared into the faces of the people whose bloodline she supposedly shared, looking for some image of herself, trying to feel a kinship with them. She told herself she felt nothing. In truth, she was swamped with feelings, none of which she could name or understand. *These are not my people.* Henry, her Black Lab, dozed at her feet. She eased her toes under his body until she could feel the beat of his heart through her socks.

She sat between two women. They could not have been more different had they come from different planets, yet each had reason to think of Peace as her daughter. One had given birth to her twenty-two years ago. The other had loved and nurtured her for all but the first week of those twenty-two years. The couch they shared was small, really just a love seat. She shifted to her left so that her shoulder touched the shoulder of Caroline Morrow, her adoptive mother. On her right was her biological mother, Holly Francis—a name that slipped strangely through the recesses of Peace's brain. Up to a few months ago, Peace had known her as Fran Walters and she still found it difficult to think of her by any other name. They were in the living room of Holly's home, a room more formal than Peace was used to or felt comfortable in.

She moved a little closer to Caroline, needing the warm presence of her mother, her *real* mother.

She felt the pressure of Caroline's hand on hers and looked at her. Caroline tilted her head ever so slightly to the right, reminding Peace to tune in to the words of the woman on her other side.

Holly's face glowed with pride. Her fingertip rested on the image of an elegant woman in one of the photos. "...your grandmother." She paused, looking at Peace, apparently expecting a response.

Unfortunately, Peace had no idea what had been said. True to the Quaker training Caroline had given her, she decided it was better to own up than try to fake it. "I'm sorry," she said. "I guess I drifted off. I'm a little overwhelmed."

"Of course you are," Holly said. The hurt in her eyes was unmistakable, but it was obvious she was trying to mask it. She smiled and tilted her head toward the album. "Once you get to know them, you'll like them. I promise. They're very down to earth."

Peace looked at the book that weighed so heavily in her lap. *Down to earth?* Those were the last words she'd use to describe these people. *Well-dressed. Confident. Privileged.* Those were some of the words she'd have chosen.

Caroline chimed in, "They're certainly a handsome bunch. Doesn't look like there's a horse thief in the lot."

After the briefest tic of hesitation, Holly laughed. "Well, who knows? I guess every family has a horse thief or two hidden away."

She's trying. Really trying. So should I.

Peace pointed to an exceptionally pretty girl who appeared in many of the photographs. "Who's this?"

"Flannery. Your cousin." Holly's expression softened and she caressed the face in the photo with a manicured fingertip. Flannery was clearly a favorite of hers.

A stab of jealousy took Peace by surprise. "Tell me about her," she said.

"She's my sister's daughter. A little younger than you. Seven months actually. Her birthday was just a couple of weeks ago, December first. Her mother's my twin. I've told you about your aunt Noelle. We're very close." She stopped to look into Peace's eyes and reached for her hand. "This is a lot coming at you all at once. I …" Her voice trailed into nothingness. Tears filled her eyes and threatened to spill down her cheeks.

Again, it was Caroline who saved them. "Flannery … pretty name, unusual."

"After the writer, Flannery O'Connor." Holly laughed and brushed the tears from her eyes. "Noelle's an English teacher."

Caroline nodded.

Holly looked down at the album again and turned to Peace. "When Flan was growing up, I used to look at her and wonder about you … what you were doing, how you looked. I imagined the two of you playing together, sharing secrets, being great friends." She smiled. "Maybe that will happen now.

I hope so." The last words came out in a wistful puff that sounded like a prayer.

Peace had her doubts. The girl in the photo looked way too perfect, the kind of person who made her feel like her clothes were on backwards.

Holly glanced at her watch. "They should be here soon. I'm glad you're finally meeting. I've dreamed of this day so often." There was a catch in her voice when she added, "Ever since the day I gave you up. To tell the truth, I didn't really believe it would ever be more than a dream."

Caroline said, "It's a big day for all of us."

"Yes," Peace said. "A big day."

Henry must have heard the doubt in her voice. He stood up and eased his nose into Peace's lap, upsetting the album.

Pinpoints of restless energy prickled Peace from head to toe. She'd had about as much blended family camaraderie as she could handle. She closed the album and passed it over to Holly. "I should take Henry for a walk before everyone gets here."

At the word *walk*, the big dog padded to the corner where his leash had been dropped and came back with it in his mouth. Peace fastened it to his collar and stood. "I won't be long," she said, and headed for the door before anyone could stop her.

Outside, she lifted her face to the sun and took a deep breath, filling her lungs with the crisp air. It was unusually warm for mid-December in Pennsylvania. Dappled light filtered through the few leaves still clinging to the branches of the massive oak that formed a canopy over the sidewalk. Under foot, dried leaves crackled with every step, as if punctuating Peace's conflicted thoughts. Self-conscious, she walked quickly, sure the two women were watching her through the window. What would they talk about in her absence? They had so little in common—actually nothing she could think of except her. Would they discuss her? Would they talk about the coming meeting? Were they nervous about it?

They can't be more nervous than I am.

Two

Rachel Woodard stared out the train's clouded window, trying not to flinch as blunt fingertips caressed the side of her neck.

The fingertips moved up to trace the line of her jaw and chin. Rachel recognized the tenderness in their touch, but felt none of the tingling response it had once elicited. Despite her best effort, a small shudder escaped.

"What's wrong?" Tony asked.

She faked a laugh and leaned forward. "You're tickling me."

Obliging as always, he moved his hand from her neck to her shoulder. "This okay?"

"I guess."

"You guess?"

The train slowed, then lurched to a stop. The seats on their side of the car were wide enough to comfortably accommodate three people, but Rachel and Tony shared the space with an overweight businessman in a voluminous overcoat too engrossed in his phone to realize he was squashing the young couple beside him. Tony seemed to welcome the forced intimacy, but it had long since begun to fray on Rachel's nerves. She glanced at the sign above the station at which the train had just stopped. *Lansdale. Only another half hour.*

She watched passengers turn off their gadgets and gather their belongings. On this Saturday afternoon in mid-December, there were more shoppers than commuters. Plastic bags with bright logos predicted a prosperous holiday season for Philadelphia merchants. Glancing sideways, she saw the businessman tuck his phone in a pocket, stand up, and button his coat around his ample form. She flexed her elbow, hoping Tony would take the hint and give her some space. It was a short-lived hope. Darren Wright, Tony's best friend since they were kids, came up from the rear of the car and lowered his chunky frame into the empty spot, squeezing them closer than ever.

The train eased back into motion and Rachel prepared herself for the non-stop chatter that was Darren's trademark. She was relieved when he said, "So, what's gonna happen with the Eagles? Think they'll get the quarterback situation worked out in time to make the playoffs?"

"Dunno. Depends on ..."

Rachel heard only the first few words of Tony's reply, grateful that football talk would keep the guys happy and leave her alone to reflect on her new life—a life transformed by glimpses of a world beyond the safe confines of her childhood.

# # #

Loosen up, Rach. Go out on a limb. Step outside the box. Break some rules. Clichés all. As old as time itself, but a new way of thinking for Rachel. She'd spent her entire eighteen years under the watchful eyes of adults who took great pains to see that she did *not* go out on any limbs. That had changed a few months ago when she began her freshman year at Penn State's main campus, her first experience away from home overnight without a family member except for sleepovers at girlfriends' homes. At first she'd been disappointed that none of her friends would be there to share the experience with her, but she soon recognized that as a blessing. Alone, adrift in an alien world, she'd been forced to make new friends. And what friends they were—smart and funny, curious and daring, and, most important, challenging her to look at life differently. She smiled, thinking of them, especially one. She imagined introducing him to her parents. Would that ever happen?

Brendan Richards, affectionately called B.R. by friends who teased him, suggesting that the initials really stood for Brash and Reckless. An apt designation. Chills danced down Rachel's spine when she thought of the night he'd *borrowed* the car of an unknown patron of a bar on College Avenue. She knew, of course, she shouldn't venture into this new, dangerous life, but couldn't deny that being with B.R. made her feel alive in a way she never had before.

"See?" he'd said, when they returned the car and miraculously found an empty space half a block from its original parking place. "Nobody ever remembers exactly where they left their car. They'll never know. No harm. No foul." Another cliché. Rachel knew that, but coming from B.R., trite sayings sounded fresh as spring rain. Of course he'd found a parking place. Things worked out for him. Always. That was part of the thrill of being with him.

She knew none the old gang from high school would understand about B.R. He was nothing like Tony. Tony was tall, with a muscular physique that broadcast his non-stop participation in sports. B.R. was compact—an inch or so shorter than Rachel's five feet, six inches, and rail-thin; "built for speed" is how he laughingly described himself. Tony's hair fell in dark, gentle waves over his forehead; B.R.'s was carroty red and Brillo pad curly. None of this mattered to Rachel. She was too entranced by those dancing, mischievous eyes. Green, a mesmerizing combination of emerald shades that changed according to his mood—those eyes took Rachel's breath away. Even better was his conversation. B.R. didn't talk sports. He spouted poetry, quoted long passages from Russian novels, and could answer the most obscure questions on Jeopardy.

# # #

The train lurched, slamming Tony against her side, a reminder that she was not at school now, but back in the mundane world she'd always known. He leaned into her, forcing her even closer, and grinned. She shrugged free, wondering what he would say if he knew about her life at school. Not that he ever would. She planned to tell him about some of it, but not all. Definitely not about joyriding in a *borrowed* car. She pushed thoughts of B.R. away and turned to look at Tony. He was undeniably beautiful, the stereotypical tall, dark, and handsome male that all women were supposedly seeking. She couldn't help comparing him to B.R.—Roman god versus leprechaun. And, inexplicably, it was the leprechaun who haunted her dreams.

Tony seemed to feel her eyes on his face. He leaned his head against hers.

Rachel tried to relax, to be part of the group, the same as she'd always been, but Tony's hand was heavy on her shoulder. She leaned forward, pretending that something outside had caught her attention, and managed to free herself. Not for long.

He leaned forward too and gently kissed her cheek.

Darren half rose from his position, held one hand over the heads of Rachel and Tony, and sang out in his clear tenor voice: "Lovebird alert."

The friends they'd gone to Philadelphia with, seated further back, hooted and applauded.

Tony stood up and bowed.

Rachel remained seated, but turned to face their friends and nodded.

An elderly woman across the aisle looked up from her book and smiled.

It seemed to Rachel that everyone in the car was looking at them. All were smiling. No. Not all. Amanda stared out the window, her expression aloof. No surprise there. Amanda was Darren's younger sister, the perpetual tag-along, only fourteen, but she'd had a crush on Tony for as long as Rachel could remember.

Another lurch. The train stopped and the conductor called out, "Last stop. Doylestown."

Three

Peace had known since she was a toddler that she was adopted and couldn't remember a time when she hadn't been curious about her biological roots. She'd grown up part of the Quaker community in Philadelphia, attending the Green Street Meeting on Sundays and, from kindergarten through eighth grade, had gone to their school. She and her classmates were a racially mixed group, her education one that stressed respect for all people and conflict mediation rather than the more aggressive behavior she'd come to know existed in the rest of the world. It was a good life, idyllic in many ways. Peace knew this and was grateful, but it didn't stop her from wanting a family–a big family with grandparents, aunts, uncles, cousins–the whole nine yards, as they say. Now, her wish granted, she had a family–and was about to meet them. "Be careful what you wish for." How often her mother had said that to her and how foolish she'd thought it at the time.

She remembered Holly's words: "You'll like them once you get to know them."

But will they like me? She thought of all those smiling faces in the photo album, the elaborate birthday cakes topped with candles, the picnics, the hammock filled with laughing children, and, most of all, the posed shots of multiple generations in front of a Christmas tree. *Christmas. Two more weeks.*

This one promised to be different from others she'd known. Last year, she and Caroline had donated money to purchase a door and a window for a local Habitat for Humanity project. The year before, they'd funded a flock of chickens for Heifer International. This year, at Caroline's suggestion, they'd be joining Peace's new-found family in their traditional gift-giving and attending Christmas Eve service at the church that Holly attended. Would Peace fit into this different tradition? Did she want to?

With these thoughts swirling in her head, she followed the familiar streets leading to her apartment. She stopped when she came to the corner of Pine and Ashland, studying the labyrinth laid out there, a red gravel path outlined with white stones. It was a relatively new landmark in an old town, inspired by a woman seeking solace from her grief after the violent death of an adopted daughter. From the first moment she'd heard it, the story had touched Peace. It echoed the bond between her and Caroline Morrow, the only woman she'd ever thought of as *mother*. When she learned that Holly Francis was her birth mother, Peace had been filled with resentment, even revulsion. She shared the news with Caroline, assuming she'd feel the same, but instead, Caroline had said, "We have to move over and make room for her in our lives. Even learn to love her. Anything less will destroy us all." Peace was past the resentment. She'd grown to like Holly well enough, but ... *love* the woman who'd abandoned her?

She stared at the labyrinth. Could it fulfill its promise and help her find the answers she needed? Did it really have the power to quiet her mind? Dare she take time to walk its path? Tempting as the prospect was, the call of home was stronger. She'd spent most of the day looking at pictures and listening to stories about strangers who made up the family she'd always longed for. What she wanted most now was the cozy nest she'd built for herself. She turned from the labyrinth and headed to her apartment. Before she met the people in the photos in the flesh, she needed time with the familiar things that made up the life she knew.

A train was pulling in when Peace and Henry reached the station. A group of young people got off and sorted themselves into couples. One twosome lagged a little behind the others. They crossed the street and stepped onto the sidewalk, apparently oblivious to the rest of the world. Even the presence of a large black dog directly in front of them escaped their notice. Peace pulled the leash up short to avoid a collision. Half-amused, half-annoyed, she looked into the young faces as they passed.

The boy was smiling, seeming to breathe in the essence of the girl beside him, his love so obvious it was almost palpable. He bent down as if to kiss her.

She turned her head. Her scarf flared out and struck him in the face. A bright yellow flag.

Seemingly unaware of the cautionary message, he kissed the top of her head.

Four

Rachel had to turn away from the love in Tony's eyes, lest it burn a hole in her face. She ducked her chin and his kiss landed on the top of her head.

# # #

Rachel Woodard and Tony Rosino had been a couple since fifth grade when he'd invaded the girls' side of the playground and she'd kicked him in the shin, letting him know in no uncertain terms to go back where he belonged. It hadn't taken long, though, for her to respond to the persistent teasing with which ten-year-old boys declare their interest. By the end of the school year those big brown eyes, so quick to broadcast everything he thought or felt, had won her over. It didn't hurt that all the other fifth grade girls, and even a fair number in sixth grade, agreed that Tony was *cute*. By the time they were freshmen in high school, *cute* had become *hot*, and by their senior year, he was, by consensus of all grades, ages, and classes, the best-looking male in town, maybe in all of Bucks County. And, in spite of all this, in spite of the fact that other girls were constantly throwing themselves at him, Tony had eyes only for Rachel. He told everyone who would listen he'd made up his mind that day on the playground, even while he was still smarting from the blow to his shin, that he was going to marry Rachel Woodard some day.

# # #

I have to tell him. How? When? she asked herself. *Tonight.* The decision made, she quickened her step.

"Hey!" Tony held tightly to her arm. "What's the rush?"

She nodded to the rest of the group, who had already crossed Ashland and were headed up Main Street. "We're falling behind."

"That's okay. They understand we want to be alone." He stopped, still gripping her arm so she was forced to stop too. "I haven't seen you since Thanksgiving."

She didn't know if she should laugh or cry. "How about the times you came up to school?"

"They don't count. So many people. Always part of a crowd. It's not the same."

"Of course, it's not the same. It's not supposed to be. We're adults now. I need to focus on college and you need to–"

"Don't you miss me?" His face assumed the woeful Cocker Spaniel look that was his specialty. "Even a little?"

"How can I miss you when you text me half a dozen times a day?" She struggled to keep the irritation out of her voice.

He caressed her cheek with his thumb. "That's not half as often as I think of you."

Rachel knew most of her friends considered her lucky and, until just a few months ago, she had agreed. Now ... She looked up at him. He smiled down at her. The smile was the same as always, a dimple appearing in his left cheek, his brown eyes crinkling with good nature and hinting at secrets to be shared. She waited for the familiar lurch in her stomach. It didn't come. All her life she had believed in the magic of love. All the books she'd read, all the songs she'd hummed … all were about falling in love. Somehow, until now, she'd missed the part about falling *out* of love. She had to tell him. She renewed her resolve. *Tonight.*

His smile faded as he continued to stare into her eyes. "What's wrong?"

To avoid answering, she tilted her head toward their friends. "I want to spend time with them too." She pulled her arm free and jogged away. He caught up and, together, they joined the rest of the group.

Darren said, "Ah ha, the lovebirds decided to mingle with us ordinary birds."

Amanda shot her brother a dirty look and snapped, "Hurry up. It's getting chilly."

Rachel said, "You guys go ahead. I should get home. Big family get-together tonight. Everyone wants to know how I'm doing at college."

Tony rolled his eyes.

Rachel relented and kissed him on the cheek. "You're coming over after work, right?"

"Yeah, I already told Dad I'm leaving early. I'll be there about eight. Eight thirty. Soon as the dinner rush is over."

"Okay." She turned her cheek for a quick kiss and started to hurry away.

He caught up and grabbed her hand. "I'll walk you home."

She didn't pull away this time. *Tonight.* She wasn't looking forward to telling him it was over. He'd be hurt. She knew that. She had to do it anyway. It was time.

###

Rachel stood between her parents and watched the last car back out of the drive, conscious of Tony standing behind her. How could she not be? His hands rested on her shoulders as if she were a prized possession. *Which is exactly how he thinks of me.*

Her father checked the grandfather clock that guarded the Woodard's foyer and turned to Tony. "Still time to catch the end of the Flyers game."

"Sure," Tony said. He didn't look thrilled, but he was always respectful to Rachel's parents.

Her mother stepped in. "Why don't we catch it upstairs? I think the kids might like some time to themselves." She took her husband's elbow and guided him firmly toward the staircase, pausing to give Rachel a brief, encouraging nod. "You're not being kind to pretend to love someone you don't," had been her advice when Rachel had confided in her earlier that day. "Every day that you don't tell him, you're lying to him."

As soon as they disappeared, Tony settled into the corner of the couch, one arm over the back, creating the perfect nesting place.

Rachel settled on the ottoman across the room. "We have to talk."

"Okay." He grinned and patted the couch next to him. "I can hear you better if you sit here."

She shook her head.

The grin disappeared, replaced by the Cocker Spaniel expression.

Stop looking at me like that. She tried to speak and couldn't catch her breath. *How do I say it?*

Straight out is best. She lifted her chin. "I think we should see other people."

"What do you mean?"

"I mean … date others."

"Why?" He started to rise.

"No." She shook her head and put her hands out. "Stay there." She took a couple of deep breaths and, after he eased back into the cushions, went on, "Think about it, Tony. We've never dated anyone else. How do we know we're right for each other?"

"I know what I feel."

"Maybe I don't."

"What're you saying?" He was on his feet now, pacing. He stopped in front of the ottoman, looming over her. "You don't love me? Is that it?"

"No … I mean … not exactly. I'm saying I don't know how I feel."

"Is there someone else? Somebody you met up there?"

She hesitated.

He put his hands on her shoulders. "Think of all the fun we've had together. All our plans. We have a history. A future. You can't throw that away." He let her go and spun around, then turned to face her again. "I won't let you."

Five

Peace gave Henry a treat and wandered through the apartment, waiting for him to finish. In the living room, she opened the drawer where she kept important papers, reached for a well-worn envelope, removed the pages, and read the words written on the pale blue paper:

My Dearest Peace (what a lovely name),

One of my most ardent wishes has come true. My daughter just shared the wonderful news that, after all these years, she has found you. Surely now some day we shall meet—only when you are ready, of course. I realize this has all happened very suddenly and unexpectedly. The unveiling of your ancestry may not be welcome to you, but, for me, it is the answer to a prayer, a realization of a favorite fantasy. I hope that one day, when you have had a chance to become accustomed to the idea, you will be as eager to get to know your grandfather and me as we are you.

Holly tells me you have your grandfather's eyes. You can have no idea how that pleases me. While I am proud of my three children and think both my daughters quite lovely and my son the handsomest man I've ever seen (with the exception, of course, of his father), I confess to being disappointed that they did not inherit my husband's blue eyes and, alas, neither have any of my other grandchildren. (That doesn't keep me from doting on them, as I hope to one day dote over you.)

There are so many things I want to say, I don't know where to start, so I will save them for a later time when we can meet face to face. By way of introduction, I am sending along two photographs. The old one with the curling edges is of me as an infant at my Christening ceremony. I am confident you will recognize the dress and bonnet. I was thrilled when Holly told me these items have been given a place of honor in your home up there in Pennsylvania. The other is of your grandfather and me, taken some months ago at the beach house where our family has summered for most of our lives. It is not a particularly flattering picture, but it is a good enough likeness and I believe captures something of the affection we still feel for one other after nearly fifty years of marriage.

Your affectionate

(and most impatient) grandmother,

Karalee Francis

P. S. My other grandchildren call me Snap-snap. I like it much better than any of the other strange grandmotherly names one hears. When we meet, if you like, I'll tell you how I came to be called that. As for you, my dear, you may call me anything you like. Please just let me meet you some day–when you feel the time is right. It can't come soon enough for me.

# # #

Peace ran her fingers over the words, the long sentences, neatly written in old-fashioned, flowery script–so different from the terse notes Caroline left for her from time to time in no-nonsense block printing.

Her cell phone rang. She knew without looking who it was.

Caroline's voice: "They're here."

"Okay. I'll be right there."

In a lower voice: "Where are you?"

"Home." Silence at the other end told Peace this worried her mother. "We were right here, so I came in to give Henry some water and a treat."

Softer still: "Are you okay?"

"Yes. I had to get away for a few minutes. I'll be right there."

The same voice, this time a whisper of loving concern: "It's going to be fine."

# # #

Peace saw the battered van in front of Holly's house as soon as she turned onto the street. She was glad Kirk had offered to pick everyone up at the airport, grateful that he would be there when she met these strangers who were supposed to be family. No matter what they thought of her, she knew there would always be at least two people to approve of her: Caroline Morrow and Kirk Buchanan. Her mother and her best friend.

She saw Kirk's lanky figure emerge from the house and raised her hand in a wave. Apparently, he didn't see her. Instead of returning her greeting, he half-turned and said something to the girl by his side. Peace recognized the pretty girl from the pictures. *Flannery. My cousin.*

Watching Kirk wrestle with the sliding door to the back of the van, she had to smile. That door always stuck. Even from this distance, she knew he was making a joke about it. She waited for him to notice her. He didn't. He was too busy removing luggage from the back and talking to Flannery, who stood idly by. Peace continued to observe while they entered the house, both relieved and disappointed when no one looked her way. *She's even prettier than her pictures.* Kirk struggled to manage the bags alone. As far as she could tell, there was no offer of help from Flannery. She smiled again, anticipating how they would joke about that later. Kirk was famously disapproving of helpless females.

Minutes later, she followed them into the house, stepping into a symphony of voices: overlapping, melting together into a harmonious whole that was in sharp contrast to the strained conversation she, Caroline, and Holly had shared while looking at the photo album. Her eye sought and found her mother, standing before a tall, distinguished-looking man. Caroline said something Peace couldn't hear.

The man turned around.

Their eyes met.

A jolt of emotion almost buckled Peace's knees. *My grandfather.*

He crossed the room and spoke. "You must be Peace." His voice was low, his words slightly blurred, softened by the accent of the aristocratic south.

The other voices stopped abruptly and, one by one, everyone turned toward Peace. Unable to speak, she nodded and looked around, identifying the room's other occupants: the dear, familiar figure of her mother; the elegant woman from the album, smaller and daintier in person than she had appeared in the photographs. *Snap-snap.*

Holly appeared from the kitchen. She looked nervous, but happy–happier than Peace had ever seen her. And proud. So proud it scared Peace a little. Automatically, she looked toward Caroline, her *real* mother.

Caroline nodded, and closed one eye in a wink, her usual signal of encouragement.

She looked back at the handsome gentlemen before her, squared her shoulders and extended her hand. "Yes, I'm Peace. You must be …" She hesitated, unsure what to call him.

He stepped forward, his arms spread wide. "Ben Francis. My grandkids call me Poppy." When Peace failed to step into his open arms, he took a step back. "It's too soon. For you, I mean. Not for me." His manner was so open, his face so kind, it should have been easy to accept the invitation of his arms, but something in Peace held back. She looked over his shoulder and saw her mother watching her, encouraging her.

Not yet, Peace told herself and remained frozen, her right hand still extended, her left arm at her side.

Ben took her extended hand and enfolded it in both of his. "I'm delighted to meet you. Some day I hope you'll learn to think of me as Poppy. For now, how about Ben?"

Peace looked into his eyes, so very blue, so like the eyes that stared back at her when she looked into a mirror. It was her first inkling that she really might belong in this family. The icicles in her heart began to thaw. She smiled back at him. "I guess we can go straight to Poppy." Before Peace could say more, a tiny slip of a woman appeared at Ben's side.

"I'm your grandmother," she said. "Karalee." She tilted her head and, after the briefest pause, added, "Or we can go straight to Snap-snap."

Her expression, so eager, reminded Peace of Henry standing in front of the cabinet that held his treats. She laughed in spite of herself. "Okay. Poppy and Snap-snap." This was going better than she had dared hope. She stepped into her grandfather's hug. He extended one arm to include both her and her grandmother. She looked over his shoulder into her mother's approving eyes.

Laughter from the kitchen distracted her, a hearty sound that could only be Kirk. She saw him in profile. He was leaning forward, his gaze intent on something just out of sight. Peace moved slightly to the left to see what had so enthralled him. *Flannery.* The girl was sitting on the counter, biting into an apple and staring into Kirk's eyes. Peace couldn't decide if she looked more like Eve or the wicked queen from Snow White.

"Hey," she called out to catch Kirk's attention.

It took a few seconds for him to respond. "Hey yourself," he called back when he finally tore his eyes from Flannery's face. "I'm getting to know your cousin."

"That's nice." Peace hoped no one noticed the coolness of her reply.

Holly came forward. "See. I told you you'd like them."

Peace acknowledged the remark with as much attention as she could muster, distracted by the image of Kirk and Flannery, laughing and remaining a little apart from everyone else.

The rest of the afternoon went by in a blur. Peace felt herself the center of attention and knew how hard her grandparents were trying to put her at ease. Flannery remained on the perimeter of the group, always close to Kirk. After dinner, they went over the sleeping arrangements for the next two weeks. Ben and Karalee had booked a room at Highland Farm, the former home of Oscar Hammerstein that had been turned into a bed and breakfast. Flannery would stay with Peace, an arrangement Peace had agreed to when Holly proposed the plan, saying, "This will give you two young people a chance to get acquainted."

It had seemed like a good idea at the time. Now, Peace was not so sure.

The time came for noisy goodbyes. Peace, Caroline, Flannery, and Kirk trooped out to the van. When Kirk opened the door, Flannery deposited herself in the front seat, smiling sweetly, leaving Peace and her mother no choice but to climb in the back. Kirk went around to the driver's side, leaving them to struggle with the stubborn door.

The ride home was only a few blocks, with a stop at the station so Caroline could take the train to her rowhouse in Philadelphia. The whole time Flannery kept up a string of bright chatter. Kirk laughed at every other word. Peace looked out the window, trying to ignore the obvious chemistry between the two. Not that she cared, of course. She and Kirk were best friends and neither wanted it any other way. *Never had. Never would.*

SUNDAY

Six

Alone in her room, Rachel stood before a bulletin board filled with high school memorabilia, slowly tracing the outline of each item with a fingertip. Programs. Ribbons from corsages. Notes passed in study hall. Photographs. So many of those. In most, Tony was front and center, laughing, bursting with vitality, overshadowing the slight girl who stood beside him. She studied the photographs. *Why did I let him?* Not that she hadn't enjoyed basking in his glory, but it was time to find her own light. Staring at a picture of Tony in his football uniform, she re-lived last night's scene, unable to erase his expression from her mind. She'd never seen him so angry. No. Not angry. Confused. Disbelieving.

She turned from the bulletin board and saw a small brown bird take flight from the ledge outside her window. She watched it soar out of sight and become swallowed up by the cold, gray sky. *It's so tiny and so fearless.* She continued to look into the now empty sky and came to a decision.

Her mother was in the kitchen, covering a plate of brownies with foil.

"Mom, I need the car for an hour or so. Okay?"

"Sorry. I have to take all this,"–Lisa waved her hand over three more foil-covered packets on the counter–"to the Blakeleys."

"Can't you do it later?"

"Why do you need the car?"

With only the smallest tic of hesitation, Rachel gave the reply she'd rehearsed upstairs in her room: "Christmas shopping. I don't have anything for Dad yet."

"That can wait. Sonia is in the hospital and I promised I'd bring dinner and stay with the kids while Jeff visits her."

"I could drop you off."

Paul Woodard wandered in from the living room. He looked from mother to daughter. "Drop off? Where?"

"Shopping center." Rachel kept her tone light and hoped she sounded sincere. She wasn't used to lying to her parents.

Still crimping the foil edges around the cookies, Lisa said, "I'll drop you there and you can walk home."

"That won't work for me." Rachel turned to her father. "How about your car?"

Before he had a chance to answer, Lisa Woodard turned from the food on the counter and gave her daughter a searching look. "What's up? All of the sudden you can't you walk three blocks?"

Rachel hesitated, chewing on her lip, and finally said, "I need to talk to Tony."

Both parents went still.

Paul said, "I thought you settled everything last night."

"He was upset when he left. I don't want to leave it like that."

Lisa said, "Honey, you didn't do anything wrong. You did what you had to do, probably should have done a long time ago."

"Then why do I feel like an axe murderer?"

"Because you're a sweet, good person." Lisa reached out and brushed her daughter's cheek with chocolate-scented fingertips. "That's fine. Wonderful, in fact, but don't let it make you do something that's not right for you."

"He looked so hurt."

"He'll get over it. If you don't want to spend the rest of your life with Tony, don't let him guilt-trip you into it. You have a right to your own life."

Paul came to stand behind Rachel and kissed the top of her head. "She's right, honey."

She twisted away and stood glaring at her parents, knowing there was nothing she could say that would make them understand. Their lives were settled, uncomplicated. She couldn't believe they'd ever been confused or uncertain. If they had, it was so long ago ...

Paul broke the silence. "Listen to your mother. She gives good advice." When Rachel didn't answer, he went to the refrigerator, and, after a few seconds, added, "But sometimes she forgets to buy beer."

"You can't buy your own beer? Have some cranberry juice." Lisa aimed a playful swat at his backside.

He danced away.

Lisa laughed out loud when his sock-clad feet slipped on the polished wide plank floor and he had to grab a chair to remain upright.

Rachel watched her parents, recognizing their exchange as an attempt to lighten the mood. There was a time when it would have worked. She'd have joined in. Now, their antics just seemed trivial.

Paul returned to the refrigerator and pulled out a bottle of cranberry juice. "Gonna need more than this to get me through the game. The Eagles aren't exactly flying high today."

Lisa said, "If you get tired of the game, you can always fix that bookcase."

"Fix it? How?"

"I don't know. Maybe bolt it to the wall. It's topheavy. I'm afraid it's going to topple over and hurt somebody."

He sighed and poured a glass of juice. "I'll take care of it after the holidays."

"Let's hope nothing happens before then."

Rachel half-listened to her parents, thinking how cautious they were, how small their lives, and vowed never to be like them. She heard her name and realized her father was speaking to her.

"I agree with your mother. Give Tony time to cool off."

"If I wait, he'll brood and get even more upset. I have to talk to him. The sooner, the better."

Paul and Lisa exchanged coded looks. He nodded in apparent agreement to whatever signal his wife had sent and left mother and daughter alone.

Silence grew until it seemed like a physical presence, cold and ominous, at odds with the space it filled—a large, cozy room with walls the color of cider, a shade that evoked an image of cinnamon-dusted apples. It had once been two small, cramped rooms, but Rachel's parents had removed the wall dividing kitchen from dining room, thus creating an expansive area where most of the milestones of Rachel's childhood had been marked. More recently, in honor of their twenty-fifth anniversary, they'd purchased a seven-foot Shaker trestle table from a furniture maker in Vermont. An assortment of almost-matching chairs in varying shades of pale oak set off the hand-rubbed cherry finish. A crazy quilt in rich earth tones hung on one wall; a brick fireplace took up most of another. Except for the table, there was nothing distinguished about the furnishings, but together, they created a feeling akin to being wrapped in a warm embrace, an embrace Rachel shunned at the moment.

She took a deep breath, determined to make her mother understand. "He'll be riding his bike now. He always says riding is when he does his best thinking. Puts him in the zone. This is the perfect time."

Lisa shook her head. "Wait a day or so. Talk to him when his feelings aren't so raw." She spoke slowly and gently. "You may think it's the right time, but believe me, honey, it's not. Especially not out there on some country road. I can't allow you to do that. Not if he's as angry as you said."

"Mom, don't be silly. You know Tony."

"Maybe you don't know him as well as you think you do."

"But—"

"No buts. I need the car and you need to stay away from Tony. At least for a few days."

"But–"

"I said 'no buts'. End of discussion."

Rachel knew her mother too well to continue the argument. She flounced to the foyer, grabbed her coat and stormed out of the house, slamming the door.

Seven

Peace sat on the couch with a magazine in her lap, trying to think of something to say to her cousin, who was, alternately, perched on the edge of a chair and springing up to prowl the perimeter of the room. Henry sat at Peace's feet, watching Flannery, then looking up at Peace with his ears drawn slightly forward, his brow wrinkled, as though asking, "What's *she* doing here?"

Peace stole a look at the clock. *Two fifteen. We'll never make it to four.*

The family had elected to go to Meeting with Peace and Caroline that morning instead of attending the service at the Methodist Church where Holly was a member. It was clear they, particularly Flannery, were not accustomed to the quiet reflection of a Quaker Meeting. Flannery had fidgeted through all but the first five minutes and still seemed bursting with suppressed energy.

Peace watched her stop to examine the shadowbox frame that occupied the most prominent space on the wall.

"So this is the famous Christening dress."

Peace nodded, uneasy about where the conversation might be going.

Without looking away from the framed dress and bonnet, Flannery said, "You do realize you're the only grandchild who ever got to wear it."

Peace felt herself go rigid and the threat of tears stung her eyes. She swiped her hand over her face, brushing them away, determined that the interloper not see her distress.

Flannery stepped closer to the framed clothing articles and picked up the tiny pillow resting on the shelf under them. She ran her fingertips over the words embroidered on the pillow as she read them aloud: "Peace Be With You". She was quiet for a moment, then, still without looking at Peace, she said, "Aunt Holly said that's where you got your name."

Put that down!

Almost as though she had heard Peace's silent scream, Flannery put the pillow back on the shelf. She leaned closer to inspect the silver cup next to it, but turned away without touching it.

Peace watched, taking deep breaths, willing calm, not trusting herself to speak.

Flannery sat back down and smiled at Peace, then resumed her examination of the room. She picked up a small carved figure from the table beside her chair, looked at it, then at Henry. "Looks like him," she said.

Peace said. "Actually, it is him. Kirk made it."

Flannery perked up. "Kirk?"

"Umm hmm. He carved it from a scrap of wood. The day I moved in, he came over to introduce himself. The place was a total mess. It had just been converted from a single family home into two apartments. The contractors were still finishing up when I started bringing my stuff in. There was a scrap of wood in the kitchen sink. Kirk picked it up, asked if I had any use for it. When I said I didn't, he stuck it in his pocket. A couple of days later, he showed up with that." She pointed to the little wooden dog Flannery was holding.

"So ... he's creative? I had him pegged as more of an outdoorsy type. He was telling me about all the canoeing he does."

"He's both. Anything hands-on, he'll try."

"You ever go canoeing with him?"

"Sometimes."

Flannery looked at her with an arched eyebrow. "You're dating?"

Peace shook her head. "Just friends."

Flannery put the little dog back on the table and drifted over to the window. "Anything to do in this town?"

The change was so abrupt, it took Peace a minute to answer. "Sure. There's a lot to do. Very historical. We could take a walk. Maybe visit the book store, then stop at one of the coffee shops."

"How about shopping? Do you have a mall?"

"There're a lot of little shops in the center of town. And a shopping center at the north end."

"Let's ..." Flannery started, then stopped and smiled brightly at Peace. "You probably don't want to go. Maybe I could borrow your car and check it out?"

"You don't need a car. It's not that far. You just walk to the corner, make a left. and go right up Main Street 'til you get there."

Flannery seemed to consider this, but not too seriously. "What if it starts to rain? Besides, I don't have that much time. We have to be at Aunt Holly's at four."

Peace was too anxious to be rid of her cousin for a couple of hours to argue. "All right. Want me to draw you a map?"

"Already got one." Flannery retrieved her purse, an oversized, overstuffed pouf of buttery leather, from a chair and, after a bit of digging, pulled out a folded rectangle. "Aunt Holly sketched one out for me last night. Showed me where her house and yours are. And the B and B where Poppy and Snap-snap are staying." She unfolded the paper and smoothed it flat on the end table next to Peace's chair. "You said it's just up Main Street, so …" she traced a line with her finger, then looked at Peace. "Right?"

Peace nodded.

"I've got my cell. I'll call if I have a problem."

"You have my number?"

Flannery pulled out her phone. "What is it?"

Peace gave Flannery the digits and watched her program the number into her phone.

Peace handed over the keyring containing her house and car keys along with a tiny replica of Robert Indiana's LOVE sculpture.

Flannery skipped out the door like a bird who'd been freed from a cage.

Peace watched through the window. She held her breath when Flannery narrowly missed a pickup truck as she executed a u-turn instead of going around the block as Peace had suggested. She felt vaguely guilty for sending her off on her own, but rationalized that it was for the best. *She needs to get away from me as much I need to be rid of her.*

Eight

Rachel wandered the aisles of the Bon Ton, trying to banish Tony's forlorn expression from her thoughts while she looked for a Christmas present for her father. Gloves, shirts, ties. Blah, blah, blah. Boring, boring, boring. Her thoughts drifted to B.R. If only he were here. He'd know what she should do. Maybe even find a car to hot wire. No. Best to leave that thought alone. Not that she'd ever do such a thing.

She left the store and cut across the parking lot toward Music and Arts. She still had no idea what to get her dad, but he loved music, so they were bound to have something he'd like. He'd played trumpet in his younger years and was a big jazz fan. Maybe at least they'd be able to suggest something.

She slogged through the rows of cars, head down, her scarf pulled tight against the biting wind. Shopping was the last thing she felt like doing. The argument with her parents rankled. Maybe they were right, but the memory of the crushing hurt in Tony's eyes last night wouldn't stop haunting her. She had to make him understand and was convinced her best chance was now, while he was involved in something he loved almost as much as he loved her. *I really, really need a car.*

Absorbed in her conflicted thoughts, she bumped into a young woman coming from between two cars.

"Sorry," Rachel said. "My fault. I wasn't …"

The other woman waved a dismissal, and hurried on her way. Rachel watched her go, saw her juggle a suitcase-sized purse in one hand and slip the other into her pocket. A set of keys fell onto the parking lot. Rachel picked them up and called out, "Miss ..."

The woman walked on without a backward look and disappeared into the doors of the Bon Ton.

Rachel started after her, then stopped, an idea worming its way into her consciousness, a dangerous idea, something so unlike her customary behavior that it felt unreal, like a scene from a movie or ... A smile turned up the corners of her lips. She moved her hand, savoring the tantalizing heft of the keys. The image of Brendan Richards danced in her head. *Brash and Reckless.*

She looked at the two cars from between which the woman had emerged. To the left was a silver BMW. To the right, a dark blue Hyundai Elantra. *It won't take long. Half an hour, tops.* She looked toward the row of stores, the people scurrying in and out of the doors. *With the crowds, there's no way she'll be out that soon. She won't even miss it. No harm. No foul.* Rachel flipped aside the LOVE charm and pressed the key fob. The Elantra's lights went on. *That's it.* She put her hand on the door handle. Pressed. Not even locked. She took that as a sign that the universe approved and pushed away the thought that her parents most definitely would not. That's okay. She wasn't like them. She'd learned sometimes you have to take a chance and listen to the universe.

She got into the car and turned the key. The Elantra hummed to life. She backed out and headed north on 611. This being Sunday, she knew exactly where he'd be. Tony Rosino was the most dependable person in the world, one of the many things everyone admired about him. Everyone else, that is. It drove Rachel crazy.

She turned right on Saw Mill Road and spotted him immediately, bent over his bike, legs pumping, a bullet-shaped helmet covering his head. He must have heard the car coming up behind him; he moved closer to the shoulder, leaving plenty of room for a car to pass, but didn't slow down or look back. She pulled even with him, slowed to a crawl, and tapped the horn. He glanced sideways and squinted into the vehicle. The light in his eyes when he realized it was Rachel was almost as painful to her as last night's anger had been.

He stopped peddling, removed his helmet and hung it over a handlebar. The wind ruffled the dark waves of his hair, pushing them away from his face, accentuating his profile, making him look like a statue come to pulsing life.

Rachel pulled over to the shoulder.

Tony bent down to look in the passenger side window. His face looked like Christmas morning.

She took a deep breath, determined to stand her ground, before she pushed the button to lower the window.

He leaned in and extended an arm toward her.

She leaned back against the driver's side door, beyond his reach.

The brightness went out of his face. "You haven't changed your mind?"

She shook her head.

"Then why're you here?"

"I didn't want to leave it like last night. Not after all these years. You've been an important part of my life. I want you to know that. It's just..." Her voice drifted as realization dawned. *Mom was right.*

Tony's knuckles stood out, sharp and white against the handlebars. "We're meant to be together. We've always said so."

"No, Tony. *You've* always said so. I just ... kind of went along."

He swung his leg over the bike frame, eased it to the ground, walked around to the driver's side, and leaned down so their faces were level. His eyes were slits in his face. "You never loved me?"

"I didn't say that."

"So, you did love me, and now, all of a sudden, you don't."

She didn't answer.

He lifted his hands to the sky and shook his head. The motion sent the dark curls dancing. "It doesn't work that way. Love is forever."

A car approached. It slowed and swerved to the center of the road before it drove on.

When Tony spoke again, his tone was quiet, reasonable, as though he were addressing a recalcitrant six-year-old. "You're getting all kinds of crazy ideas in your head at college. I was afraid this would happen."

His patience was salt in a wound to Rachel. Suddenly, all the resentment she'd pushed away for the past year flooded over her, demanding to be spoken aloud. "Right! You wanted me to throw away a scholarship. A chance to learn about something that fascinates me. Something I'm good at." The suffocating anger rising in her throat threatened to choke her.

"You didn't have to go all the way up to State College."

"Do you know how lucky I was to be accepted to the main campus? Tony, this is my dream. You say you love me, but ..." She searched for words to make him see that he had to let her go so she could find her own path.

He pounced on her hesitation. "I thought I was your dream. Everything we talked about since ... geez ... since fifth grade!" His patient tone disappeared. He leaned into the window, his face inches from hers.

Seeing him loom over her, Rachel knew there was no point in prolonging the breakup by trying to explain. Her mother was right. A quick, clean break was the only way. "Tony, I'm sorry. It's over."

She reached to start the car.

He grabbed her hand, and pulled the keys from the ignition.

"Stop it!" Her scream came from deep within, so deep it burned the back of her throat as it escaped. "Give them back!"

His face contorted. He reared back and threw the keys over the top of the car into the open field.

She unlatched the door and pushed with enough force to send him stumbling backward.

He landed, sprawling in a half-seated position, supported by his elbows, in the road.

Rachel dodged past him and ran into the field, keeping her eyes on the spot where the keys must have landed, terrified that she wouldn't find them. She kept her head down, scuffing the ground with her shoe as she made a slow circle in the area, anger and fear causing her heart to pound.

Clods of dirt broke apart, rose a few inches and then fell back to earth, creating small mushroom clouds of dust. Finally a bright glint shimmered in the dark earth. The word LOVE looked up at her, a mockery of everything she'd always believed. She stooped, picked up the keys, and gripped them tightly, prepared to fight rather than surrender them. She stood and looked toward the road, unsure what to expect.

Tony had gotten up and moved out of the road. He was standing by his bike, watching her. He looked as shocked as she felt.

She went back to the car.

He reached out to touch her as she passed.

She twisted away, giving him a wary glance, and saw that his eyes were filled with tears.

"Please," he said. "Can we at least talk about it?"

"The time for talk is past." Struggling to control the fury that threatened to explode within her, she got into the car and started the engine, looking at the road ahead.

Tony moved off the shoulder. He went to the front of the car. There he stopped and spread his arms wide.

"Get out of the way!"

"Not until you talk to me."

"There's nothing more to say."

He stared at her, but did not move.

"I'll run over you if I have to."

He didn't budge.

Rachel started to shake. "I mean it. I will."

"You know you won't." And then he sealed his fate. He grinned at her, the same grin he'd used to win every argument since fifth grade.

Rachel's foot was on the accelerator. She leaned back, gripped the wheel, and moved the gear shift lever, intending to put the car in reverse. She felt the car move.

Tony moved with it. His eyes widened, his mouth formed a large oh, his head moved side to side. He stumbled back, but still, he remained squarely in front of the car.

Rachel felt her body tense and, unbelievably, as if of its own volition, the car shot forward. She watched as Tony seemed to dive onto the hood, then slide, slow motion, off to the side.

His feet went up. His body flipped sideways and disappeared.

She stared through the windshield, to the spot where, seconds ago, Tony had stood, grinning at her, blocking her way. Now there was nothing. She looked to the side where he'd fallen, waiting for him to get up.

He didn't.

She got out of the car and walked around to the other side.

He lay face down by the side of the road, next to his bicycle, still as a broken doll.

"Tony?"

No answer.

Rachel knelt beside him and touched his arm with tentative fingers. "Tony?"

No response.

"Tony!"

Still no response.

She stood and took a step backward. *He's okay. He'll wake up.* She drove away, the hurt expression that had haunted her earlier replaced by the image of the unnatural angle of Tony's head and neck.

Nine

Four twenty-five. We were supposed to be there at four. Peace punched in the number for Flannery's phone again. And, again, there was no answer. *Where is she?* She slipped the phone back in her pocket, only to have it ring immediately. She checked the identity of the caller. Her mother.

"What's up?" Caroline asked.

"Flannery's still not back." When there was no response, she added, "I guess Holly's worried and she's probably blaming me. Believe me, I–"

Caroline interrupted. "Calm down. She's not blaming you. Or Flannery either, for that matter. She's laughing about it. Saying she should have warned you. When Flannery goes shopping, she loses track of time."

"In other words, she thinks it's cute."

"That's pretty much how it's going down over here."

Peace heard the combination of disapproval and amusement in her mother's voice and said, "I guess I know what you think of that."

"Yep."

"What do you think I should do? Walk over there? I can leave a note on the door for Flannery."

"It's probably best if you stay put. We can't go anywhere until she shows up anyway."

"Holly could go up to the shopping center and see if she can find her."

"I'm not calling the shots here. You and I need to sit back and let the family do whatever they do."

"What about Poppy and Snap-snap?"

"They're still at the B and B. Holly called them and explained why we're running late."

"Are they upset?"

"Not as far as I can tell. Everybody's taking it in stride. You should too."

"All right. I'll call if I hear from her. If she calls over there, let me know. Okay?"

"Will do."

After she hung up, Peace fumed, alternately angry with herself for not insisting on accompanying Flannery to the shopping center and angry with Flannery for being irresponsible and making everyone wait for her. Henry lay on the floor, his head between his paws, watching his mistress, his mood attuned to hers.

It seemed like years before the phone rang again. Peace checked caller i.d. *Finally!* She waited a second to answer, squared her shoulders, breathed deeply, and swallowed her resentment, determined to be nice, no matter how she felt. "Hi. Did you run into a problem? Or find lots of bargains?"

"Oh, Peace, I'm so sorry." The words erupted in short bursts. "Your car is gone."

"Gone?"

"Somebody stole it." Sniffling sounds, then, a heart-rending: "I'm so sorry."

Peace took a minute to answer, pushing away angry thoughts while she told herself to be fair. "You don't have to be sorry. It's not your fault if somebody stole it."

More sniffles.

"Have you called the police?"

"Not yet," Flannery said. "Snap-snap said I should call you immediately."

"Snap-snap? Where are you?"

"Aunt Holly's. When I couldn't find the car, I walked to the B and B where Snap-snap and Poppy are staying. They called Aunt Holly and she picked us up and brought us here."

"Oh." Peace took a few minutes to let this sink in. "I'll walk over there and we'll call the police. See what we should do next." She listened to Flannery relay this to the group at her end of the exchange and to what she could hear of their responses. After some discussion, the consensus was that it would be best to meet at Peace's apartment.

She paced while she waited.

They arrived about fifteen minutes later. Five minutes after that, Peace was on the phone with the police.

Flannery stood by, wide-eyed and sniffling.

Ten minutes later, a police car pulled up to the curb.

When Peace went to the door, a very young cop held up a badge and introduced himself as Sergeant Edward Shepherd. Peace explained that she was the owner of the missing vehicle, but that she hadn't been driving. She gave him the information about make, model and color, then nodded toward Flannery. "She drove the car to the shopping center."

Sergeant Shepherd shifted his attention to Flannery. "Your name, please."

"Flannery Donahue."

"Residence?"

"I live in Richmond, Virginia. I'm just visiting here."

"May I see your license?"

There was an awkward quiet while Flannery rummaged through her humongous purse until she found her driver's license and handed it to the policeman. Her dark eyes looked huge and a little scared beneath the fringe of thick lashes that, seemingly, she could not keep from fluttering.

He scanned the license quickly, handed it back, and nodded at Flannery to continue.

Poppy stood by his granddaughter's side, his arm around her shoulder, while she explained in detail about coming out of the store and not being able to find the car. "At first I thought I'd forgotten where I parked," she said. "But I went up and down every row of cars and it wasn't there." She looked around as though inviting sympathy.

She got none from Peace.

Shepherd asked, "What about the keys? Any chance you left them in the car?"

"I don't think I did, but I can't find them." She started to sniffle again.

Snap-snap came over to hand her a tissue.

Poppy patted her shoulder. "You checked your purse? Your pockets?"

"Yes, especially my coat pocket. That's what I usually do when I go in a store and don't think I'll be long."

The policeman looked at her like he expected more.

She said, "I put my keys my pocket so I don't have to hunt for them in my purse."

"Could someone have picked your pocket?"

Flannery shrugged and opened her eyes wider. "I guess it's possible." Her chin started to quiver, her eyelashes to flutter faster. More tears seemed imminent.

Sergeant Shepherd, apparently as dazzled by those fluttering lashes as Kirk had been, said, "I'm sure we'll find it. We ..." His phone beeped. "Excuse me." He answered it and, after listening intently for a moment, said, "Have to go. Busy day. Most of the time, nothing much happens around here. Especially on a Sunday. Today ..." He paused, shaking his head. "Chief's checking out a developing situation north of town. Thinks it could be related."

Peace walked out onto the porch with him. "You'll be in touch if you find the car?"

"Yes." The one-word response was clipped, brusque.

After he left, the family stood there, looking like an army waiting for a general to take charge.

"It wasn't my fault." The words burst from Flannery.

Poppy said, "Of course not, Sweetie. Nobody blames you." Then everyone chimed in, assuring Flannery that she had done nothing wrong.

Peace couldn't help noticing they were all treating Flannery like a tragic heroine, wronged by circumstances beyond her control. *I'm the one without a car. Why doesn't somebody think about that?* She looked toward her mother.

Caroline was sitting quietly in a chair by the window, her face composed and noncommittal. When things calmed down a bit, she said, "Don't we have dinner reservations at seven?'

"Oh, that's right," Poppy glanced at his watch. "We better get going. I think we could all use a good meal. A stiff drink wouldn't hurt either." He looked a little embarrassed and said to Caroline, "If you don't mind, that is."

"Not a bit," she said. "All things in moderation, that's the Quaker belief." She paused a few seconds, looking around. "Unless I'm mistaken, we have a transportation problem. One small car and six good-sized people."

"Right," Holly said. "My little Prius really only seats four."

While they were deciding how to handle this, the doorbell rang.

Peace answered it to find Sergeant Shepherd once again on the porch, this time accompanied by the Chief of Police, Louis Grimaldi. She called over her shoulder. "Maybe we don't have a problem after all." She looked at the chief's face and changed her mind. "You didn't find the car, did you?"

He stepped inside, with Shepherd close behind him. "I think maybe we have," he said. He introduced himself and showed his badge. "Where's the young lady who last drove the car?"

Flannery stepped forward. "That would be me."

"I need you to go over exactly what happened." He looked stern. "Don't leave anything out."

Poppy approached the chief and held out his hand, "I'm Ben Francis, Flannery's grandfather." He waited for the chief's acknowledging nod, then asked, "If you have the car, why is this necessary?"

Grimaldi said, "We'll get to that in a minute. First, I'd like to hear what ..." he paused to look down at his clipboard and went on, "... Miss Donahue has to say."

Flannery told her story again.

The chief never took his eyes off her face as she spoke. When she stopped, he asked, "You're sure that's all?"

"Yes."

Poppy stepped protectively between the police chief and his granddaughter. "What's this about?"

Grimaldi looked at him through half-closed eyes.

Peace knew that look and didn't have a good feeling about it. She asked, "Where's the car now?"

"Fanny Chapman parking lot."

Poppy tilted his head toward the chief. "Fanny Chapmen?"

Grimaldi said, "The community swimming pool. I understand Miss Donohue ..."–He paused to look at Flannery– "...walked from the shopping center to Highland Farms Bed and Breakfast when she couldn't find the car."

"Yes," Poppy said. "My wife and I are staying there."

The chief looked at Flannery again. "You're not leaving anything out?"

She shook her head.

"Fanny Chapman's between the shopping center and the B and B. You had to walk right past the car."

Flannery opened her big eyes wide and looked directly at the chief. No fluttering eyelashes this time. "If I passed the car, I didn't see it." When he continued to stare at her, she added, "I was pretty upset."

Poppy put his arm around Flannery's shoulders. "When can we have the car back?"

Grimaldi chewed on his lip, staring at Flannery, for what seemed an eternity. He finally turned to Peace. "There was an accident up north of town and there's a strong possibility your car was involved."

It was like someone had taken a giant vacuum and sucked all the air out of the room.

Caroline asked, "A bad accident?"

Grimaldi nodded. "As bad as it gets. A young man was riding his bicycle. Looks like someone ran him down and left him there to die."

Ten

Paul Woodard looked at the ceiling above his head, then at his wife. "What's up with Rachel?"

"What do you mean?" Lisa went on slicing a pepper into thin strips.

"Don't you think it's strange? Her staying in her room like this? It's like she's hiding."

"She needs some time alone."

"That's not like her. She's usually right here helping us with dinner, chattering a mile a minute." He picked up a thin green strip of pepper and bit into it. "She's not a loner by nature. Something's wrong."

Lisa rested the tip of the knife on the cutting board and returned his look. "She feels bad about Tony."

"Oooh." He was quiet for a moment. "That's to be expected, right?"

"I think so. She knew he wouldn't be happy, but she didn't expect him to take it this hard. She's never dated anyone but Tony. Never experienced a breakup." She picked up the knife and resumed her preparations.

"Think she has regrets?"

"I hope not. As for me, I'm glad it's finally happened. I was afraid they'd drift along and get married without testing other waters." When he didn't answer immediately, she asked, "Agree?"

He shrugged and took another strip of pepper. "That doesn't explain her moping in her room all afternoon."

"It's not all afternoon. She's only been home an hour."

"Where was she? With Tony?"

"No. Not with Tony. She said something about Christmas shopping." Lisa paused to look at Paul with a lifted eyebrow and added, "For a difficult person."

He grinned. "Did you give her any hints?"

"Not telling."

They slipped back into the comfortable camaraderie that comes with twenty-plus years of a happy marriage.

A shrill ring cut short the exchange.

Lisa wiped her hands on a towel and grabbed the phone resting on the counter. She looked at Paul and mouthed "Angelo" when she saw the name in the caller i.d. window, but her voice was neutral when she spoke. "Hello."

Her hand started to shake and the color drained from her face. "Omigod. I am so sorry." She listened a few minutes more. "I'll tell her." Then, again, "I am so sorry. If there's anything … Yes, of course … Not tonight. She'll need time to absorb this. So do you, of course. We'll come by tomorrow."

She laid the phone back on the counter and turned to her husband. "Tony's dead."

He choked on the pepper slice and, when he stopped coughing, said, "What happened?"

"An accident. Hit and run."

They both looked toward the ceiling overhead and, without speaking, went upstairs together.

# # #

Rachel lay on her bed, staring at the ceiling. Waiting. *Have they found him yet? Maybe he's not dead.* Trying to pray. *Please ...* Afraid to pray.

She heard the phone ring downstairs and her mother's muffled voice. She clenched her hands into fists when she heard them on the stairs. Two sets of footsteps, one quick and light, one firm and solid. The tempo changed. She knew her parents had reached the top of the stairs and were coming down the short hall to her room. She turned on her side, her face away from the door, struggling to compose herself.

A soft knock. The door opening.

She turned for the news she already knew and forced a smile. "What's up?" She hoped her voice didn't sound as phony to her parents as it did to her.

Her mother sat on the bed and folded her hands in her lap. She seemed to be searching for words. Her father stood beside her, shifting his weight from one foot to the other. It was he who finally spoke. "There's been an accident and ..." He paused, taking his lower lip between his teeth.

Her mother finished for him. "Tony was out riding this afternoon and he was hit by a car." She spoke carefully and distinctly, but her voice quavered. After she finished, she reached over and smoothed the hair away from Rachel's brow.

Rachel sat up. "Is he okay?"

Her mother hesitated, then said quietly, "He's ... dead.

"Oh." Rachel didn't have to fake the shock she felt when she heard her worst fear spoken aloud. "Dead?" The word felt heavy in her mouth. "Are they sure?"

"Apparently so," her father said.

Her mother reached out and wrapped her in a tight hug.

Her father sat down and enfolded both of them in his arms.

They sat like that, rocking slowly to and fro for what seemed an eternity to Rachel. Finally, she could stand it no longer. She had to tell someone. "I didn't mean to hurt him."

Her mother pulled away and looked into her eyes. "Oh, honey." She wiped the tears from Rachel's face with her thumb. "It's not your fault. It was an accident. It has nothing to do with you breaking up with him." She was crying too.

"A coincidence," her father said, reaching into a pocket for a handkerchief and handing it to his wife.

They don't understand.

"I guess," Rachel said aloud and told herself she'd tell them later. Then, unbidden, the thought came: *Maybe they don't have to know. Some crimes are never solved.* She tried again to pray. *Please ...* But could get no further than the one vague word. Practical thoughts began to emerge. "Who called?" she asked. "Was it the police?"

"No," her mother said. "It was Angelo."

Tony's dad. Rachel pictured the round face, usually so jolly. She imagined the dark eyes, so like Tony's, filled with pain. "How did he sound?"

"Not good."

Rachel could only nod. The image of the kindly old face, distorted with grief, hung in the air before her. Unshed tears filled her eyes.

Her father patted her shoulder.

"Did he ask to speak to me?"

Lisa shook her head. "No. He just said he wanted us to know. I told him I'd tell you. He asked us to come over tonight. I said tomorrow would be better."

Rachel nodded, accepted the handkerchief that her mother handed over, and wiped away her tears. A curious calm settled over her. "Tomorrow's better. Thank you." Questions filled her mind. She looked at her mother. "Did he say anything about Tony and me? About us breaking up?"

"No." Lisa said quickly, then seemed to think about it. "I wonder if Tony told his parents. Angelo sounded like he still thought of you as a couple."

"Should I tell them? I mean if they don't already know?"

Her mother said, "I don't see any reason to. What difference would it make now?"

"Who found him?"

"Someone driving by saw him and the bicycle on the shoulder and called the police."

"Oh." Rachel was aware of the look that passed between her parents over her head.

Her father stood. "Why don't we go downstairs and talk."

Her mother said, "We should have something to eat." She looked at Rachel. "I know you don't feel like eating, but you'll feel better if you do."

"You guys go on. I'll be down in a minute."

"You sure you're okay?" Paul asked.

"Yeah."

Lisa said, "You're not okay. Not now. But you will be. No matter how you felt about Tony toward the end, he was a part of your life for a long time. This is a shock." She signaled to her husband that they should leave. At the door, she turned back to Rachel. "Don't be too long. It's not good to sit up here and brood. Daddy and I will help you through this."

"I know." She watched them slip their arms around each other's waists after they passed through the door. *They don't know. It'll break their hearts when they find out. Tony's parents too. I hurt so many people today.*

After a few minutes, she rose to follow her parents downstairs. A flash of yellow caught her eye. *The scarf.* She stared at it, wondering if it had left traces when she'd wiped the car clean with it. She picked it up, went to her closet and pushed it to the back of the shelf, behind of jumble of seldom-used items. Her only conscious thought was *I'll never wear it again.*

# # #

Downstairs, Lisa resumed her preparations for dinner. Paul set the table, then prowled the kitchen. "What do you think?"

"I don't know. At first her reaction was exactly what I would expect … then, she seemed to go numb. I couldn't tell what she was thinking."

"I know. That's not like her." He stopped pacing, put his hands on his wife's shoulders and, after a few seconds, said, "She's strong. She'll be okay."

"Yes," Lisa agreed, and hoped it was true, but couldn't get her daughter's zombie-like demeanor out of her mind.

Eleven

In the silence after the police left, Flannery stood in the center of the room, looking from one face to the other. "I didn't do it. I swear I didn't." She went to her grandfather. "You believe me, don't you?"

He wrapped her in a tight hug. "Of course I do."

Peace noticed that he looked across the room, seeking his wife's face. She couldn't tell from his expression if he believed Flannery or was merely offering the support she so obviously required. The family seemed to do that a lot. Well, Peace had been brought up by a different standard. She said, "I don't know what happened but, if you did run into that guy, you're better off admitting it now."

Flannery pulled away from her grandfather's hug and whirled to face Peace. "I didn't–"

"I'm not saying you did, just ..." She let her voice trail.

In the quiet that followed, the doorbell rang, sending shock waves through the room. Everyone looked toward the door, but no one moved. Peace went to the window, looked out and saw Kirk's van in the space that, until a few minutes ago, had been occupied by Grimaldi's vehicle. She let out the breath she hadn't known she'd been holding and called out, "Come on in. It's not locked."

Kirk had his guitar case in his hand. He looked around the room, focused on Peace. "I just got home from practice and saw a police car pull away."

Flannery reclaimed her position center stage. "I'm so scared."

Kirk looked briefly at Flannery, then at Peace. "What happened?"

Before she had a chance to answer, Flannery said, "I've been accused of murder."

Ben patted his granddaughter on the shoulder and said, "No one has accused you of anything."

"Maybe not in so many words."

Kirk looked bewildered. "What happened?"

This time Caroline chimed in, explaining the situation succinctly and calmly, ending with: "The police have to look at all possibilities. I'm sure, once the dust settles, the truth will out." Despite, or maybe because of, the fact that she spoke in a voice not much above a whisper, no one interrupted. Everyone, including Flannery, seemed calmed by the older woman's serenity. Only Peace, who knew her mother so well, suspected the doubt behind her soft-spoken reassurances.

Peace couldn't tell what Kirk thought. The smile he directed to Flannery seemed tender, almost adoring.

He said, "No one could think you're capable of leaving a man in the road to die."

Voices seemed to erupt as everyone chimed in to assure Flannery that he was right.

Caroline interrupted the chorus. "What should we do about the dinner reservations?"

Ben looked at his watch. "We should go. Now."

Caroline looked around the room. "Since we're missing a car, how do we get there? Piper Tavern is too far to walk."

Silence.

Kirk looked embarrassed. "My van has a drum set and a couple of amplifiers in the back. Otherwise, I'd …" He scrunched his face and let his voice trail.

"Please," Karalee said. "Don't worry about it. We'll cancel the reservations. There must be a restaurant we can walk to." She looked at Peace. "Right?"

"The Freight House is across the street."

"Perfect." Karalee smiled at Kirk. "You're welcome too, of course."

"That's nice, but no thanks."

Caroline said, "I think I'll beg off too. I have to get back to the city."

Peace said, "If you don't mind, I'll stay here and see Mom off."

After what seemed endless discussion, the family accepted the fact that Peace and Caroline weren't going with them. They cancelled their reservation and trooped across the street to the Freight House.

# # #

After they left, Peace, Caroline, and Kirk found themselves alone in a house that suddenly seemed much larger and blissfully, though ominously, quiet.

Kirk looked at Caroline. "What do you think?"

She hunched her shoulders. "As I said, 'the truth will out.'"

He looked surprised. "You don't really think Flan would lie about something that serious, do you?"

"I hope not," was her noncommittal reply.

He looked at Peace. "How about you?"

"I hope not too." She declined to express her opinion that it seemed like exactly the kind of thing Flannery would do. She had yet to see anything to indicate that her cousin was used to having to face consequences. If anything, she was the prototype for a damsel in distress and was accustomed to being rescued.

# # #

After her mother took the train into Philly, Peace had time to reflect on the complications that accompanied having an extended family. She had been adopted as an infant and raised by a single woman, a woman of uncompromising integrity who expected no less of her daughter. She marveled at the way everyone seemed more intent on making sure that Flannery wasn't upset than on the tragedy that had occurred.

She reflected on the day's events, evidence that the seeming bad luck of having been abandoned as an infant had given her a far different life than she would have known with the people whose DNA she shared.

Henry padded over with his leash in his mouth, interrupting her reverie.

She rubbed his silky ears and snapped the leash to his collar. "You win, boy. There are things that have to be taken care of, no matter what else is going on."

Walking him in the crisp night air, she thought about how little she resembled either her adoptive or biological mother. She might have a choice which family she would take her values from, but as to her physical appearance, she was undeniably the child of her father, a man she'd known only a few weeks before he met a violent death. She relived her devastation when she learned he was a petty crook, who thought more of his own skin than the wellbeing of his fellow man.

MONDAY

Twelve

Rachel stared through the windshield, her fingers frozen on the latch to the seatbelt. A drizzle that threatened to become a downpour left tear-like trails on the glass. She turned her head to the right and focused on the only spot of color in a world that this morning was dull gray: a red door leading into a white two-story house. She turned to her mother. "I can't go in there."

"I know it's hard, honey, but we have to." Lisa Woodard touched Rachel's cheek, then gently pried her fingers from the latch and clicked it open. She guided the seatbelt away from her daughter's body as gently as she had when Rachel was a small child. "We don't have to stay long."

Rachel avoided her mother's eyes. "I don't know what to say."

"Everyone feels that way. It doesn't matter what you say. No one will remember anyway. It only matters that you're there."

Her eyes burned, but no tears fell. Her legs felt like tree trunks, rooted. Getting out of the car seemed an impossibility. "I have to tell them."

Lisa was quick to respond. "What good would it do?"

She still doesn't understand. Rachel didn't set her straight. Instead, she said, "Why did the paper say we were engaged?"

"His parents probably told them you were. Maybe it makes them feel better to think of him having a future."

"But it's a lie."

"A lie that can't hurt anyone now. I think the less we say about that, the better. Mostly, our job is to listen. Let them believe whatever helps them through this."

The less we say, the better. The words resonated in Rachel's head. *There's nothing I can do now anyway. Maybe no one will ever know.* She forced her body to move, her muscles to propel her out of the car, her legs to carry her toward the door. She saw the curtains part. A face appeared in the opening. Seconds later, the door jerked open, revealing the short, softly-rounded figure of Bella Rosino, with her husband, Angelo, looking over her shoulder. Bella stepped out and enfolded Rachel in an embrace that felt more desperate than affectionate. Angelo wrapped his arms around both of them and guided them into the house. Rachel heard her mother's footsteps behind her and wished she could escape into those more familiar arms.

Inside, Rachel and Lisa Woodard faced Bella and Angelo Rosino. After an awkward few minutes, Rachel heard her mother say, "I'm so sorry." She managed to echo the words in her own halting voice. She felt tears on her cheeks. Surprised, she reached up to touch them. How could she be crying when she felt nothing? She focused on her surroundings, trying to orient herself.

Random, irrelevant memories washed over her:

The day Bella had shown her a sample of the bright, floral wallpaper she'd chosen for the foyer. At the time, Rachel had thought it cheerful. Now the curling vines snaking their way to the ceiling made her dizzy.

The afternoon she and Tony had rescued a tiny bedraggled kitten from the restaurant parking lot. This morning a fully-grown, overfed orange tabby rubbed against her ankles, begging to lifted into her arms.

The way music—loud, passionate music—always filled the house. This morning the stillness was broken only by low voices and stifled sobs.

The aroma of food offered by a family who poured their souls into its preparation. This morning, the fragrance of freshly-baked bread enveloped her. She was startled to realize that this was not a memory, but real. *Bella would cook no matter what.*

Something poked at her arm. She looked down and realized it was the corner of a tissue box that Bella was thrusting toward her. She took a tissue and dabbed her eyes.

Bella extended her arm toward the living room.

Angelo said, "I'll get coffee."

Bella fussed with pillows on the sofa and gestured for Rachel and Lisa to sit. When they were settled and Angelo had returned with tiny cups redolent with the aroma of strong coffee, she held up one finger. "I'll be right back," she said and went to the stairs.

Angelo sat facing Rachel and her mother, sipping the aromatic brew, making no attempt to check the tears sliding down his cheeks.

Lisa said again, "I'm so sorry," squeezing Rachel's hand as she spoke.

Rachel knew it was a cue. She tried to say something, but burst into tears.

Angelo nodded at her. "I know," he said. "You don't have to say it." His eyes narrowed and his expression hardened. "The police will find the monster who did this. If they don't, I will. It will be my life's work!" He looked at Rachel as though for reassurance.

Before she could respond, Bella came back into the room. "For you," she said, and thrust a small square box into Rachel's hand. She visibly fought tears as she added, "Tony was going to give it to you for Christmas."

Not knowing how to avoid it, Rachel opened the box with shaking fingers. It contained, as she feared, a ring. The tiny diamond sparkled. She looked from her mother to Bella, unable to speak.

Bella said, "It was my mother's. From Italy. She gave it to me to keep for Tony." She broke down when she pronounced her son's name.

Rachel reached out her hand, holding the box toward Bella. "I can't ... take this."

Bella was crying too hard to answer.

Angelo said, "It was always meant for you. Since fifth grade. Our Tony knew you were the one."

Rachel looked at her mother, pleading with her eyes.

Lisa took the box from her daughter's hand and placed it on the coffee table. She looked at the velvet-covered cube for a moment, seemed about to comment on it, then changed the subject. "Do the police know who was driving the car?"

Angelo said, "No, but they found the car. In the parking lot by the swimming pool."

Lisa said, "You mean Fanny Chapman? Right here in town?"

Angelo nodded.

Rachel asked, "What about fingerprints?" She held her breath.

"No fingerprints. Not on the steering wheel. Not on the outside of the car. Not anywhere. None." As he spoke, he thrust a finger in the air, adding emphasis to each word.

When Rachel expelled the breath, it came out as a gasp. She knew they all thought she was going to cry again. How could they know she felt she'd been granted a reprieve?

Angelo rose from the recliner and came to stand directly in front of them. "You know what that means? Whoever did this didn't just panic and run away. They understood the evil they had done and tried to cover it up."

Rachel sat rigidly erect, silent as a stone, remembering her frantic scrubbing at the car with the yellow scarf.

Lisa said, "That is truly awful." She touched Angelo's arm. "I'm sure they'll find him, though. Something will turn up and it will lead them to the right person."

Bella came to stand by her husband. "If they don't, we will. The person who killed my son will pay." She looked at Rachel. "You'll help us, won't you?"

"What can I do?"

"Someone knows something. You must ask all the young people. You know them. They'll tell you things they would not tell the police."

Rachel shrank back into the soft cushions, shaking her head.

In the silence that followed, her mother said, "This is overwhelming for her. I'm going to take her home." Lisa looked at Bella and Angelo. "I hope you understand."

They nodded and did not object. Even in their grief, their concern for Rachel was evident.

Bella said, "Come back tomorrow. We'll talk."

Lisa rose from the sofa and pulled Rachel to her feet. "We'll call. Later today or in the morning."

Bella focused on Rachel, "Tomorrow we have to go to the church and the funeral home. We'd like you to come too. Tony would want you to help make the arrangements."

Rachel began to sob.

Lisa guided her toward the door.

Bella and Angelo followed. Bella pressed the small box into Rachel's hand. "Take this."

"I can't ."

Bella stepped away and put both hands behind her back, shaking her head. "It's what our Tony wanted."

Lisa said, "We'll talk about it another time. Right now ..." She let her voice trail.

Bella said, "We need a plan to find the monster who did this." She looked at Rachel. Her voice softened. "In a way, you are the person who lost the most. You were Tony's life. His future. And we know that he was yours."

Rachel was shaking so hard she couldn't speak.

Her mother said, "I need to get her home."

In the car, Rachel put the box on the dashboard. When they backed out of the drive and turned onto the street, it slid to the floor and rested at her feet. She moved them as far away from it as she could.

Her mother looked at her oddly. "Pick it up. We'll find a way to deal with it, but you can't just leave it there."

"I should have told them."

"Maybe. It wouldn't help them, but it might help you. We'll talk about it later with Daddy. In the meantime, let yourself grieve, but don't punish yourself. What you did was normal. If this hadn't happened, Tony would have gotten over it."

"But it did happen."

"And you're blaming yourself. I know how you feel."

No, you don't. You don't know anything!

Thirteen

Peace crept out of the bedroom and closed the door gently, not wanting to wake Flannery, whom she suspected had not fallen asleep until shortly before dawn. She retrieved the newspaper from the porch and headed for the kitchen to start the coffee. The hazelnut blend smelled so good she decided to forego her usual tea this morning and made enough coffee for both of them. She spread the paper on the table while she waited and was not surprised that news of the hit and run accident took up most of the front page.

Cyclist hit by a car and left to die screamed the headline. The face under the words looked vaguely familiar. It took her a minute to recognize the young man she'd seen leaving the train station on Saturday. Shocked, she got up and went to look out the window. She didn't know him, of course, but the feeling of connection wouldn't go away, the horror of knowing it was her car that had cut short his life. She remembered the expression on his face as he bent to kiss the girl by his side. She went back to the table, sat down and studied the photo, not a snapshot, but a formal picture. So young. Scarcely more than a boy. *Looks a school picture.* Dark hair was swept straight back from a high forehead, like unruly curls that had been brushed into submission for the photograph. Beautiful eyes. Dark and full of laughter. A prominent, square chin thrust slightly forward. Good looking. Peace scanned the article.

Yes, his senior picture. He graduated from high school last spring. The coffee pot stopped gurgling, signaling that the coffee was ready. She got up, poured herself a cup, spooned in some sugar, and returned to the paper.

Anthony (Tony) Joseph Rosino was struck by a vehicle while riding his bicycle on Saw Mill Road and left to die by the side of the road yesterday. Tony, a lifelong resident of Doylestown, graduated from Central Bucks West High School last spring. He was vice-president of his class and a running back on West's football team. A talented athlete, many were surprised when he turned down a football scholarship and chose to work in his parents' restaurant, Rosino's, on North Main Street. He's been a familiar figure to patrons of the restaurant since he began serving as an unofficial greeter at age ten. More recently, Tony had been honing his skill as a chef. "Tony loved to cook. He loved everything about the restaurant," his mother, Bella Rosino, said. "Everything. From going to the market in Philadelphia with his father, to ..."

A separate item near the bottom of the page caught Peace's attention. Her own face. Looking as though she hadn't a care in the world. *Wonder how they got that.* Looking closer, she realized it was a picture the museum had used in one of their advertising campaigns. She focused on the verbiage under the picture, identifying her as the owner of the car that had killed the young man. The disconnect between her smiling face and the grim reality of the words made the incident doubly shocking. Sounds of life from the bedroom distracted her. She put the paper aside, turning it over so that the front page story wasn't the first thing Flannery saw when she came in.

"Morning." Flannery padded into the kitchen on bare feet, wearing an over-sized University of Virginia tee shirt. Her chestnut hair fell over one shoulder in soft, glossy waves, beautiful even in its disheveled state.

Peace's first thought was *I'm glad Kirk isn't here to see her.* Her second was a guilty *Where did that come from?*

Flannery said, "Thought I smelled coffee." She looked at the mug in Peace's hand. "Where do you keep those?"

Peace pointed to the open shelving above the sink.

Flannery selected an extra large mug and filled it with coffee, then looked around. "Cream?"

"There's milk in the fridge," Peace said. "It's two percent." She watched her cousin pour milk into the coffee and take a tasting sip. She thought she detected a slight curl to her lip and added, "I'll pick up some half and half later." She pushed the sugar bowl across the table.

Flannery shook her head and pointed to the paper. "Any news of the accident?"

Peace turned the paper so that the headline was clearly visible.

Flannery winced and dropped heavily into a chair. "Have they caught the person who did it yet?"

"I don't think so. I just started reading. I'm pretty sure they'd mention that first thing if they had."

Flannery nodded her agreement.

Looking closer, Peace saw the smudged darkness under her eyes and felt a reluctant sympathy.

"You mind?" Flannery asked, reaching for the paper.

Peace pushed the front section across the table.

Flannery read silently, finally looked up. "Did you see this?" Her finger was poised above a paragraph half-way down the page.

"I didn't get that far. What's it say?"

"Apparently he wasn't dead when they found him. He died in the ambulance. He was semi-conscious. Kept saying a name over and over. Rachel." She seemed to be waiting for Peace to say something. "Maybe that's who ran him down."

"Maybe," Peace mumbled, remembering the young woman she'd seen him with on Saturday night, the love that had been evident even to a casual observer and thought it more likely he was thinking of her. She didn't say this to Flannery. *Why argue? The truth will come out eventually.* She was more than half convinced that Flannery had lied about the car and wondered how the family would feel when they learned the truth about their darling. She recalled the look that had passed between their grandparents. *If they don't already know.* She remembered the mixed feelings she'd had about this visit from her new-found family, thought it was too bad that, just when things seemed to be going well, this had to happen.

Flannery's voice intruded, "It says here Rachel was his fiancée."

Peace looked at the photo. "He looks a little young to be engaged."

Flannery shrugged. "My parents got married while Mom was still in college." She glanced into the living room, to where the framed Christening dress hung. "Both of us were born when our mothers were only nineteen." When Peace didn't answer, she said, "Sorry. Maybe you don't like to talk about that."

"It's okay," Peace said. After a minute, she added, "It's a little weird for me to have someone refer to Holly as my mother. I don't think of her like that."

"Does it bother you? I mean ... seeing all of us?"

"No. My mother ... when I say that I mean Caroline Morrow ... gave me a wonderful childhood."

"But didn't you ever wonder? About ... you know."

"No," Peace pronounced the word firmly, vowing she would never tell this pampered darling about the fantasies she had invented to explain her abandonment. It was true that Caroline Morrow had given her a childhood as close to perfect as possible. Still, yes, she had wondered. She looked at the beautiful girl sitting across the table from her, thinking, *Does she ever wonder about anything? Has anything bad had ever happened to her before?* Looking at Flannery, it was easy to believe nothing had. *Did she really leave a human being to die on the side of the road?* It seemed entirely possible to Peace that she had. Almost as bad, the family seemed more interested in protecting their darling than in discovering the truth.

Fourteen

Paul Woodard kissed his wife's forehead. "You're sure you don't mind my going in?"

"No," she said. "This meeting is important. I understand that."

"Nothing's more important than our daughter. If you think ..."

"I'll be with her," Lisa said. "It might be better for us to have some one-on-one time. Don't worry. We'll be fine." She pointed to the antique railway station clock mounted on the wall. "Better get going."

Paul was a vice-president of one of the large pharmaceutical firms in New Jersey, a forty-five minute commute and was in the habit of leaving by six thirty to avoid the heaviest traffic. He picked up his briefcase but didn't move toward the door. He stood before his wife, shifting his weight from one foot to the other, the movement causing the case to swing ever so slightly. "You're sure?"

"I'm sure." She put her hand on his arm and walked with him to the door leading to the garage. "Scoot. Or you'll spend an extra half hour in traffic." He nodded and gave her another kiss on the forehead, then pulled her close and pressed his cheek against the top of her head.

They remained like that for a few seconds before Lisa pulled away and opened the door leading to the garage. "I'll call if anything comes up."

She watched the car leave the driveway. Only when it was no longer in sight did she allow her shoulders to slump. She leaned against the doorway for a moment and bit her lip, determined not to cry. She'd watched Tony grow up and felt his death as a physical pain, but this was not the time to indulge her grief. Her daughter needed her to be strong. She looked toward the ceiling. Rachel's room was just above. No sound came from there. She hoped that meant Rachel was sleeping, but doubted it. She thought about going to her, decided to wait. She poured another cup of coffee and reached for the paper. She read the article about the accident again. She and Paul had read it together earlier. She put the paper in the recycle bin, retrieved it a few seconds later, and placed it on the table. It was no use trying to shield her child. This was a reality she had to face sooner or later.

She waited until nine to call her office. Lisa worked in the District Attorney's office and she knew they would be investigating the accident. She briefly considered going in for a short time in the hope she would pick up information not released to the public, but decided such knowledge could wait. She was needed here today. Any information she might learn would not affect Rachel. The only thing important to her was that Tony was dead and she was blaming herself. Knowing the name of the person who had driven the car was irrelevant. Her job as a mother was to convince her daughter that she had no reason to feel guilty.

Eschewing the main office line, Lisa punched in the numbers taking her directly to Sally, a fifty-something matron who had worked in the office for most of her adult life and who was the first to know everything about anything that went on—both the facts and the rumors that surrounded any criminal investigation.

"Hi," Sally said before Lisa could identify herself. "I figured you'd be calling. Such a shock about Tony. A real tragedy. How's Rachel taking it?"

"Not good. I'm not going to be able to come in today."

"Nobody expects you to."

"Thanks." Lisa hesitated, then asked, "Anything that hasn't made it to the papers? Any leads as to the driver?"

"Not yet," Sally said. She lowered her voice. "Looks like it's not really a hit and run."

"Really?"

"Yeah. There's bruising on the body that doesn't match up with him being struck while riding a bicycle. Besides, the bike is intact. No damage at all."

"So ... what do they think that means?"

"Not sure yet. But indications are there was malice involved."

"That doesn't make sense. Tony didn't have any enemies."

"Well, something happened out there. There's more to this than meets the eye. More than a careless driver panicking and driving away. At least that's how it looks at this point."

Lisa couldn't help wondering how this would affect Rachel. She said, "That puts things in a different light, doesn't it? Guess there'll be an autopsy."

"Yes."

"Do me a favor. Give me a call if anything else comes up today. I'll be in tomorrow."

"Take your time," Sally said. "You've got personal days coming. May as well use them. Everyone knows Tony was practically part of your family."

Lisa didn't tell Sally that Rachel had broken up with Tony the night before the accident. If it *was* an accident. She just said, "Thanks, but I plan be there tomorrow. I'll let you know if I change my mind."

"Okay. Give Rachel a hug from me."

"I will."

She hung up, thinking about Sally's statement that there was doubt about whether it was really an accident. Could that be true? Had someone deliberately run down Tony, the town hero? She sipped her coffee, pondering this, and wondering if she should have mentioned the breakup to Sally. No, she told herself, that's up to Rachel. If it comes up, Bella and Angelo should hear it from directly from her. She felt sure that, to them, it would be like salt to a wound. They would know their son must have been unhappy at the time of his death and that would deepen their pain. But what about *her* child's pain. She suspected part of Rachel's anguish was the feeling she was an imposter by not telling everyone she and Tony were no longer a couple when he died. *What difference does it make now? Why do anything that might make a bad situation worse?*

These tangled thoughts were interrupted by the musical tones of Rachel's phone. It was not the cheerful tone she was used to hearing–something different. Harsher. *She changed her ring. Not surprising. My little girl is growing up. College does that.* While these thoughts were running through her head, Rachel strolled into the kitchen, still in her pajamas and with her thick, chestnut-colored hair falling into her face. "Morning, baby," Lisa said.

"Morning," Rachel said. She tucked her hair behind her ears and held up her phone. "Darren just called. He's devastated."

"Of course. He and Tony were like brothers."

Rachel nodded. "He doesn't know we broke up either." She looked away and, after a few seconds, added, "I thought he might. He's the first one Tony would tell."

"Honey, I don't–"

Rachel interrupted. "I'm beginning to think you're right. There's no reason to tell anyone now. Let them believe whatever makes them happy." She laid the phone on the counter, went to the refrigerator and brought out a dish of left-over macaroni and cheese.

"Not the best breakfast in the world," Lisa said mildly.

"Not the worst either."

Lisa watched Rachel put the dish in the microwave, thinking she seemed calmer. She looked better, too. In fact, except for the dark smudges under her eyes, she looked remarkably well.

The microwave buzzer sounded and Rachel removed the dish and grabbed a fork. She took a couple of bites, then looked at her mother as though seeing her for the first time. "How come you're home?" she asked. "Aren't you supposed to be at work?"

"I called in. I didn't want to leave you alone all day." She slid the newspaper across the table toward Rachel. Tony's picture and the oversized headlines were impossible to miss.

Rachel glanced at it, shuddered, and looked away. "You didn't have to call in. I'll be okay." She pushed noodles around with her fork and finally asked, "Is your office going to investigate the accident?"

"Of course. Hit and run is a serious crime."

"I know." Rachel turned her head so Lisa couldn't see her face, but her voice quavered, hinting at suppressed tears.

Tears or not, Lisa thought she better tell her what Sally had said. "Very serious. And this looks like it might be even worse."

Rachel set the bowl on the counter. "How can it be worse?"

"When I called in this morning, I talked to Sally ..." She paused and put her hand on Rachel's. "You realize this is confidential. You can't tell anyone. Not Darren. Not anyone."

"Yeah, yeah. I know. What'd she say?"

"The bike wasn't damaged. It couldn't have been struck by a vehicle. Plus, there were bruises on Tony's body that are inconsistent with that type of accident."

Rachel stared at her, wide-eyed, chewing on her thumbnail. "What does it mean?"

"I don't know. That's the investigator's job. To find out what happened."

Lisa reached for her arm, but Rachel turned and bolted for the stairs.

After numerous unsuccessful efforts to get Rachel to open up, Lisa decided she may as well take advantage of an unexpected day off and get a couple of errands out of the way. She grabbed her keys off a hook by the door and yelled up the stairs, "I'm going out for a while. You know how to reach me if you need me."

Rachel's voice floated, ghost-like, down the stairs. "Yeah."

# # #

Alone, Rachel roamed the house, wondering if they would find anything to link the car to her. The phone rang. Before she picked up, she looked at caller I.D. When she saw Angelo Rosino's name, she covered her mouth with her hand and let it ring, not daring to speak with him.

The shrill tones seemed to go on forever before the machine kicked in. After the beep, Angelo said, "This message is for Rachel. We cannot go to the church and the funeral home today. We're not sure when we can. They're not releasing Tony's body." His voice cracked on the word *body*. He hesitated and added, "God bless you, little daughter. Mama and I are thinking of you."

She glared at the instrument. *I am not your daughter.*

Fifteen

Peace refused to look at the clock, but she couldn't control her thoughts. *Move hands. Move! Point straight up.* When the clock reached that magic position, Snap-snap would appear and she—Peace Morrow, who'd never in her twenty-two years, had any family except her mother—would experience an event all her friends took for granted—lunch with a grandparent.

The rest of the family had taken the train into Philadelphia to visit the historic sights, but her grandmother had stayed behind, saying the trip and all the excitement had worn her out and she wanted nothing more than a day to herself.

"Oh?" Ben had looked surprised and a little concerned.

Karalee was quick to reassure him. "Okay, I really want to stay behind and have lunch with my granddaughter." She stretched her diminutive form and planted a kiss on his chin. "Sorry, but you're not invited. You'll have to schedule your own date. I've waited forever for this opportunity and I don't intend to share our lovely girl."

He'd laughed and stroked her cheek before he looked at Peace. "I'll wait my turn, but I insist on equal time."

Peace had thrilled to the love and acceptance their words indicated they felt for her. She had been afraid to meet these people and they were making it easy. At least the grandparents were. She'd been hoping for time alone with her grandmother ever since she'd received the letter. *Snap-snap.* Peace smiled to herself whenever she thought of that name. She still had reservations about her cousin. Try as she would, she couldn't help wishing that Flannery had stayed home in Virginia. She forced a smile, determined not to think of the cloud hanging over them.

The visit was going so well except for the accident. She wondered if she dared ask Snap-snap if she believed Flannery was capable of lying about the episode. When it was as simple as the car being stolen, Peace had been sure that Flannery was lying, but hit and run was the equivalent of murder. Surely, even someone as spoiled as Flan would not leave another human being by the side of the road to die.

Her thoughts were interrupted by a gentle tapping on the doorframe of the office where she was working. She looked up to see her grandmother's face.

"They told me to come on up." Karalee looked at the assortment of small, oddly-shaped implements spread on the desk in front of Peace. "Am I too early? Are you in the middle of something?"

"No." Peace laughed and admitted she'd been forcing herself to keep her eyes on her work, to not look at the clock. "To make the time go faster," she explained. "Mom always says, 'Watched clocks are like watched pots. If you want to hurry them along, ignore them.'"

"A good trick. I'll have to remember it."

The words were spoken with a smile, but Peace thought she noticed a suppressed frown when the other woman heard the words "my mother". She knew the Francis family would always think of her as Holly's daughter, whereas, in her own mind, there was no question that she was the daughter of Caroline Morrow, the woman who had loved her unconditionally her whole life. Hoping to bridge the fissure, she said, "I hope you're going to tell me how you came to be called Snap-snap.

"I'll tell you all about it while we're having lunch. Until then ..." She put her fingers to her lips and made a zipping motion.

Peace wrapped each of the items on the desk in a soft cloth, then carefully placed them in a flat, rectangular box.

"Ready?" her grandmother asked.

"Yes."

Peace shivered a little when they stepped outside. The temperature had dropped since she'd left home that morning. She looked at the sky; it was overcast, but no rain was falling. "The Michener Museum's just across the street," she said.

"How convenient to have the two museums so close," Karalee said. She pointed to a nearby building, one that had a long, covered walkway leading to it. "Is that another museum or part of this one?"

"That's not a museum. It's our library," Peace said.

"How nice for you. Everything's right here together. An easy walk from your apartment."

Peace nodded. "That's part of the reason I chose it. Quakers were thinking *green* before it was a popular thing to do."

"Umm."

Peace noted the non-committal reply and thought again how different her life would have been if she had not been abandoned and discovered all those years ago by Caroline Morrow. She said, "Is it okay to just grab a bite in the museum cafe? It's tiny so we may not be able to find a seat, but we can give it a try. It's close and you asked about Bucks County's local artists. We'll have more time to spend in the museum if we eat here instead of walking uptown to a restaurant and then having to come back."

"Perfect." Snap-snap pulled her scarf tighter around her neck and put her hand through Peace's arm. "I like the way you think."

They took the brick path past the carriage shed and crossed the street to the other museum.

Peace almost purred with pleasure as she opened the door and allowed her grandmother to enter ahead of her. "I have the afternoon off, so we'll have plenty of time to look at the exhibits after we eat."

"Wonderful."

The cafe consisted of seven small tables, each of which could seat just two people. The tables were jammed together, making private conversation impossible. The simple menu was printed on a board above the cash register.

Peace suddenly felt embarrassed, protective of what her town had to offer. "Not much choice," she said.

Gracious as always, Karalee tilted her well-coifed head and smiled. "Makes choosing easier."

Peace didn't know if she meant it or if it was part of her southern manners. She glanced at the older woman, trying to decide. She certainly looked sincere. Did it really matter? The important thing was that she had a grandmother, and that they were having lunch together.

Once they were seated and had ordered, Peace said, "Okay, I can't wait any longer. Tell me about Snap-snap."

Karalee, obviously a born storyteller who knew how to engage her audience, took a slow sip of herbal tea and set the cup down before she answered, "Well, as you know, Flannery is our first grandchild ... except you, of course. When she was little, just learning to talk, I was reading a story to her. It was about a little deer who lived in the forest. Whenever he stepped on a twig on the path, it would make a noise ... snap-snap. When I read that part, I'd make a twisting motion with my arm,"–she paused to demonstrate–"and say very dramatically, 'snap-snap'. Flannery would laugh uproariously and it wasn't long before she began saying 'snap-snap' every time she saw me and she began to ask for me by that name." She took another sip of tea. "Well, it just stuck. Now, all of my grandchildren ..." She looked at Peace ... "including you, call me Snap-snap." Her face became serious as she reached to touch Peace's arm. "I'm so glad you do. You can't imagine how thrilled your grandfather and I are to finally get to know you and to have you accept us."

A lump in Peace's throat prevented her from answering.

Karalee went on, "We were afraid you wouldn't. That you would hold it against us. Your being left like that, I mean." She paused again. "You don't mind talking about it, do you?"

Still unable to speak, Peace shook her head and took a moment to compose herself. "Flannery asked me that too. I had a wonderful childhood. I can't imagine any other life."

Karalee looked away for a moment, biting her lower lip. When she looked back at Peace, her eyes were filled with unshed tears. She reached across the table for her granddaughter's hand. "I'm glad," she said. She dabbed at her eyes with a napkin and added, "Relieved really. It was such a worry, wondering what happened after that awful man ..."

Peace jerked her hand free. "Don't call him that. He wasn't awful ... he just ..." She stopped, not knowing how she could justify the actions of the man she thought of as Jack, the man she knew was the father she had always longed for. Finally, she said, "Well, I don't really know what he was, but he was my father and ..." She stopped, suddenly aware of the people at the table next to them. An elderly couple was sitting there, quiet, their eyes averted, obviously embarrassed by the personal turn the conversation had taken. She smiled at Snap-snap and said, "We should go. People are waiting for this table."

"Of course," Snap-snap gathered her things and stood, surveying the area. Her eyes lit up when she spotted the adjacent gift shop. "Do I have time for a quick look-see?" A short laugh, then, "I guess Flannery comes by her shopping gene honestly."

Having missed out on the shopping gene, Peace watched her grandmother examine the colorful scarves and handmade jewelry and finally select a packet of note cards illustrated with one of the Peaceable Kingdom paintings of Edward Hicks, possibly the county's best known artist.

"I'll pay for this and then you can tell me all about your Bucks County painters."

Peace started to say *okay*, but was struck by a better idea. Better to her, that is. She was unsure how Snap-snap would feel about it. "Can we save that for another time?" she asked. "I'd like to show you the shed where I was found." She lifted her chin and looked the other woman in the eye.

Karalee's eyes, usually so merry, were dark pools in her face, unreadable; her lips were a tight, straight line.

Knowing this was a bridge that had to be crossed, Peace resisted the temptation to relent. "It's part of my history," she said. "I'm not ashamed of it. My mother taught me to be proud of who I am. All of who I am." The words came slowly at first, but gained momentum, and finally, spilled out in a breathless rush of emotion. "She made me feel that I'm special because I have a special history. When I was growing up, every year we visited the shed on my birthday and she told me the story of how she'd found me. She said someone had obviously loved me and she reminded me of the beautiful clothing I was wearing." Peace paused and smiled at her grandmother. "I know now I have you to thank for that."

Karalee nodded, but did not speak."

Peace went on: "Mom said whoever left me there must have needed to save me from something—just like the baby Moses—so they put me in a basket for her to find."

A small gasp escaped from Karalee.

Peace pretended not to notice and led the way to the exit.

A slow, steady rain had begun to fall in the short time they had been in the gift shop.

Peace looked toward the shed, then at her grandmother. She lifted her arm toward the weeping sky. "Maybe the universe is sending us a sign."

Karalee nodded and looked relieved. "You can show me tomorrow. I think it's supposed to clear up overnight."

Together, they ran across the grass and returned to the Mercer Museum. When they reached it, Karalee said, "Tomorrow will be better anyway. Poppy can be with us." She gave Peace a long, serious look. "I do want to hear your story. And so does he." She touched her fingertips to the corners of her eyes as though trying to keep tears at bay and, after a minute, said, "You really are a remarkable young woman. I feel very lucky that you've come into our lives."

"Thank you." Peace just managed to get the words past the lump in her throat.

TUESDAY

Sixteen

Rachel watched as her mother prepared to leave for work. "Don't worry, Mom. "I'm fine."

"You're sure? I can call in again. Everyone will understand. In fact, they'll probably be surprised to see me." When Rachel didn't respond, Lisa crossed the room and looked into her daughter's eyes. "You don't look fine. I shouldn't have told you about the investigation. Not now, when you're just starting to get used to ..." She hesitated and spread her hands wide. "Everything."

"It's kind of shocking, that's all. What if they decide he was murdered?"

Lisa shook her head. "It doesn't seem possible. Who would want to kill Tony?"

They looked at each other, neither knowing what to say.

Lisa recovered first. "If I'm going, I better get started." She paused with her hand on the doorknob. "Promise me you won't sit around and brood all day. Call someone. Maybe go out for lunch?" She took a step back, smiling. "Want to meet me for lunch? I'll treat you to—"

"Thanks, but no." Rachel saw her mother's brow wrinkle and added, "I'm not going to brood. Just do some serious thinking."

"Not too serious. Why don't you watch a movie? Something silly."

"Maybe I will."

Lisa looked doubtful, but she turned to go. With her hand on the doorknob, she said, "Honey, you did nothing wrong by breaking up with Tony. This is not your fault."

She forced herself to meet her mother's eyes. "I know."

Unable to sit still, Rachel roamed the house, going from room to room, touching each piece of furniture as she passed it. She sighed as she let her fingers skim the surface of the trestle table, so prized by her parents, remembering her disappointment when they'd bought it. She'd hoped they'd choose something modern, something that would bring the house into the twenty-first century. *Something hip for a change.*

She longed to be hip. To step outside the safe, traditional box her parents had created for her. *Stop it*, she told herself. *You tried that and look how it turned out.* Still, she wasn't ready to give up. She told herself, if she kept her head, it still might be okay. She couldn't bring Tony back, but maybe this didn't have to ruin her life. People tell lies and get away with it all the time. She knew from stories her mother told that some crimes are never solved. She made up her mind to *go with the flow*, as B.R. would say, and play the role everyone expected of her.

That determination made, she headed for the living room and the cabinet housing her parents' extensive collection of DVDs. *Something silly. Like Mom said.* That wouldn't be hard. Paul and Lisa Woodard both favored comedies. She examined the spines of the plastic cases. Lots of Woody Allen. Rachel rejected those. Funny they might be, but they provoked thought, the very thing she needed to escape. She wanted silliness, plain and undiluted. She was sitting on the floor in front of the cabinet when the doorbell rang. She leaned back so she could see through the window to the front porch.

Two figures stood by the door. Darren and Amanda.

Rachel's first reaction was relief. Despite what she'd told her mother and tried telling herself, she was finding it hard to be alone. When she opened the door and got a close look at Darren's face, the relief she'd felt evaporated. The pain in his eyes brought tears to her own. She looked away from him—to Amanda, the little sister of the group. Amanda wore her grief differently than her brother. Her eyes were more angry than sad.

Rachel resisted the urge to flee from all that raw emotion. "Come in," she said and stepped aside to make way for them.

For a few seconds that seemed like hours, the three of them stood looking from one to the other.

Darren broke the silence. "Oh, Rach," was all he could get out before his voice cracked. He held out his hand, presenting to her a single, perfect rosebud. "How can we stand it?"

She shook her head and bit her lip. "I guess we don't have a choice." Unable to look at Darren, she closed her eyes, brought the rose to her face and let its velvety petals caress her cheek. After a moment, she forced herself to open her eyes. "Thanks."

He attempted a smile. "Think of it as from Tony."

Not knowing what to say, Rachel nodded.

Amanda brushed past them, marched into the living room and plopped down on the sofa.

Rachel and Darren followed.

Darren said, "We went to see Tony's parents this morning."

Amanda said, "We gave them a rose too." She leaned forward, her hands resting on her knees, and stared directly into Rachel's face. "They said they called you and left a message, but you didn't call back." The words were simple, but fiercely spoken.

"I haven't had a chance yet." Rachel hated that she felt the need to defend herself to a fourteen-year-old. "Mom and I went to see them yesterday."

"Yeah, they told us." Darren said. He remained standing, shifting his weight from one foot to the other. "Tony was planning to propose to you on Christmas Eve," he said. "He even had a ring." He moved closer to Rachel. "His parents and I were the only ones he told." He searched her face. "Maybe you guessed?"

"I didn't exactly guess," Rachel said, "but I wouldn't have been surprised."

"Did you know he was going to give you his grandmother's ring?"

"No, I didn't know that. Not before ..." She stopped, debating whether she should tell them, decided they'd find out anyway. "I have the ring. His mom gave it to me yesterday."

Amanda popped up from the sofa, grabbed Rachel's left hand and looked at it. "Why aren't you wearing it?"

Silence.

Rachel pulled her hand free. "I don't know." When the quiet became oppressive, she added, "It doesn't seem right. Obviously, I can't marry him now. Wouldn't it be dishonest?"

"Not if you really loved him."

Darren broke in, "Amanda, stop! You're too young to understand."

Amanda kept her eyes on Rachel. "Where is it?"

"Upstairs. On my dresser."

"Can we see it?" Amanda asked.

Rachel nodded. "I'll get it." She went upstairs, glad for an excuse to get out of the room even for a few minutes. When she came back, she held the box containing the ring out toward Amanda, who, against all logic, seemed to be in charge.

Amanda accepted the box, opened it and let out a small whimper. She gently removed the ring and slipped it on her finger. Tears were flowing down her face.

Darren grabbed for his sister's hand, obviously appalled at her action.

Amanda turned away from him and thrust the ring-clad finger toward Rachel. "If you loved Tony, this would be on *your* finger."

"Stop it, Amanda! Everybody knows she loved Tony. They were a match made in Heaven."

"She never loved him as much as he loved her."

Darren grabbed Amanda's hand. "Take it off! You don't know anything about love."

"I know more than she does. "Amanda twisted away from him, but she took the ring off. She darted a poisonous look toward Rachel, held the ring between her fingers for a few seconds, then slipped it back into the box and handed it to Rachel. Her anger seemingly spent, she went back to the sofa and slumped into the cushions.

Darren put his arm around Rachel's shoulders. "I'm sorry," he said. He turned to his sister. "You owe her an apology too."

"I'm sorry," Amanda whispered.

"It's okay," Rachel said. "I know you're upset. We all are."

Amanda's mood suddenly changed, became almost businesslike. "Did you read this morning's paper?"

"No," Rachel said. "I read about the accident in yesterday's. Mom was still here when I got up and we were talking. I haven't seen today's."

Darren said, "Does your mom know if they have any idea who drove the car?"

"I don't think so. She wouldn't say anything even if she did. She never talks about work. Everything that goes on in that office is confidential."

Amanda said, "They found the car that ran him down. The person it belongs to works at the Mercer Museum. She loaned it to someone who was visiting and they said it was stolen from the shopping center parking lot. Everybody knows that's a crock."

Suddenly, it was too much for Rachel. She started to shake and sat down on the ottoman.

Amanda kept talking, her voice droning on, repeating the words from the newspaper as though she had memorized them.

Rachel covered her ears with her hands. Tears flowed, unchecked, down her cheeks.

"That's enough, Amanda!" Darren seemed almost as upset as Rachel.

Amanda stopped and went to stand before Rachel. "Crying won't help Tony. We have to do something."

Cowed by the fury in her voice, Rachel asked, "What can we do?"

"Go to the museum with me tomorrow." Amanda paced as she spoke, seemingly clarifying her plan with each step. "We'll find the person who owns the car and make her tell us what really happened."

"But the paper said she wasn't driving it. She probably doesn't know any more than we do."

"I don't believe that. I think she's helping her friend cover it up. If she loaned her car to this person, she must know them pretty well. She can make them confess."

Rachel shook her head. "We should leave this to the authorities."

"No!" Amanda was relentless. "We owe it to Tony to find his killer."

Finally, they left.

Rachel watched their departing figures for a moment before she went back to the living room. She picked up the rosebud from the ottoman, intending to put it in water, but it was already beginning to wilt.

Seventeen

Peace stood with her grandparents at the entrance to the carriage shed and pointed toward a dark corner in the back. "There," she said. "Behind the old hay wagon." Looking at the space through her grandparents' eyes, she found herself wishing the cobwebs had been swept away and the antique conveyances shined or at least dusted. She wondered if it had been cleaner when her father left her there.

There was a small gasp from Snap-snap. "He left you there? Alone? A tiny infant?"

Peace nodded.

"And you still defend him?"

"Karalee," Ben pronounced the name softly, but with a cautionary note that couldn't be missed.

Peace hated the pity she knew had prompted their responses and was determined to dispel it. "He wasn't a monster. I know you think he was, but ..." She paused a moment, then went on, careful to keep anger out of her voice, but refused to back down. "I don't know why he left me, but he must have had a reason. He was not an evil person. He wasn't perfect, but he wasn't all bad. I know that in my heart."

Karalee turned away from the shed to face Peace. She looked ready to argue, but didn't. After a moment, she said, "You do know that my daughter knew nothing of this?"

"She told me that."

"Well, it's true. He led her to believe he was taking you to a lovely home, to a couple who wanted a child but had been told they were too old to adopt. He assured her ... promised her ... they would cherish you and would give you a good life."

"Something must've happened." Peace raised her chin. "Anyway, Mom found me. And I *have* had a good life." She paused for a moment, then spoke again, telling her grandparents what she'd told herself so many times. "He must have known about the festival, that a lot of people would be around and someone would find me." Without giving Karalee time to argue, she added, "You've probably never heard that part of the story."

Karalee looked ready to say something, but Ben cut her off. "Just bits and pieces. We'd love to hear the whole story from you."

Peace flashed him a grateful smile. "Mom was at the folk fest, listening to someone play the dulcimer." She looked at both of them. "Did you know she plays the dulcimer?"

"No." Karalee whispered, still visibly upset.

"Well, she does. She's good. Anyway, a dog started barking in the shed. So loud he was drowning out the music. Mom heard a voice in the crowd say, 'Someone should do something' and she knew she was that someone. She went to comfort the dog and he led her to me." Peace continued to tell the story, unconsciously choosing the words Caroline had used through the years as she brushed Peace's hair each morning.

Karalee and Ben listened without interruption, their eyes taking in every corner of the dusty shed.

Peace said, "Mom says it was the best day of her life." She held her breath, waiting for a reaction.

For a long moment, there was none.

Finally, Karalee whispered, "It almost seems as though it were meant to be."

Peace let out a long, relieved breath. "I believe it was."

They stood quietly for a moment longer, each lost in private thoughts.

Ben glanced at his watch and broke the mood. "If we're going to Valley Forge today, we'd better get back."

Karalee said, "Do we still want to go? With everything that's happened, I'm not sure—"

He cut her off. "We're better off if we keep busy. Go about our lives. There's nothing we can do about the ... situation ... anyway." He looked at Peace. "We're not indifferent. You understand that, don't you?"

"Of course."

"Sure you won't come with us?"

"I wish I could, but I'm meeting Kirk. His band is playing for a holiday sing-along at the museum this weekend and I have to go over the set-up with him."

# # #

Peace stood back pretending to study the rows of chairs but really to look at Kirk who'd been unusually silent all afternoon. She couldn't read his face.

In an attempt to gain his attention, she moved a chair back a few inches. "What do you think?" she asked. "Should we move the first row back a little?

Like this? So you have more space to move around and interact with the crowd?"

"It's fine like it is." His answer was terse. His face remained closed.

"Okay, then. See you Friday." When he didn't respond, she turned to leave but changed her mind. This elephant wasn't going away. Best to confront it head on. She gathered her courage, something she'd never had to do before with Kirk. "Wanna talk about it?"

"About what?" His tone was flat, as devoid of expression as his face.

"Whatever it is that's bothering you."

He shrugged and looked away.

Peace grabbed his sleeve. "Come on. We're friends. I thought you were my best friend. Now, all of the sudden, you won't even look at me. I'm going through a crisis and you act like–"

"*You're* going through a crisis! How do you think your cousin feels?"

She stared at him, open-mouthed, before she responded. "So, that's it. This is all about Flannery."

"Yes, it *is* about Flannery. She thinks you believe she ran over that guy and left him there to die. How would you feel?"

"I don't think–"

"Yes, you do."

"Okay, maybe I do. To tell the truth, I don't know what to believe. You have to admit her story's pretty far-fetched."

Kirk hunched his shoulders. "But not totally unbelievable."

"So you believe her?"

"I'm willing to give her the benefit of the doubt. Obviously, you're not."

"That's what you're mad about?"

"I'm not mad." He heaved a huge sigh. "Just disappointed."

"Disappointed?"

He nodded and, when Peace kept looking at him, he said, "It's not like you to be harsh."

"I haven't said one harsh word to that girl!"

"You haven't said a kind one either. Everybody else is rallying round, trying to make her feel better. And you stand there, looking like it's Judgment Day and you're in charge of the prosecution."

Something inside of Peace snapped. "Boy, you nailed it when you said everybody's rallying round Flannery. Dear. Little. Lamb. Flannery." She spun around, took a deep breath, and went on, "It doesn't seem to occur to anybody to wonder how I feel that my car killed someone." She took a step toward Kirk. "Do you think I'll ever drive that car again without thinking of that poor boy? Assuming I ever get it back from the cops."

"Okay! Okay!" He held out his hands as though to keep her from coming closer. "But you weren't driving it. And everybody knows that." He dropped his hands to his sides and put them in his pockets. "It just happens to be your car. This isn't about you. Nobody's blaming you."

"Apparently nobody's blaming Flannery either."

"You are. At least she thinks you are. And she's really upset about that."

"You'd think she'd be upset that somebody died because of her carelessness. Not the fact that one person in her whole acquaintance isn't rushing in to hold her hand and tell her what an innocent little lamb she is."

Kirk opened his mouth as if to say something but closed it, creating a silence more eloquent than any words he could have spoken. Then he turned and walked away.

"Kirk," she called after him.

He waved one hand above his head and kept walking.

Eighteen

Rachel heard the garage open and, seconds later, a car door slam. She waited for the sound of the back door opening. There it was. Next, her mother's voice sang out the obvious announcement. "I'm home."

She took a deep, composing breath and headed for the kitchen. "Hi," she said, turning her cheek for her mother's quick kiss. "Any news?"

"Not yet. Should be something soon. They're making Tony's death a priority."

"What does that mean?"

Lisa held up one finger, signaling Rachel to give her a minute, as she shrugged out of her coat. She tossed it over a chair before answering. "It means they're pulling out all stops to find out who was driving the car that killed him. An accident reconstruction expert's coming in tomorrow."

Rachel felt tiny beads of perspiration pop out on her upper lip. "What can he do?"

"He met with the coroner today to examine the bruises on Tony's body. Tomorrow, he'll check over the car, then go out to the accident scene to see if he can figure out what happened."

Tony's body. The words echoed in Rachel's brain, paralyzing her for a moment.

Her mother didn't seem to notice. She slipped off her shoes and started pulling dishes out of the refrigerator.

When Rachel was able to speak again, she asked, "Think he'll be able to?"

"Those guys are pretty good. You'd be surprised what they can learn from the smallest thing."

Rachel's heart was pounding so hard she had to grab the back of a chair.

Her mother looked at her curiously. "You okay?"

"Yeah, it's just ..." She stopped, looked at the dishes Lisa had set on the counter. "Need help?"

"No. Leftovers tonight." She snapped her fingers and added, "Zap these things and add a salad. No fuss." She went back to the refrigerator and removed a container of lettuce. "You can wash this."

"Okay." Rachel took the lettuce from her mother's hand but didn't move toward the sink. "Darren and Amanda came over," she said.

"Poor Darren." Lisa turned on the faucet and waved Rachel nearer. "How's he taking it?" When Rachel didn't answer and didn't move, she looked at her again. "Oh, honey." In one fluid motion she turned off the faucet, moved to her daughter and enveloped her in a tight hug. After a few seconds, she loosened her arms and stepped back so she could look into her face. "That must have been brutal."

"Yeah, kinda."

Lisa gently pushed her into a chair. "Want to talk about it?"

"Darren's taking it hard. So's Amanda, but you know her. I told them about the ring and she started screaming at me that I never loved Tony." By the time Rachel finished the sentence, her voice was a high, thin squeak.

"That's Amanda. When she's upset, she attacks. She doesn't mean half of what she says. Try not to take it too seriously."

Rachel sat rigid in the chair, staring at the strange green object in her hand.

Lisa took the lettuce from her and placed it on the counter. "This can wait. We need to talk."

Rachel knew her mother was right, but couldn't stand the thought of saying what she knew had to be said. "Not now, Mom. Right now, I just want to go upstairs. Later. Okay?"

Lisa studied her and, finally, nodded. "Okay. After dinner then. When Daddy's here too. In the meantime, stop blaming yourself. Your breaking up with Tony had nothing to do with his death."

# # #

Rachel lay on her bed, staring at the ceiling, testing possible scenarios for the coming days. She imagined herself confessing, accepting the consequences, whatever they might be. She wondered if she would survive being locked up. *Yes*, she told herself. *If I have to, I can. I will.* How long would it be? How old would she be when she got out? Her parents? What would happen to them? That's where everything broke down. Worse than being locked up, worse than the destruction of her dream of a career in medical research, was the thought of being led away in handcuffs with her mother and father watching. Not just them. Tony's parents. All her friends. How to tell them? She tested combinations of words to explain how it had happened. None were adequate. The loss of her freedom seemed small compared to the loss of the good opinion of everyone she loved–people she'd so taken for granted that, until now, she'd had no idea how much she loved them, how much she needed their respect.

Confession was not an option, but what other option was there? What would happen if she continued to pretend innocence? Could she get away with it? Might Tony's death be added to the list of unsolved cases? It seemed possible. No one suspected her. Why should they? What about the scarf hidden in the dark recess at the back of her closet? The one she'd used to wipe her fingerprints off the car. Had it left fibers that could be traced to her? Even if the scarf were found, would it be tested? Would anyone ever make that connection? She rolled over and punched her fists into the pillow. Could she keep the secret? Alone? Never tell another soul? She told herself that would be punishment enough. Surely the best course was to protect her parents. Whatever she had done, they didn't deserve to suffer. And Tony's parents. Even for them, this would be better. Nothing she could do would make it right for them. She couldn't bring Tony back. Yes, guarding the secret was ...

She heard the door from the garage open. Her father's voice floated up the stairs: "I'm home. How're my girls?" Then, softer: "Where's Rachel?"

Her mother's voice: "Upstairs."

With her door closed, Rachel didn't hear the actual words. She didn't have to. Her father said the same thing every day when he came home from work and her mother's answers were equally predictable.

Next she heard the mingling of their two voices, hushed and careful. Again, she couldn't distinguish words, but their cadence left no doubt that they were spoken with concern.

And, finally, her mother's voice, loud and firm: "Rachel. Dinner."

She took a moment to still her troubled thoughts before she answered. "Coming." She stopped before the mirror to run trembling fingers through her tangled hair.

The aroma of the comfort food her mother specialized in enveloped her as she descended the steps and entered the dining room.

Her father was setting a platter of beef, carved into thick slices and covered with onions that had been caramelized to a dark golden hue, on the table. He looked up when Rachel came into the room. "Your mother's a genius," he said. "The queen of gourmet leftovers."

Rachel nodded and sat down.

Her mother joined them, carrying bowls of side dishes made up of combinations of leftovers from the family dinner on Saturday night.

Looking at the mismatched assortment of serving pieces, many of them handed down through multiple generations, Rachel flashed back to the gathering, made up of her grandparents, a favorite great aunt, her parents, and Tony. A collection of people she had thought boring at the time. Now she would give anything to be able to rewind her life and return to the camaraderie she'd found so tedious just a few days ago.

The meal was begun in silence, which Paul finally broke. Looking at Rachel, he said, "Your mom tells me Darren and Amanda came by and Amanda gave you a hard time." He glanced at his wife before he went on. "Try not to take it to heart. She's young. We all know she had a crush on Tony. She's lashing out at you because she doesn't know what else to do."

"I know," Rachel said. She looked from one parent to the other. "Amanda thinks we should help find Tony's killer."

Paul responded with a grim laugh. "What's she think you can do?"

"She wants to go to the museum and confront the owner of the car. Make her tell us what really happened." She watched her mother's face for a reaction.

"No!" Lisa leaned forward, gripping the table's edge with both hands. "That's the worse possible thing you could do." She paused, looking at Rachel. "Do not interfere with the investigation. Not if you want the truth to come out."

Rachel had no intention of going with Amanda, but her mother's statement set off a chain of possibilities in her head. "Why?" she asked. "How can it hurt?"

Lisa said, "I don't know, but I do know the investigators hate it when lay people take things into their own hands." She stopped to look at Rachel. "If you know anything you think might help, go directly to the investigating officers. But don't try to solve this yourself. You'll only make trouble."

"But if they don't have any leads ..."

Lisa let her daughter's statement hang for a moment before she said, "Actually, maybe they do. A woman called the office today. A possible witness."

Rachel felt herself go cold. She lay her fork on the table so her parents wouldn't see how her hands were shaking. "Witness? So she'll be able to tell them who was driving the car?"

"I don't know. She's coming in tomorrow."

Nineteen

Peace held the small carving in her hand and ran her thumb over its surface, marveling at the details of the tiny ears and face, savoring the sensation of the satiny finish against her skin. She thought about the patience it must have taken to coax the oddly-shaped scrap into a miniature replica of Henry, the sanding required to ease the rough-grained wood to its present glossy finish, but, mostly, her thoughts were about Kirk. *He never does anything halfway.* She thought, too, of her response when Flannery asked if she and Kirk were dating. Should she have given a different answer? *We do spend a lot of time together.*

At the beginning of their relationship, Kirk had sent signals of romantic interest, signals that Peace carefully diverted in a different direction, one that had resulted in their present status of best friends. *That's the way I want it.* Why, then, did the memory of Flannery's fluttering eyelashes and Kirk's obvious interest cause such a hollow feeling under her breastbone? Had she been kidding herself? She stared at the tiny dog in her hand and thought again of the day she and Kirk had met.

# # #

"Hey," he'd said when she opened the door for the first visitor to her new apartment. "I'm Kirk Buchanan. Saw you moving in and thought I'd introduce myself." His smile was the most genuine she'd ever seen.

She held out her hand. "Peace Morrow."

Then they'd both stood for a moment, smiling awkwardly, assessing each other.

Peace spoke first. "Thanks for coming over."

"No problem." Another smile, even brighter than the first. "I think it's customary to bring a casserole or something when you meet new neighbors, but..." He paused and hunched his shoulders. "I don't cook."

She'd laughed then and laughed again now, thinking about it.

He'd added, "I'm pretty good at fixing things though, so if you need help along those lines, I'm your man. I live over there." He jerked his thumb over his shoulder, indicating the house next door.

"Thanks. You may be sorry you told me that. I'm not very good at stuff like that."

# # #

The scene played out in her head, as clear as if it had happened yesterday. She looked away from the tiny figure in her hand to the big dog who had inspired it.

Henry was sitting in his favorite chair by the window, his dark shape a dim silhouette against the light of the buildings across the street. It was not quite five o'clock, but already dark. The family should be back from Valley Forge soon.

Peace moved restlessly through the house. *I should change. Get ready for dinner.*

In the bathroom, she examined the jars and tubes that took up most of the surface of her small vanity. *Kirk should see this.* What would he say? Would he care that Flannery's fresh-faced, natural beauty was the result of artifice? *Probably not.*

She examined her reflection in the mirror. Frowned. Looked again at the clutter of the other girl's cosmetics. *Where's my comb? Must be in here somewhere.* She found it hidden under a crumpled tissue and forced it though the tangle of her hair. She checked the mirror again. Frowned again, and shrugged. *Best I can do.*

She started to go, but turned back and picked up a small, star-shaped jar filled with a rosy beige substance. She unscrewed the lid and sniffed it. *Nothing.* She held it out and read the label. *Fragrance free.* She rubbed one finger over the surface. *Creamy. Almost like butter.* She swiped the finger across her left cheek and leaned closer to the mirror. The freckles were still there, but less obvious than those on the other side. Feeling guilty, she dipped her finger into the makeup again and spread a thin film over her face. She checked the mirror again. *Too much.* She took a tissue and wiped most of it off. Another look into the glass. The freckles did seem less obvious and her skin had a flattering rosy glow. She replaced the jar and walked away, feeling guilty. *Why*, she asked herself, *should I feel bad?* Would Flannery hesitate to use her makeup if she had any lying around? *No.*

She surveyed the contents of her closet, pondering what to wear. This newfound family of hers worried about such things more than Peace and her mother did. *Something nice. Not too dressy. Not on a weeknight.* She settled on a fresh pair of jeans and a soft fuzzy sweater in a shade of blue that matched her eyes, remembering the line in Snap-snap's letter about how glad she was that Peace had inherited her grandfather's blue eyes. There, at least, she had Flannery beat. *Stop*, she told herself. *It's not a competition.* So, why did she feel that it was?

She was pulling the sweater over her head when Henry took off for the front door. She yanked the sweater the rest of the way down and followed him, knowing he'd heard activity on the porch. Sure enough, there they were: Snap-snap, Poppy, and Flannery.

"Hi," she said as the three of them trooped in. "How'd you like Valley Forge?"

"Inspiring," Poppy said. "Sacred ground. Brings history to life. Makes me proud to be an American."

Snap-snap slapped him playfully on the arm. "Almost everything makes you proud to be an American."

"Yes, it does," he said. "I don't take our history for granted. The sacrifices made. Seeing firsthand the conditions those men had to endure that freezing winter ..." He looked at Snap-snap and Flannery, who were laughing at him. "I'm not ashamed to be a patriot." He shrugged as though a little embarrassed, and added, "A hungry patriot." He turned to Peace. "Any suggestions for dinner?"

She hesitated a few seconds, not sure of the preferences of her newfound family. "Mom and I like ethnic foods. There's a Thai restaurant on State Street. We haven't eaten there yet, but I've heard good things about it. It's close enough that we could walk."

Snap-snap said, "Sounds perfect."

The decision made, they called Holly, who was still at work, and arranged for her to meet them at the restaurant.

Flannery said, "Should we invite Kirk?"

"I doubt he'd want to go," Peace was quick to say.

"But—" Flannery started to object.

Snap-snap interrupted her. "I think Peace knows him better than we do, dear."

# # #

Dinner was a jovial affair, but there was a dark undercurent. Poppy, a born raconteur, kept the conversation lively. Peace and, she suspected, everyone else, knew he was deliberately steering talk away from any mention of the stolen car and the young man's death. Even so, Peace thought the laughter seemed forced. She noticed stolen glances directed toward Flannery by other family members. Snap-snap sat between her two granddaughters and seemed determined that both enjoy themselves.

The only reference to the serious matter was a rather oblique one. It came when Peace excused herself to go to the ladies room.

"Wait. I'll go with you," Snap-snap said. When they were washing their hands, their eyes met in the mirror and Snap-snap said, "I suppose you think we spoil Flannery."

Peace started to protest, but Snap-snap stopped her. "You're right, of course. We do. Always have." She looked away as though distracted by a distant memory. "She came along so soon after we learned Holly had given up a child." She smiled sadly and looked back at Peace. "Our first grandchild. You.

Whom we thought we would never see." Another sad smile, then, "You could say we were spoiling for two."

Peace nodded, torn between conflicting emotions. She knew Snap-snap's intent was to convey to Peace how much they were prepared to love her. That realization almost wiped out the resentment she felt toward her pampered cousin. Almost.

After dinner, they walked back to Peace's apartment and said their good-byes without coming in.

Peace watched them drive away in the car they had rented, conscious of Flannery standing by her side. It was not quite nine. Too early for bed. How would they get through the rest of the evening?

Henry made his usual fuss when they went inside, distracting Peace for a few minutes, returning her to the world of normalcy.

Flannery's defiant voice brought her back. "The car really was stolen." She stopped, and when she continued, her voice had collapsed into a whisper: "And I didn't kill that boy." She sank into a chair and covered her face with her hands.

Again, Peace's feelings were conflicted. She had no idea how to comfort this virtual stranger who was supposed to be of the same blood, but she was relieved that, finally, someone was acknowledging the cloud that hung over them. She said, "I'll make some tea."

Flannery took it wrong. Her body snapped into an upright posture. "Tea won't fix it. This isn't Victorian England."

After a moment of stunned silence, the ridiculousness of the situation struck Peace. She began to laugh.

Flannery watched her, unamused.

"I'm sorry," Peace said. "I know it's not funny. I guess I'm just nervous."

"I know. I'm sorry too. That I snapped, I mean."

Peace tried to explain. "I wasn't trying to change the subject. That's what my mother does when we have a problem. She makes tea. And we talk it out. That's what we should do now."

Flannery took a deep breath and blew out the air. She pointed to the kettle. "I can't think of anything else to do."

Over steaming mugs of chamomile tea, they rehashed the events of the past few days, with Flannery reiterating in minute detail her actions of the day that had sent their world into a tailspin.

Peace zeroed in on the fact that Flannery said she had probably slipped the keys in her coat pocket. She remembered Chief Grimaldi's question to Flannery and repeated it to her: "Could someone have picked your pocket?" When Flannery didn't answer right away, she added: "Do you remember anyone bumping into you?"

"It's possible. You know how the stores are at Christmas. A lot of people probably bumped into me. None that I remember. All I know is that when I went to get the car it was gone. I looked all over the parking lot for it. I didn't know what to do so I walked to the B and B where Poppy and Snap-snap are staying. I knew everyone would be mad at me and I wanted them to help me tell Aunt Holly and you."

She told the story with such conviction and in such detail, Peace began to believe her. Almost. She wasn't totally convinced, but had reached the point of *wanting* to believe. What she wanted most was to *know*. Was Flannery the victim of a horrible set of circumstances? Or was she the consummate liar? It had to be one or the other. There was no middle ground. While Peace was weighing the two possibilities, an idea struck. "We should visit the crime scene."

"Do you know where it is?" Rachel asked.

Peace went to get the paper. "I can find it from this." She pointed to the article on the front page. There was a small map with a heavy black arrow pointing to a section of Saw Mill Road.

"Do you think we'll learn anything?"

"We have to start somewhere."

Flannery looked doubtful, but Peace was on a roll. "We'll ask Holly if we can borrow her car. Better yet, we'll see if Kirk can take us. He has a great eye for detail." Peace brushed aside the thought that she'd really suggested inviting Kirk because she wanted—no needed—him to know she was trying to help Flannery.

WEDNESDAY

Twenty

Rachel lay in bed, staring into the darkness, haunted by the specter of a witness. When sleep finally came, it was filled with images of gaping mouths shouting her name and skeletal fingers pointing in her direction. She awoke in the half light of predawn, shaking, drenched in perspiration. Determined to escape, she threw off the tangled sheet and headed for the shower. She stood under the water, steam rising around her, wondering who the witness could be and what they might have seen. Had any cars passed while she and Tony were arguing? She thought maybe one had but couldn't say for sure. Her attention had been totally focused on Tony's anger and denial and her dawning awareness that her mother was right. There was a side of him she'd never seen. Had there been hints of it she'd missed in all the time they'd spent together?

She massaged shampoo into her hair and fantasized about going back and doing what she'd set out to do. What would be happening now if she'd taken her mother's advice and let a couple of days pass before she talked to Tony? He'd still be angry, but he'd be getting used to the idea. The word would be out that he and Rachel were no longer a couple. Someone, maybe one of his football buddies, would have set him up with a date. No problem there. All the time they'd been together, girls had practically been standing in line, waiting for a chance to be seen on the arm of Bucks County's golden boy. If she'd waited, he might have listened to her. More important, he'd still be alive.

She stepped out of the shower and dried off, still thinking of *what might have been*. When she opened the bathroom door, the smell of coffee and her parents' voices reached her, a grim reminder of *what is*. She knew they were talking about her. Worrying. Because that's what they did. Her problems were their problems. The burden and blessing of being an only child. As she'd grown up, she'd become more and more aware how much their happiness depended on hers. Their faith in her, their dreams for her, had been a large part of the reason for her success at school. Their dreams had morphed into her dreams. They were thrilled and so, so proud when she'd won the scholarship. Now this. She was about to lose it all. What would happen when they found out what she'd done? She knew the chances of their *not* finding out were slim. She slipped into jeans and a sweatshirt, telling herself she had to come up with a plan to keep that from happening. You're a scientist, she told herself. Treat it like a puzzle to be solved. Lay out all the pieces and analyze them.

The accident reconstruction expert and the witness were the trickiest pieces. There was probably nothing she could do about the expert. The witness? Maybe. If only if she knew more about this person. Mom said she was coming in today. *She. A woman.* Rachel shook her head. *Not good.* Women, at least in her experience, tended to be more detail-conscious, more likely to notice little things that would lead to Rachel. Or maybe not. She might have had a carful of kids distracting her. *How old was she?* The questions were endless and Rachel needed answers.

She finished dressing, gathered her hair into a ponytail, took three deep breaths, and headed for the stairs.

She found her parents exactly as she had known they would be: facing each other across the table, each with a bowl of cereal in front of them, a cup of coffee and a glass of juice beside the bowl. Her father was ready for his day at the office, his tie neatly knotted, his shirt starched and pristine white, and his suit jacket hung over the back of an empty chair. Her mother, who always showered and dressed after her husband left for work, was still in a robe, hair hastily finger-combed, and no makeup. Both had dark circles under their eyes. Rachel knew they'd gotten no more sleep than she had last night.

Both looked up when she entered the room. "Morning," they said in unison and with identical artificial cheer.

"Morning. Anything new?" she asked, joining them.

"New? Meaning about Tony?" Lisa asked.

"Yes. Or the witness?" Rachel pointed to the paper.

"No," Paul said, "Nothing about a witness."

"Umm." Rachel poured herself some juice and tried to sound casual.

Lisa said, "There won't be anything about that. They're keeping it quiet until they know what she has to say." She leaned toward Rachel. "And don't you say anything. Not to anyone."

"I won't. Why would I? Anyway, why do they care? Don't they usually want the public to know? So maybe others will come forward too?"

"After they talk to her, they'll probably make a statement."

Rachel's cell phone rang. She looked at the screen and froze. She mouthed, "Tony's mom," to her parents.

"You have to answer," Paul said. "I know you don't want to talk to her, but ..."

"Remember," Lisa whispered. "Not a word. Not even to her."

Rachel began to shake.

The phone shrilled on.

Paul picked it up and handed it to her.

"Hello." Her voice was as tremulous as her body.

Bella began speaking immediately, so fast that her words tumbled together and Rachel could only make out some of them, enough, though, to know what she wanted.

"I don't think that's a good idea," she said when Bella paused for a breath. When there was no response, she added, "My mom said the D.A.'s office is making this case a priority." She glanced at her mother and saw her stiffen and make a zipping motion across her lips. Rachel nodded and went on, "She said when lay people try to help, they usually do more harm than good." She listened a moment longer, then said, "I'm sorry. I can't. I really can't."

She laid the phone on the table, her hands shaking harder than ever.

"What'd she want?" Lisa demanded.

"She wants to go to the owner of the car and make her confess."

"Do you have any idea how much trouble you could get into if you do that?"

"I told her I wouldn't."

"She knows you mean it?"

"Mom, you heard what I said. I think I was pretty clear."

"What'd she say?"

"That she'll go by herself then."

"Surely not."

Rachel shrugged. "She's pretty determined."

Lisa reached for the phone. "I'll call her back and tell her myself."

Paul spoke up. "Not a good idea. I doubt you can stop her. We need to step back."

"But—"

He reached over and took both of his wife's hands in his. "Think about it. What if we were in her place? We'd want to do something ourselves. Anyone telling us not get involved would only make us more determined." He looked over at Rachel and back at Lisa. "If it were our child, would we listen to someone in the courthouse?"

Lisa grudgingly admitted he was right and turned to Rachel. "You stay out of it. I know you don't think so, but you could do something trying to be helpful that would make it impossible for the investigators to do their job."

"I understand." Rachel looked her mother squarely in the eye.

#

Lisa had been gone for a little over an hour when the doorbell rang. Rachel went to answer it, knowing who it would be. She wasn't really even surprised that Bella was accompanied by Amanda.

Both stepped in without waiting to be invited.

Bella said, "We're going to the museum. That's where ..." She paused to pull a slip of paper from her coat pocket and held it out at arm's length as she squinted. "Peace Morrow works."

When Rachel didn't answer, Amanda said, "Peace Morrow's the owner of the car."

"I know who she is, but she wasn't driving. Everybody agrees on that."

"But she knows who was," Bella said. "It was her car. She can make the driver confess."

"That might just mess things up for the investigators. We don't know what's going on behind the scenes. Mom said–"

Bella raised both hands over her head and shook them. "I'll tell her about my Tony. I'll make her understand that she must help bring justice. The person who did this needs to be punished."

When Rachel didn't answer, Amanda said, "We're going. With you or without you."

#

At the museum, Rachel stood back and let Bella do the talking. All the while she was listening, her mother's words echoed in her head: *You might do something that would make it impossible for the investigators.*

Bella was dramatic and emotional, as only she could be, but in the end, her eloquence didn't matter. They learned that Peace Morrow had taken the week off to spend time with her family who was visiting from out of town. When they asked for her home address, the woman smiled and said she was sorry, she couldn't give out that information.

Bella, with tears in her eyes, asked, "Do you have a son?"

The woman nodded and repeated how sorry she was.

"If it was you son–"

Amanda grabbed Bella's arm. "Let's go. They're not going to help us."

Rachel trailed along when they filed out.

They went into the library across the street and sat at one of the tables along the back. Amanda took out her phone and started pushing buttons. Within seconds, she looked up, triumphant. "Here it is. She lives just a couple of blocks from here. On Ashland."

Twenty-One

Peace hung up the phone and turned to Flannery. "He can't make it. Painting gig." She didn't admit to Flannery, or even to herself, how relieved she was that Kirk wouldn't be with them when they visited the crime scene.

"Painting gig?"

"He calls all his jobs gigs, no matter what they are. Makes him feel like he's a real musician."

"Well, isn't he? A real musician?"

"Sure, but he has to take on all sorts of other things ... gigs ... to pay the bills. Today, he's finishing up an outside job, a barn in Buckingham. He's pushing to get it done before the weather changes. Plus, he needs to get paid before his rent's due."

Flannery shrugged, seemingly ready to move on, not nearly as disappointed as Peace had expected her to be. Her face became tense with concentration for a half minute, then brightened. "We'll borrow Aunt Holly's car. I know she'll let us. She's desperate for us to be friends." She reached for her phone, hesitated, and looked at Peace before she pushed in the number. "Think I should tell her why we want it?"

"Probably not."

Flannery made the call, telling her aunt only that Peace wanted to show her some of the countryside. Afterwards, she grinned at Peace. "I didn't lie."

"No," Peace said, but she knew a half-truth was no better than a lie. Not that she would have done it differently, but she told herself at least she knew the difference. *Does that make me better or worse?*

They spent a few minutes with Holly when they picked up the car. "I'm glad you two are finding time to do something together." She beamed at them.

They both smiled back.

Peace headed for the shopping center, wanting to see exactly where Flannery had last seen the car. She drove up and down the rows of cars, pulled into the first empty space she found, switched off the engine, and turned to Flannery. "Tell me exactly where you left the car."

Flannery's brow furrowed as she scanned the lot. She took her time and finally pointed to the next row over, about half a dozen cars closer to the stores than their present location. "About there."

"Which store did you go in?"

Flannery looked toward the row of stores. "That one," she said. "The Bon Ton."

"Do you remember what you looked at?"

A noncommittal shrug. "Bit of everything."

"Did you try anything on?"

Flannery shook her head.

"Nothing at all?"

Another head shake, this time accompanied by a hostile stare. "You're asking more questions than the police did. Why? What difference does it make? You don't believe anything I say anyway."

"That's not true."

"Yes, it is. You don't care about helping me." Flannery's words erupted in resentment-filled spurts. "You're trying to trip me up. Prove me to be the black sheep you think I am, while you're Little Miss Do Everything Right."

The ferocity of her outburst cut short the denial Peace had been prepared to make and forced her to admit she didn't know what to believe.

They sat in stony silence, each looking out the window on her side of the car.

When they'd started this venture, Peace thought she'd felt the beginning of a possible friendship, a sense of common purpose. That was gone now. She needed to understand why. Did Flannery really believe the things she was saying? She tried to put herself in her cousin's shoes. How would she feel if the situation were reversed? *Not that it ever would be. I hope I've got more sense than to get myself into a mess like this.* Then she remembered Kirk's accusation. Was she being judgmental? Whether she was or not, she knew it was up to her to mend the fence.

She turned to face Flannery. "Let's start over," she said. "I admit I don't know how to figure out what happened, but one thing keeps coming back to me. Grimaldi's question whether someone could have picked your pocket. That's the only thing that makes sense. I'm hoping if we retrace your steps, you'll remember somebody bumping into you or, if you tried something on, maybe you left your coat in the dressing room. The keys could have fallen out of your pocket."

"I didn't try anything on." Flannery continued to stare out the window, her mumbled words barely audible, her expression that of a pouting six-year-old.

"How about someone bumping into you really hard or brushing against you?"

"It's almost Christmas. The store was a mob scene." She expelled a long breath and looked Peace in the eye. "Don't you think I've gone over it a thousand times?" Her chin was trembling, her voice shaky. "It may be your car, but I'm the one everybody thinks is a murderer."

Again, Peace remembered Kirk's chiding remarks. This really *was* about Flannery, not her. "Sorry," she said, and reached out to touch her cousin's arm. "Let's go in the store. Being in the place where it happened might make you remember something or someone. That way, you'll at least have a description to give the police."

Flannery pulled her arm away. "Like they'll believe anything I say." After a minute, she opened her car door. "Let's go. Anything to make you happy."

Peace couldn't resist snapping back, "It's not about making me happy. Whether you believe it not, I'm trying to help you. If you have a better idea, I'm willing to try it."

Inside, they walked through the crowded aisles, until Flannery said, "This isn't working. Besides, even if someone picked my pocket, how would they know which car the key fit?"

That stopped Peace but only for a minute. "They could have used the key fob. Went out into the parking lot and just kept clicking it until they found the car." She spoke slowly, making it up as she went along, trying to visualize what might have happened. "Or maybe they saw you put the keys in your pocket and followed you, then waited until you were distracted and stole the keys." Both scenarios made sense to her. "Do you remember anyone coming in at the same time you did? Or maybe seeing the same person everywhere you went?"

"No."

Peace repressed a sigh. "Okay." *Time to move on.*

# # #

Following the map in the paper, they drove north on Main Street until it became 611. When they reached Saw Mill Road, they turned right and, about a hundred yards from the intersection, they saw a black sedan parked by the shoulder. Just past it, were three men. One of them was walking along the roadside, hands in pockets, his head down. He seemed oblivious to the approaching vehicle. The other two stood in the field, watching. One of them had something in his hand, a black, squarish object. When the car was almost abreast of the men, Peace slowed down.

"Keep going," Flannery said. She slouched down in the seat and leaned over until her head was almost resting on her knees.

"What are you doing?"

"Those two guys standing there? They're the cops that came by the house. I don't want them to see me." She was whispering, as though afraid they could hear her. "They'll think I've returned to the scene of the crime."

That hadn't occurred to Peace, but it made sense so she kept driving. After checking traffic, she veered closer to the center line to avoid coming too close to the man on the shoulder. She looked toward the field and saw that Flannery was right. The two men who were watching were Chief Grimaldi and the young cop who'd responded to the stolen car report. Grimaldi was the one holding the black object, which turned out to be a serious-looking camera. Both of the watchers glanced briefly at the car as it passed, then returned their attention to the third man, who didn't even look up. It was pretty clear he was searching for something. He stooped and brushed his hand over the surface of the pavement. A low shape by the roadside drew Peace's attention. Her hands tightened on the steering wheel when she saw what it was—a crude wooden cross, a football, some plastic flowers, and a small brown mass that looked like a Teddy bear. For a moment, she had to struggle to catch her breath. When she did, she said to Flannery, "You can sit up now. They're not paying any attention to us."

Flannery sat up and looked back over her shoulder. "They must be looking for evidence."

Peace nodded. "This was a bad idea," she said. "Let's go home. Leave crime solving to the professionals." She turned right at Old Easton Road, knowing it would take them back to Route 611 without having to pass the investigators again. They drove back to Doylestown without much conversation. Peace couldn't get the makeshift memorial out of her head. It was an all-too-real reminder that, to the family of Tony Rosino, this was more than a puzzle to be solved. More than a stolen car. More than a cousin who might or might not be telling the truth. She glanced sideways at Flannery's perfect profile, but couldn't begin to guess what she might be thinking. She wondered, too, about Flannery's remark that anyone seeing her on that road would assume she was returning to the scene of the crime. It made sense, but would an innocent person be so quick to think of it?

# # #

They returned the car to the museum lot, went in to tell Holly where they'd left it, and walked back to Peace's apartment. They were almost there when they noticed three figures sitting on the porch steps.

Flannery said, "Looks like you've got company."

Peace looked closely at the women. One was middle-aged, with wisps of gray hair framing her face. The other two looked quite a bit younger. One, she judged to be in her late teens, twenty at the most, the other looked like she was still in her early teens. She didn't know any of them, but had the vague feeling she'd seen at least one of them before. The feeling was brief, a tiny flame that flickered at the edge of recognition, then slipped away. She nodded to them when she and Flannery approached the steps. All three women stood.

Twenty-Two

Amanda was the first to see them approaching. "There they are," she said. She pointed to the tall redhead. "That's the owner of the car. I recognize her from the picture in the paper."

The two women, the tall one with red hair and the other, shorter, dark-haired, and strikingly pretty, stopped not more two yards from Rachel, Amanda, and Bella.

I should tell them. Now. Rachel opened her mouth, but no words would come.

Tony's mother planted her short figure squarely in front of the two women, blocking their path to the steps. Rachel couldn't see Bella's face, but her posture broadcast the relentless determination that Rachel knew so well. Her gloved hands hung by her sides, her fingers twitching. When she spoke, her voice was surprisingly firm. "Is one of you Peace Morrow?"

Rachel stayed a couple of steps back. Watching.

"Yes," the tall one said, "I am." She smiled tentatively, her head tilted as though waiting for an explanation. After a few seconds, she asked, "Can I help you with something?"

Bella barely came to the young woman's shoulder and, standing so close, had to tilt her head back to look into her face. "I'm Bella Rosino. Tony's mother."

Rachel held her breath while she waited to see if the woman understood what this meant. For a few seconds she seemed not to, then her eyes widened and Rachel could see that she did.

The other young woman, the shorter of the two, lowered her chin so her hair cascaded forward, hiding her face behind its dark curtain.

"I'm so sorry," the redhead said. "For what happened. For your loss." She reached out as if to touch Bella's arm.

Amanda stepped forward and shouted, "Sorry's not good enough. We want justice." She linked her arm through Bella's, pulling her away from the redhead. She turned to the other woman, the one with the bowed head. "Are you the friend she loaned her car to?"

The redhead answered for her. "She's my cousin."

After a minute, the other woman raised her head. "I'm Flannery Donohue." She lifted her chin and went on, "And, yes, I am the one who drove the car to the shopping center that day." She spoke firmly, but something in her eyes told Rachel she didn't expect to be believed.

"Oh? And where else did you drive it?" Amanda's face contorted with rage. She let go of Bella's arm and moved closer, focusing on the woman who had spoken last. They were about the same height, but Amanda's chunky body made her look twice the size of the slender brunette. Only the childish pitch of her voice hinted at her youth.

"Nowhere. When I came out of the store, the car was gone. Someone stole it." She looked over Amanda's shoulder, to Bella, and said, "I didn't kill your son. I didn't even know him."

Rachel watched, unable to speak. *I'm the only one here who knows she's telling the truth.* She held her breath, wondering if the girl would recognize her from when they'd collided in the parking lot. *She doesn't even see me. She's too focused on Bella.* She expelled the breath. *If she did see me, would she make the connection?*

While these thoughts careened through Rachel's brain, the argument escalated.

Amanda screamed, "Liar!" She reached out as though to push the terrified girl.

Rachel grabbed the back of her coat, trying to pull her back.

Amanda wrested free and spun to face Rachel. "You want to let her get away with it?"

"What you're doing won't help."

"It's better than doing nothing. Like you!"

They were standing so close, Rachel felt Amanda's breath on her face. She took a step back. The two of them stood like that, facing off, panting, for what seemed an eternity to Rachel.

Bella's voice broke the spell. "Somebody saw something."

Those words drove every other thought from Rachel's mind. Had news of the witness broken? She looked toward Bella and saw that she was only inches from the dark-haired girl, the one who had admitted to driving the car.

Bella went on, "Somebody knows something. They'll call the police and tell them what they saw." She leaned closer to the dark-haired girl. "And you will be found out." Her words erupted in short bursts, punctuated by half sobs. She stopped to catch her breath, then added, "Why don't you admit what you did? It'll be easier for everyone if you do."

"I didn't kill your son," the smaller woman said. "I told you someone stole the car while I was in the store." By the time she finished the sentence, her voice was shaking.

If Rachel didn't know better, the girl's demeanor would be proof that she was lying. She sounded desperate, as if she knew she wouldn't be believed, as if she didn't deserve to be. Rachel felt a reluctant sympathy, followed by a guilty hope. Her heart pounded against her ribs.

Then Bella and Amanda both started shouting, their voices drowning each other out, making their words unintelligible.

Suddenly Bella stopped shouting. She spat at the ground by the young woman's feet.

The woman's face crumpled. She bolted past her accusers, up the stairs and onto the porch. She stood by the door, pleading with her eyes for the redhead to come.

The redhead brushed past, ran up the stairs, and unlocked the door.

The dark-haired girl scurried inside.

Amanda started screaming again. "Coward! Murderer!"

The redhead turned back to face the accusers. She looked first at Bella, who was standing quietly at the foot of the steps, then at Amanda, still screaming, and finally, at Rachel, who had, so far, remained an observer.

Rachel couldn't read her expression, but she felt as though the woman could see into her soul.

Their eyes caught and held. There seemed to be a question in the redhead's eyes. What was she asking? *It's like she knows.* Unable to remain silent under the unwavering gaze, Rachel joined Amanda in her shrill cries. "Coward!" she shouted, then, gaining courage from the sound of her own voice, she added, "Murderer!" Hearing the words, she almost came to believe them and shouted louder, as if a lie shouted loud enough would become truth.

The redhead continued to study her. She looked more perplexed than angry and Rachel was more than ever convinced that she *knew.* Determined to beat down the woman she'd begun to think of as her enemy, Rachel continued her tirade, adding epithet after epithet until she hardly knew what she was saying and her throat burned from the effort.

The redhead turned and went into the house.

Rachel realized that Amanda and Bella had become quiet and were staring at her, Amanda in apparent admiration, Bella with tears streaming down her cheeks.

"Wow!" Amanda said. "I didn't know you had it in you."

Bella came over and put her arm around Rachel's waist. Tears filled her eyes. "We'll find a way to make her pay for what she did to our Tony," she said. "Don't worry, little daughter."

At the last two words, Rachel began to shake.

Bella patted her shoulder and repeated them.

It was all Rachel could do to remain upright.

She felt Bella's arm tighten around her waist.

Twenty-Three

Trembling, shaken to the core, Peace closed the door and leaned against it. Never had she been the target of such rage. Never had she witnessed such undiluted hatred. She took a minute to calm herself before she moved to the window. She remained off to one side and peered around the drape, not wanting to draw the attention of the women on sidewalk. From this vantage point, they were nowhere in sight. She moved tentatively to the center of the window, looked out, and saw them getting into a white SUV parked halfway down the block. She waited until the car turned left onto Main Street, then turned to Flannery. "They're gone."

"Thank God." Flannery huddled in a corner of the sofa, her knees drawn up against her chest, her chin resting on them. After a few seconds, she raised her head. "They really believe I'm a murderer. The way they acted. What they said. I've never had anyone look at me like that. Or spit at me! What kind of people act like that?"

Peace made an effort to re-focus, to put herself in Flannery's shoes. "Try not to take it to heart. They don't know you and−"

"That's right!" Flannery looked at Peace like she'd been thrown a lifeline. She leapt off sofa and began to pace, her humiliation changing to outrage. "They don't. So what right have they to judge me?"

"Try to look at it from their point of view. They're hurting. They need someone to blame."

Peace marveled at her own words, so sensible, so like the advice she knew Caroline would give if she were here. "And you're the only one in sight."

"Too much in sight. Are the police even looking for anyone else?"

"I'm sure they are." That's what Peace said, but, privately, she wondered the same thing. Were the police looking at other suspects or were they so convinced of Flannery's guilt that they failed to consider other possibilities?

The image of the young woman who had at first seemed a spectator, then erupted into a venomous attack, flashed before Peace. She couldn't shake the feeling she'd seen her before.

Flannery's voice droned on in the background like the buzz of an indignant wasp.

Peace closed her eyes and blocked her cousin's words, concentrating, trying to bring an elusive image into focus, until suddenly, there it was: a group of young people leaving the train station, two of them falling behind. Letting the scene replay in her head, Peace saw the boy lean down to kiss the girl, her turn so that his kiss landed on the top of her head. Most of all, Peace recalled the look on the boy's face—an expression of love so vivid it was imprinted indelibly on her brain. The girl who had turned away was one of their attackers. There was no doubt in Peace's mind. She blurted it out. "I've seen that girl before."

"Who?"

"Saturday night, just before you got here, I took Henry for a walk. I saw a group of kids leaving the station. She was with them. I'm sure it was her."

"You mean ..." Flannery indicated the street outside with a sweep of her hand. "One of them?"

Peace nodded. "Yes. She was with him ... the boy who was killed. I noticed them because they were lagging behind the others. Then, when I saw the victim's picture in the paper Monday morning, I recognized him. And, just now, I realized she was the girl with him."

"Which one?"

"Not the kind of chubby one. The other one."

"You just passed them on the street and you remember them?"

"Yes. Odd, isn't it?" Peace thought about the eerie coincidence, then about the girl's behavior during the attack. "Did you notice how she acted? Different from the other two. Quiet. At least at first. Then all of the sudden she joined in."

Flannery shook her head. "I was too busy worrying about the other two. His mother. And the one who seemed really young. I thought she was going to attack me."

"I know. Then the other one stopped her." Peace hesitated, trying to put the pieces together. "I wonder if she's the fiancee." She held up one finger. "Just a minute. Maybe there was a picture of her too. I think I still have the paper."

She found it in the recycle bin and skimmed through the article until she found what she was looking for. "Here it is." She read aloud: "'Tony was engaged to be married to his childhood sweetheart, Rachel Woodard. They'd been dating since fifth grade.' No picture of her, but I think I heard the other one, the younger one, call her Rachel."

Flannery said, "If she's his fiancee, no wonder she's upset."

"But that's just it. She didn't really seem upset. Not at first. She was the calmest one."

"You'd think she'd be the most upset."

"I'm not saying she wasn't upset. But it was a different kind of upset than the other two."

"Well, if she was his fiancee, it's a different kind of a thing. Maybe she's in shock."

"Maybe." Peace couldn't quite put her finger on what she meant, so she let it go. She remained at the window, looking first at the sidewalk in front of the house, then across the street to the train station, remembering two scenes, wondering about the relationship of the young couple she'd seen on Saturday afternoon.

Henry didn't allow her to think long. He pranced over and nudged her leg, his leash dangling from his mouth.

Peace rubbed his head and took the leash from him, grateful for this small slice of normality. She snapped the leash to his collar and started toward the front door, but changed her mind, afraid their accusers might come back. "Sorry, Pal, no walkies today." She unsnapped the leash. "The back yard's going to have to do." She went to the kitchen door and clapped her hands lightly a couple of times. "Where's your ball?"

The big dog bounded out the door, did what he needed to do, then started nosing around under the forsythia bushes along the fence line. Seconds later, he let out a triumphant yip and came racing back to

Peace. In his mouth was an old tennis ball which he dropped at her feet.

She picked it up and tossed it to the middle of the small yard. Henry was there by the time the ball landed and back to Peace, tail wagging, the ball in his mouth, before she had time to catch her breath.

It's probably true that there's no problem so great that playing with a dog won't make it seem manageable. Tossing the ball, watching the big black dog retrieve and return it, repeating the sequence of mindless actions again and again, cleared Peace's head and enabled her to think. She replayed the scene with the three women, running it through her mind, until she was able to put aside the emotion and focus on the words spoken, especially by the woman who said she was Tony's mother.

One statement stood out: "Somebody saw something."

"Okay, Henry. Time to go in." She ignored the woeful look on his face when he nudged the ball he had dropped at her feet. "Sorry. That's it for today." She gave his head a consoling rub and headed for the door.

He looked at her standing by the half-open door for a moment, then, with the doggy equivalent of a shoulder shrug, he picked up his ball, returned it to the spot under the forsythia bush, and bounded to her side.

Flannery was nowhere in sight. The living room was empty.

Peace heard the shower running and put on water for tea. She puttered while she waited, gathering her thoughts, eager to talk about the encounter now that the raw emotion of it had subsided. She'd had time to think while she was throwing the ball for Henry and had an idea she wanted to run past Flannery.

She didn't have to wait long. Just as the kettle started to whistle, Flannery appeared, wrapped in a fluffy pink robe, a towel wound turban-style around her head, smelling of lavender, and looking none the worse for the recent ordeal.

Peace was impressed with the transformation. "Feeling better?"

Flannery shrugged. "Not really, but there's no use brooding about it. There's nothing I can do to change what they think." She loosened the towel, freeing her hair, and gave her head a brisk rub. "It's up to the police to do their job."

"Right," Peace said and moved on, curious to see if Flannery's take was the same as hers. "One thing the boy's mother said kind of stuck out for me."

"Like when she called me a murderer and spat at me?"

"Try not to think about that. Like you said, you can't change what they believe. Not unless you give them a reason to believe differently. I'm talking about when she said somebody saw something." Peace waited for a response. When all she got was a blank look, she added, "Could there have been a witness? Is that what she meant?" She watched Flannery, thinking her reaction to that possibility would say a lot.

Flannery stopped pacing and let the damp towel drop to her shoulders. "If there is a witness ..." She paused, tilting her head to one side, staring into space, then looked at Peace. "How can I find out? Will you help me?"

"Sure," Peace waited to see if Flannery had a suggestion. When none was forthcoming, she said, "One thing I thought of ... you could go to the police and offer to be part of a lineup. At the very least, that would tell them you have nothing to hide."

Flannery looked at Peace for a few seconds, then turned and headed for the bedroom. Over her shoulder, she said, "That will prove I'm innocent. Especially if I volunteer. I'll get dressed."

Though Peace had suggested the trip, she was uneasy with the idea of the two of them going to the police alone. She called after Flannery, "Want to call your grandparents and ask them to go with you? You know, for moral support?"

Flannery waved one hand above her head, dismissing the idea. "They're strangers, outsiders, to the police here. It'll be better if you go with me. You're from around here. They know you." She disappeared. Five minutes later, she was back, sans makeup and with her still-damp hair swept back in a ponytail. She grabbed her coat from the chair where she'd tossed it and motioned for Peace to do the same.

Twenty-Four

"Rachel?"

She heard her name and looked around. She was home now, sitting in her own living room, though she didn't remember the ride through town with Bella and Amanda.

Bella asked, "Are you sure you'll be okay?"

The question, spoken with such kindness, cut through Rachel like a knife. "Yes." She barely managed to get the word out.

"Do you want me to stay until your mother gets home?" Bella paused. "Or you can come home with me." Another pause. "That would be better. I'll cook you something."

"No," Rachel said. "I'm fine. Really."

Amanda watched, quiet for a change. In fact, she'd been unusually quiet ever since Rachel had launched into her tirade in front of the house on Ashland Avenue. She seemed to regard Rachel with a new respect.

Rachel felt like an exhibit in a freak show with both of them studying her. She knew they were concerned for her and wanted to help. If only they knew how much worse they made her feel. She suppressed the urge to shout *just go!* She dared not let them suspect how much their presence added to her distress. She made a monumental effort not to cringe under Bella's touch and repeated, "I'm fine."

Bella didn't look convinced.

Help came from an unexpected source. Amanda touched Bella's arm and said, "She's finally realizing Tony's gone. She needs to be alone."

Bella ran a caressing finger across Rachel's cheek. "Is that what you need?"

She nodded.

Amanda took Bella by the arm, turned her around, and guided her toward the door.

Rachel heaved a huge sigh when the door closed behind them, a sigh that expressed both relief and dread. Amanda couldn't know how right she'd been. She needed time alone. Time to think. Her breath escaped in ragged bursts. She closed her eyes, forced herself to take deep, cleansing breaths, and tried to concentrate, but her thoughts flew back and forth like an out-of-control trapeze, no net in sight. She rode the sickening arc, holding tight, as she imagined telling her parents the truth and, when that became too painful, all the way to the other end, hanging on, maintaining the lie, hoping she didn't get caught. What were her chances? She was pretty sure no one suspected her so far, but the prospect of a witness terrified her. Bella's words came back to taunt her: *Somebody saw something*. Had that been a random statement? A hopeful shot in the dark? Or had the witness given the investigator a description, enough to create a drawing? *Composite. That's what they call them.* If so, would they share it with Tony's parents, hoping they would recognize the person? Would Bella and Angelo know it was her? Would such a thought even occur to them? How good were those things anyway?

She was suffocating. Beads of perspiration dripped from her forehead into her eyes. She reached to wipe them away, caught a glimpse of her arm, and realized she was still wearing her coat and gloves. That brought a grim laugh, but no relief. She removed the outdoor clothing and went to the closet in the foyer to put it away. The physicality of the action−standing, walking the few steps, opening a door, selecting a hanger, stuffing gloves into a pocket−brought some relief. Motion was simple; it required no thought, no decision.

She tried to think of something else to do, something to keep reflection at bay until her mother got home, an event she anticipated with equal parts dread and longing. Doylestown, for all its self-perception of sophistication, is, at heart, a small town. Rachel was certain news of the afternoon's confrontation had reached the courthouse by now. If it had, her mother knew. There were very few secrets in the beehive of county government. She tried to relax, but could not. She held her phone in her hand, waiting for a call from her mother, trying to still her racing thoughts and concentrate on what she would say. She framed sentence after sentence that trailed off into nothing. How could she explain something she did not understand herself?

As much as Rachel dreaded her mother's call, she was desperate to talk to someone. Who? There was no one with whom she dared share her secret. No one in Doylestown. If she were at school ... As if of their own volition, her thumbs pressed keys, sending a message to B.R. "Need 2 talk 2 U" and waited for a response.

None came.

She stared at the phone, not surprised. B.R was an out-of-sight-out-of-mind kind of guy. Unlike Tony. But Tony was gone. As she had wanted him to be. No. She hadn't wanted him *gone*. Just out of *her* life.

B.R., on the other hand, she definitely wanted in her life, especially now. He was the only person she could think of who might understand what she'd done. B.R. could tell her what to do. She shut her eyes and held them closed for a count of twenty, telling herself he would answer her message. *One, two, three* ... He'd know it was urgent. ... *nineteen, twenty*. She opened her eyes and looked at her phone. Nothing. Maybe he hadn't seen her text. She shook her head, fighting panic. "It's okay," she whispered to herself. She hadn't said anything about urgency. He probably thought she just wanted to chat. She looked at the phone again. Still nothing. *Maybe it's for the best*. This wasn't a problem that could be solved over the phone.

The doorbell startled her. *The police!* She took a few seconds to compose herself before she went to the door. Not the police, but almost as bad.

"Amanda. Come on in."

Amanda nodded, but didn't say anything until they were in the living room. "I've been thinking. We had those women scared. We need to keep up the pressure."

Rachel waited for more, suspecting Amanda had a plan, afraid to think what it might be.

Amanda went on, "I called a bunch of my friends and we're going to picket that house until she confesses. If you call your and Tony's friends, we can get a huge crowd. She'll cave. She almost did today. I could see it in her eyes. She's on the edge. We're going to push her over."

By the time the words were out of Amanda's mouth, Rachel was shaking her head. "I can't do that."

Amanda waved both hands furiously, as though erasing from the air the words Rachel had spoken. "Yes, you can," she said. "Today, at first you were too scared to say anything, but then, all of the sudden, you got brave. You were wonderful. You're the key. When you started screaming, even the redhead bolted. She won't be able to stand us outside her house. She'll make her cousin confess." She paused to lift her chin. "We'll have justice. It won't bring Tony back, but ..." Another pause, this one even more dramatic. "Because of us, she'll be in jail. How does that make you feel?"

Rachel just managed to make it to the bathroom before she threw up.

Later, after Amanda had gone and she was alone, Rachel remembered the girl's wild enthusiasm, her praise: "You were wonderful," she'd said, her eyes filled with awe, and, more to the point, her conviction that Rachel could help put the scared stranger in jail. She clutched the sides of her head and moaned. *How do I stop this?* The only answer that came to her prompted another moan, deeper and more primal than the first.

Twenty-Five

Peace glanced sideways at her cousin. She looked different with no makeup and without a mass of luxuriant hair framing her face. Was that her intent? Had she deliberately changed her appearance? Almost involuntarily, Peace reached out to touch the ponytail. "Shouldn't you at least dry your hair first?"

Flannery jerked to a halt. "It's fine."

"You'll catch cold if you go out with wet hair." Embarrassed when Flannery looked back at her with a quizzically-cocked eyebrow, Peace mumbled, "My mom's always telling me that."

Flannery surprised her with a grim laugh. "Finally, something we have in common." She stood by the door tapping her foot. "Come on. Get your coat. I want to get this over with."

# # #

They found Chief Grimaldi in the station's outer office, apparently giving instructions to the receptionist. He looked up when they entered.

Peace knew the moment he realized who they were. His eyes narrowed and his body tensed. She waited for Flannery to speak up.

She didn't. Instead, she took a step backward and darted a scared look in Peace's direction, her demeanor a far cry from her earlier *I want to get this over with.*

The police chief remained silent, but he nodded and favored them with a half smile.

Afraid Flannery might bolt, Peace said, "We heard there might be a witness."

"Witness?" Grimaldi's slitted eyes were almost closed now. "Where'd you hear that?"

Peace looked at Flannery, willing her to say something. Wasn't that what this was all about? Standing there, pressed against the door frame, Flannery looked guilty as sin. Peace knew it was up to her. She said, "We didn't exactly hear there is a witness, just something that made us think there might be."

"Oh?"

Finally, Flannery spoke. "We were attacked on the street."

"Attacked?"

Flannery nodded.

When she didn't elaborate, Grimaldi looked at Peace.

She said, "Not physically. Verbally. We were ... out ..." She hesitated, unwilling to prompt questions about where they'd been. "When we got home, three women were sitting on my porch steps. Waiting for us."

"Three women?"

"Yes. One of them said she was Tony's mother. The other two were younger. I'm pretty sure one of them was his fiancee."

"And they attacked you?"

Flannery said, "Yes."

"The nature of the attack?"

"They called me a murderer. Spat at me."

"Did they threaten you?"

"Not exactly."

"What, exactly, did they say?"

"Mostly, it was the way they acted."

"What made you think there might be a witness?"

"One of them said so. She said, 'Somebody saw something.'"

"That's all?"

Flannery nodded.

Grimaldi seemed to give this some thought. "Which one said it?"

Flannery moved closer and said, "The old one. His mother."

He studied her for a moment, glanced at Peace briefly, then looked back at Flannery. "Maybe you better tell me what happened. Everything they said."

Flannery launched into a blow-by-blow account of the encounter, gaining confidence as she went along, indignation replacing her earlier hesitancy.

Grimaldi listened quietly, never taking his eyes off her face. When she finished, he said, "I understand this is upsetting, but it's not sufficient to warrant my becoming involved. If it happens again, let me know and I'll—"

Flannery interrupted him. "That's not why we're here. I came to volunteer to be part of a lineup. The witness can look us over and see if I'm the person she saw."

"She?"

"Or he. Whoever."

Grimaldi looked at her for a long time without speaking.

Peace, standing quietly to the side, wondered if he was taking stock, comparing the make-up-free, hair-skinned-back look that was Flannery today with the picture-perfect image she usually presented to the world.

As the silence grew, Flannery began to fidget, sliding the zipper of her coat up and down. "Well?" she finally said.

Grimaldi said, "I'm still not sure why you think there's a witness."

"I just told you. She said so. The boy's mother, I mean."

"You said she told you that somebody saw something. Is that all she said?"

Both Flannery and Peace nodded.

Grimaldi said, "You don't think she could have been speaking generically? Hoping somebody saw something?"

Peace said, "I guess that's possible."

Flannery shot her a dirty look and said to the police chief, "Well, just remember, I offered to be part of a lineup. I'm cooperating in every way I know how."

"I'll keep that in mind. Thanks for coming by." Grimaldi turned back to the counter and the papers he'd been studying when they'd come in. His face was expressionless.

After a moment that seemed an eternity, Peace said, "Okay. I guess that's it." She nudged Flannery, edging her toward the door.

# # #

"He must be one heck of a poker player," Flannery said when they were back out on the street.

"Yes," Peace said, then, "What do you think? Is there a witness or not?"

Flannery shrugged. "Who knows? I've done all I can."

They walked the next block in silence, giving Peace time to think and analyze Grimaldi's reaction to Flannery's offer. By the time they reached home, her conclusion had changed half a dozen times, ranging from: *there is no witness* to *there is a witness and they described someone who could be Flannery and he's playing his cards close, hoping she'll panic and make his job easier.*

They were inside with the teapot whistling before Flannery announced her conclusion. "There is no witness." She said it smugly, with, Peace thought, a touch of relief.

"So?" Peace said "Where does that leave you?"

"I don't know. Poppy said he was going to call his lawyer in Richmond and ask what he thinks we should do. He's thinking maybe we should talk to someone local." She stopped to look at Peace. "Do you have a lawyer or know one?"

Peace shook her head and, after a minute, said, "My mom probably does. She works at American Friends Service Committee in Philly. I'm sure they have lawyers on staff, but I doubt if they do much criminal work."

Flannery's face contorted. "I am not a criminal." With that, she flounced out of the room.

Left alone, Peace thought back to the scene she and Flannery had just reported to Chief Grimaldi. She couldn't get the behavior of the young woman who was supposedly the fiancee of the victim out of her mind. It still seemed *off* to her. Flannery had suggested that she was in shock. Logical as that sounded, shock didn't seem quite the right term to Peace.

She sat down, folded her hands in her lap, closed her eyes, and cleared her mind of everything except those few minutes. *She was quiet. Watchful. Then she went crazy. When did that happen?* She got up and paced the room a couple of times, still thinking, ignoring Henry's hopeful glance toward the kitchen and his leash. *When did she change?* Then it hit her with a force that almost took her breath away. *She saw me looking at her. That's when she started screaming. It was almost like she was putting on an act for the others.*

She stopped at the window, staring at the spot on the sidewalk where Flannery's accusers had stood. She was confident she was on to something, but had no idea what it might be. Should she contact Grimaldi and add this to what they'd told him earlier? What would she say if she did? She shook her head. The impression was too tenuous to put into words.

Twenty-Six

Five forty-eight. Rachel paced the kitchen, always managing to keep one eye on the microwave clock, willing its numbers to roll over, willing her mother to walk through the door. *She should be here. She's never this late.* Not that she thought her mother would have good news. She didn't delude herself. The news wouldn't be good. How could it? But, at this point, she was desperate for *any* news. She had to know what was going on.

The sound of the garage door going up stopped her. She went to open the door.

Her mother came in, brushed by her without a word, and went straight to the dining area, where she stood at the head of the long table. "Rachel! Here! Now!" Lisa pointed to a chair.

Seldom in her eighteen years had Rachel heard that tone in her mother's voice or seen that degree of anger in her eyes. She put aside her questions and seated herself in the indicated chair.

Lisa didn't speak for a minute. Instead, she stood a few feet from Rachel, shaking her head, her lips compressed into a grim line. Her body trembled as though it were filled with a liquid about to boil over.

Afraid to ask, but more afraid not to, Rachel managed to get out one word. "What?"

"What do you think?" Lisa rested her fingertips on the table and leaned toward Rachel. "I want an explanation, young lady."

"Explanation of what? I don't know what you're so mad about."

"No? You betrayed me. That's what. Anything that happens in the D.A.'s office is confidential. You've known that since you were old enough to know where I work." Lisa removed her hands from the table and clasped them in front of her. "I shouldn't have told you about the witness, but I thought it would make you feel better. I never dreamed you'd tell anyone. Especially after I specifically told you not to."

Rachel was too shaken by the ferocity of her mother's anger to respond.

"Why?" Lisa leaned closer. "Just tell me why."

"Mom, I didn't say anything. Not to anyone. I swear on a stack of Bibles I didn't."

"Then how ..." Lisa straightened up and took a step back without taking her eyes off Rachel's face. After a few second, she said, "Don't lie to me! This is serious."

"I'm not lying. I don't know what happened, but−"

"I'll tell you what happened." Lisa pulled out a chair and dropped heavily into it. She placed both hands on the table edge as though she needed an anchor. "I just spent a good forty-five minutes on the carpet." She paused for breath. "Chief Grimaldi called the office this afternoon, just as we were getting ready to leave, and said he'd had a visit from the young lady who claimed her car was stolen from the shopping center." She looked at Rachel. "Yes, that car. The one that ran down Tony. Seems she heard there was a witness and she volunteered to take part in a lineup."

"Omigod!" Rachel closed her eyes and put her head down on the table.

"My boss wanted to know if I'd said anything to Tony's mother."

"What did you tell him?"

"The truth. That I told you, but that you understand the confidentiality of this office and would not betray it." She reached over and put her hand under Rachel's chin and lifted her face, forcing her to make eye contact. "Are you lying to me? You know how I feel about that. Not only do I believe it's wrong, it doesn't work. The truth eventually comes out. I believe that and I thought I'd taught it to you."

"Apparently you lied when you said you had faith in me not to betray you." Rachel's lower lip quivered as she faced her mother.

Lisa looked toward the ceiling and expelled a long breath, the worst of her anger spent. "I do have faith in you, but after spending a long three-quarters of an hour in the boss's office, I started having doubts."

There was a long moment of silence.

Rachel finally spoke, "Mom, I swear I didn't tell anyone, but I think I know what happened."

Calmer now, but still a far cry from the understanding mother Rachel was used to, Lisa said, "Let's hear it." Then, in a voice close to a whisper, almost a prayer: "I want to believe you."

Rachel explained how she, Amanda, and Bella Rosino had visited the museum looking for the owner of the car that had killed Tony, how Amanda had found her address, and their subsequent visit to her home. She spared no detail in her account of the ugly encounter. She admitted that, although she'd at first tried to hold the others back, she'd been drawn in and said some nasty things herself.

"What sort of things?"

"I don't remember everything I said, but I know I didn't say a word about a witness. At one point Tony's mom was trying to make her confess and she said, 'Somebody saw something' or something like that. I think she just meant that there's almost always someone around, kind of wishful thinking, but maybe the two women interpreted it to mean there actually was a witness." She paused to rub her hand over her forehead. "Turns out there was."

Lisa sat rigidly erect, biting her lips, looking at her daughter. "You're sure that's all?"

"Absolutely." Rachel hesitated. "If Mrs. Rosino knows about the witness, she didn't get it from me."

Lisa continued to look at Rachel for what seemed an eternity before she reached for her hand. "Sorry I doubted you, baby." There were tears in her eyes.

Rachel choked back her own tears and asked the question that had been torturing her all day: "How about the witness? Did she come in?"

Lisa said, "Yes, she came in today, but I don't know what she said. She was in the office for quite a while."

"So," Rachel said, "you don't know any more than you did this morning?"

"Well, I've read the accident reconstruction report."

"Oh?" Rachel was having trouble breathing. "Do they have any idea who was driving the car yet?"

Lisa held up one hand. "Wait a minute. I'm going to call the office and let them know I'm sure you didn't say anything."

A good five minutes later, Lisa put down the phone with a relieved sigh.

Rachel, who had listened to her mother's side of the conversation, said, "They believe you?"

"Yes. I told them ... well, you heard what I said." She paused and leaned closer to Rachel. "They believe me, but they're not happy that you tried to take matters into your own hands." She let that sink in, then added, "I warned you about that too."

"I know. I'm sorry. I just got caught up ..." She let her voice trail.

Lisa reached out to touch her cheek. "I can guess what happened. Both Bella and Amanda can be pretty persuasive."

Her touch brought tears to Rachel's eyes. "What else did he say? I mean, are they any closer to figuring it out?"

"That's interesting. Charlie's−"

"Charlie?"

"Charlie McNeal. He's the lead investigator on this case. I told you that."

"Yeah, I guess. Anyway, go on."

"He's convinced it was the girl who said the car was stolen. He's talked to several people in the shopping center who remember seeing someone of her description, but they can't give a time. Everything points to her, but it's too vague to be much help."

"Does he think she was driving the car when it hit Tony?"

"He's pretty sure she was, but doesn't have anything to prove it. No hard evidence. So far, everything's circumstantial."

"But if she offered to be part of a lineup, doesn't that−?"

"You'd think so," Lisa said. "But Charlie's theory is she's bluffing. She thinks she can throw them off by offering to help. Chief Grimaldi said she looked different when she came by his office than when he saw her the day of the accident."

# # #

The family opted for take-out for dinner. Lisa and Rachel, in turn, related their day for Paul over potstickers and Chinese coleslaw, punctuating the dramatic parts with chopstick flourishes.

He listened quietly, taking it all in like the scientist he was. He looked at Lisa. "You said this morning there were bruises on Tony's body that made them suspect a deliberate act. In other words, murder. Assuming it was the girl who said her car was stolen, what do they think her motive was? She's a stranger in town. Apparently didn't even know Tony. Why would she kill him?"

Lisa said, "That's got everybody stumped. Not only that, but why would she be up there in the first place?"

"Any theories?"

"This is speculation, but one explanation is, not knowing her way around town, she turned the wrong way when she left the shopping center. Then she got lost. When she saw Tony on his bike, she stopped to ask for directions."

"That sounds logical." Rachel hated herself for saying that, but justified it, thinking she didn't deserve to be labeled a murderer any more than the other girl did.

"Maybe." Paul thought a minute, then added, "But why'd she kill him?"

"They must have gotten into an argument," Lisa said. "The reconstruction report indicates that Tony was leaning into the car, talking to the driver. She opened the door for some reason ... must've gotten mad about something because it looks like the door was opened with enough force to knock him down."

"They can tell all that?" Rachel whispered.

Lisa nodded and went on. "Again, this is speculation. When the car door hit him, he landed on his backside in the road. That would be consistent with the location of the bruises. And there were abrasions on his elbows that look like he landed on them. Then, for some reason ... no idea why ... Tony went around to the front of the car. She hit the accelerator. She didn't run over him. It looks like the car barely struck him. Hit him with just enough force to make him fall onto the car. He slid off the hood, landed on his head and broke his neck."

The explanation was so eerily close to what had happened, Rachel started to shake.

Lisa got up and put her arms around her daughter. "Oh, honey, I'm sorry. I know this is painful for you."

Rachel gripped the seat of the chair, trying to gain control of her body.

Paul persisted. "Why would they argue? I'm sure Tony tried to be helpful. He wouldn't make a pass at her or anything. That'd be totally out of character for him."

Lisa nodded. "You got it. Everybody knows Tony and nobody can imagine him doing anything inappropriate. What could have set her off?"

Rachel choked back the bile rising in her throat and asked to be excused. She headed for the stairs, aware of the coded look her parents exchanged.

In her room, she sat in the center of her bed, Buddha style, holding her left hand in the air, staring at the ring. The beam from her bedside lamp hit it, sending stabs of light into the air, as though broadcasting an urgent message. She'd put the ring on after the scene with Amanda, not wanting to give anyone else a reason to question her relationship with Tony.

Her mother appeared at the door. "You okay, honey?"

"Okay?" She looked up at the ceiling. "I don't even know what that means right now."

Lisa pointed to the ring. "What made you decide to wear it?"

"It seemed like the right thing to do. Mostly for Tony's parents. Just for a while. I'm still going to give it back, though."

Lisa said, "Good idea." Then: "Want to talk?"

"Not now."

"Okay. You know Daddy and I are here for you. Always." When Rachel didn't respond, she left.

Alone, Rachel thought about how much she *did* want to talk. But not to her parents. Who then? B.R's face floated into her mind. He was the only one who might understand.

What reason could she give her parents for a trip to State College? Should she ask to borrow her mother's car or offer to take the bus? She really needed the car because B.R. might be hard to find.

Her phone, lying on the bed next to her, rang. She checked caller i.d. *Amanda*. She slipped the phone under the pillow and lay there, board-still, eyes closed, until the muffled tones finally stopped. Immediately, the phone downstairs rang. She put her hands over her ears. It didn't help.

Her mother called up the stairs. "Rachel. For you. Amanda."

She descended the stairs slowly. Amanda was the last person she wanted to talk to. She could guess the reason for the call—a new plan—one Rachel did not want any part of. Midway down, an idea came to her and by the time her mother handed her the phone, she knew what she was going to do.

She listened as Amanda explained what she wanted to do, then said, "Sorry, I can't. I have to drive up to State College tomorrow. There's something I have to take care of for one of my classes.

Amanda started to argue, but Rachel stood firm.

She replaced the receiver and turned to her parents, who made no attempt to hide the fact they'd been listening to her side of the conversation."

"Let me guess," her mother said. "She wants to go back to that house."

"Yes. And you know how she is. She won't leave me alone no matter what I say. I'd like to just not be here when she calls." She focused on her mother. "I really could go to State College. I don't suppose you could do without your car for a couple of days?" She paused. "Or I could take the bus."

Lisa shook her head. "That's not necessary. "I walk to work half the time anyway. It's a good idea for you to get away. And not just because of Amanda."

Paul nodded in agreement.

THURSDAY

Twenty-Seven

Neither Peace nor Flannery had been able to sleep, so here they were, not exactly bright-eyed and busy-tailed, but awake and facing each other across a table that resembled a groaning board. True, it was a rather puny resemblance, but still ...

More to fill time than to satisfy hunger, Peace had gone all out and prepared a Pennsylvania Dutch breakfast—meager compared to the spread you'd find out in Lancaster County, but bounteous compared to her usual morning fare—scrambled eggs, a small stack of pancakes, maple syrup, orange juice, canned peaches, and scrapple. Unsure how the last item would go over, she watched Flannery's face when she tasted it. "Well?"

"It's ... okay. What'd you say it is?"

"Scrapple. It's a Pennsylvania Dutch thing. Made from bits and pieces of meat. Pork, mostly scraps, mixed with cornmeal."

"Kind of like sausage?" Flannery wrinkled her nose and pushed the rest of the crispy slab aside. She smiled apologetically at Peace and concentrated on the scrambled eggs.

Peace said, "I guess it's an acquired—"

A shrill, intermittent beeping drowned out the rest of the sentence.

Peace went to the window, pulled the drapes aside and looked out into a sky still only half light.

She glanced over her shoulder toward the wall clock. Six twenty. Almost an hour before the sun was fully risen. She knew her neighbors and couldn't think of any who would be out and about at this hour.

"What's going on?" Flannery asked.

"There's some kids outside. Five of them. They have backpacks. One of them must have bumped a car and set off the alarm." She looked closer and groaned. "This could be a repeat of yesterday."

Flannery's fork clattered to the floor and she was at Peace's side in less than a second. "What're they're up to?"

"Looks like they're going to picket the house." She nudged Flannery and pointed to the girl handing out the signs. "She was here yesterday. The others don't look familiar." She looked closer and was struck by how young they all were—early to mid teens at most.

One of the girls turned so that the words on her sign were visible: MURDERER! COWARD! in large block letters, surrounded by a border of bright red spatters that were obviously meant to represent blood.

Flannery went back to the kitchen, slouched in a chair and stared at the array of mostly untouched food.

Peace stayed by the window, standing partially behind the drape, concealing as much of herself as she could without loosing sight of the girls. She watched them shuffle into a scraggly formation. After a word from their leader, some took a step back, some moved forward, all while continuing to hold high the sign they'd been given. The ongoing racket from the car alarm didn't seem to faze them.

Movement two doors down caught Peace's eye. A man, dressed in a bathrobe, his hair sticking out in tufted disarray, appeared on the edge of his porch and stretched his arm toward the car. The alarm stopped abruptly. He yelled at the girls, watched them for a few minutes, then shook his head and went back inside.

The interruption made a shambles of the picket line, forcing the girls to regroup. Once they did, they began marching in ragged disarray past the steps leading to Peace's home. The girl who'd handed out the signs, obviously in charge, stepped in. She spaced the protesters equal distances apart and choreographed their movement into an orderly procession that proceeded to the maple tree just left of Peace's front porch, turned in a line as precise as the Rockettes, marched to the front of the house on the right, then repeated the drill.

Peace couldn't help a grudging admiration for the leader's control of her troops, all while checking her phone every few seconds. She wondered if the girl was waiting for a phone call or, maybe, keeping track of the time. Whatever she was doing, she managed it with the efficiency of a drill sergeant, even maintaining order when a car pulled up to the curb.

No!

Peace recognized the car Poppy and Snap-snap had rented for the duration of their stay. Why were *they* here so early? The world seemed intent on proceeding at fast forward this morning. She steeled herself, prepared to hold on tight, and watched.

Ever the gentleman, Poppy exited the car and went round to open the door for Snap-snap, who emerged, carrying a large bakery box. She looked toward the parade of placard-carrying teenagers and said something to Poppy as he was closing her door.

He turned to look at them. A frown wrinkled his brow when he saw the signs. He froze for a moment, apparently assessing the situation, then trotted over to the picket line.

Peace couldn't hear what he said, but his waving arms dispelled any idea that it might be a friendly exchange.

The leader, with an aplomb amazing in one so young, stood her ground.

A girl carrying a sign bearing a roughly-drawn skull and crossbones and a broken bicycle stopped in front of Poppy.

He reached as though to take the sign from her, but the girl stepped back, eluding him.

Peace saw the leader hold her phone out and knew the incident was being filmed.

Snap-snap raced over, grabbed Poppy's arm and pulled him toward the porch.

Peace scurried to the door and held it open.

Snap-snap darted a thankful look toward her and coaxed her husband inside.

When Flannery, who had been sitting at the table, saw her grandparents, she was up like a shot and in Poppy's arms. "That's them," she said. "The people we told you about."

Snap-snap, calm, at least on the surface, said, "I thought you said there were three of them."

"Looks like they got reinforcements. Only one of those ..." Peace nodded toward the window. "Is from yesterday. The one who seems to be in charge. Yesterday she was with two older women. One was the boy's mother. The other was about my age."

Poppy paced and sputtered. "Hooligans."

Snap-snap tried to placate him. "They're not hooligans. They're children. Grieving children."

"Then why aren't they in school?"

"I imagine they're being given some latitude, considering what happened, especially if they were close to the boy who was killed."

"Latitude? They don't need latitude. They need discipline! A good kick in the pants. That's what I'd give them." He jerked open the door and yelled, "My granddaughter is innocent. Go home! Or go to school, where you belong."

The leader said something Peace couldn't hear and the line stopped. The girls moved closer together and stood shoulder to shoulder, holding the accusing signs over their heads. Together, they began chanting: "Mur-Der-Er. Mur-Der-Er. Mur-Der-Er."

Ben slammed the door. He stood, red-faced, uttering unintelligible comments under his breath, but only for a moment. He squared his shoulders, spun around, and made a beeline for the kitchen. He grabbed a pitcher from one of the open shelves near the sink, filled it with water, went back to the door, and yanked it open. In two quick strides he reached the edge of the steps. He took a few seconds to plant himself, then reared his upper torso back and swung his arm in a wide arc, sending a spray of water over the girls.

The line collapsed into chaos amid a chorus of sputtering gasps.

Ben stood looking at their shocked faces, brandishing the empty pitcher over his head.

The indomitable young leader held her cell phone in front of her. She said something. The line reformed and the girls resumed their chant: "Mur-Der-Er. Mur-Der-Er."

Snap-snap raced out, seized Ben's arm and, somehow, managed to get him inside. Once the door was closed, she leaned against it, shaking her head. "You realize you were just filmed throwing water on children in the dead of winter?"

Fire in his eyes, he lifted his chin and looked at her. "I'm not ashamed to be seen defending my family."

"Whether you're ashamed or not, no good can come of this."

New activity on the street caught Peace's eye and distracted her from Poppy's response.

Barely above a whisper, she said, "TV people are here."

Twenty-Eight

It was a few minutes before seven but Rachel was packed and ready to go. Her parents urged her to hurry instead of delaying her departure with last-minute advice as they usually did. They obviously wanted her out of the house before Amanda called. Again.

# # #

The determined teenager had called twice more last night, pleading with Rachel to cancel her trip to State College, insisting that nothing could be more important than her joining the picketers the following morning. The first time she called, she'd stated, with typical Amanda drama, that Rachel's presence just might be the arrow that would pierce the conscience of Tony's killer and make her confess. Amanda's choice of words was more apt than she knew. Her statement pierced Rachel's conscience and caused her hands to shake so badly that she dropped the phone. Her mother picked it up and replaced the receiver in its cradle.

Minutes later, it rang again.

Lisa started to reach for it, but Rachel shook her head. "It's okay, Mom. I'll handle it." and into the phone, "Hi, Amanda. Sorry about that."

"Don't hang up," Amanda said, then, "You have to come. I called the TV people and they're sending one of their teams. They'll be here at seven. You're the one they'll want to talk to."

"No! I'm not talking to them." Rachel held the phone against her chest and looked toward her parents. "She called a TV station. They're sending a reporter tomorrow morning."

Paul Woodard took the phone from her.

"Amanda," he said, "I know you mean to help, but you might be jeopardizing the investigation." He listened for a moment, his mouth tightening into a straight, stern line. "No. Rachel is not going to–" More listening, then, "Stop it! You're heartbroken about Tony. I understand that. So is Rachel. So are all of us, but what you're planning won't help." A brief silence. "You have no right to make Rachel feel guilty she's still alive. Please do not go through with this." More listening. "You should have checked before you called the station. Rachel is not going to speak to them. Not tomorrow. Not until this case is solved. It's in the hands of the D.A.'s investigator. He's the professional." He slammed the phone back into its cradle.

# # #

The memory of last night's phone calls kept goodbyes short.

Lisa kissed Rachel's cheek as she handed over the car keys. "Where's your scarf? It's cold out."

"I don't know. I must have left it somewhere."

Lisa went to the closet and came back with a bright blue scarf. "Here, wear this." She wound the scarf around Rachel's neck. "And don't forget to call me when you get there."

Her father gave her a brief hug. "Be careful, especially when you get to I-80. There'll be a lot of truck traffic. And they'll be pushing hard to get their loads to New York."

Rachel returned his hug. She longed to tell them how much she appreciated their unquestioning faith in her, but how could she? She dare not plant even the faintest suggestion that there may be a reason for them *not* to have faith. She bit her lip, feeling she would burst if she didn't tell someone. She couldn't let them suspect that she needed to get away from them as much as from Amanda. And Bella Rosino. Rachel was terrified of facing Tony's mother again. Or his father. The more distance she could put between herself and anyone who knew Tony the better.

# # #

There wasn't much traffic on the first leg of the journey. It was a different story once she turned onto I-80. On the other side of the median, huge semis whooshed eastward at speeds far in excess of the speed limit. Fortunately, westbound traffic was relatively light. The long, straight stretch of road made for easy driving, giving her much-needed time to think.

Last night, when she'd made her plan, it had seemed so right. So simple. She'd been sure B.R. could tell her what to do. Now, she wondered if she dared tell him the whole truth. Had she entered territory that even B.R. would find unnavigable? No, she told herself. *That can't be true.* It was he who had challenged her to be daring. He would understand.

A dead deer by the side of the road distracted her. The twisted angle of its neck reminded her of the last time she'd seen Tony—so different from her other memories of him. Alive, he'd been perpetual motion, bouncing with energy, full of plans, all of which had included her. Lying there, beside the road, he'd been so still. The opposing images divided her life into two distinct parts.

Before and after.

Both were dominated by Tony. It was almost impossible to remember a day without his presence. If she concentrated, she could recall random scenes of the time before she'd known him, but they were the dim, misty memories of early childhood. She'd been ten years old that day in fifth grade when he'd planted himself so firmly in her life. Thinking back, she had to admit that most of it had been fun: ballgames, victory parades, dances, parties, knowing she was part of the popular crowd, the pacesetters, looked up to by everyone.

It was just the last year that it had begun to pale. Tony's constant presence, the assumption, not just by Tony, but by everyone, that he was the center of her universe, began to feel like an abrasion to her soul. She remembered the day last summer when she'd suggested they skip the Phillies game with the rest of the gang and go to a performance of Macbeth at DeSales University. He'd pantomimed falling asleep, complete with loud fake snores. Rachel didn't laugh at him like she usually did. Instead, she'd said, "Okay. Fine. I'll find someone else to go with me."

He'd quickly backtracked, saying, "Hey, I was kidding."

She still didn't laugh. Nor did she accept his apology. Instead, she went with a friend, someone outside their usual crowd. In her mind, that marked the beginning of the end of their relationship. If Tony noticed, he didn't acknowledge it. He was his usual confident self, never seeming to realize that Rachel didn't always welcome his attention. He remained a constant presence. Charming, but always there. She'd longed to be free of him, but hadn't found the courage to tell him until that night. Saturday night, less than a week ago, marked the end of the first part of her life.

On Sunday, the second part began, but it was far different than the one she'd envisioned. Tony was still there. His death blocked the door to the new world she'd been so determined to enter more effectively than his living presence ever had.

She forced her mind to leave these depressing thoughts. There had to be a way out of this. She allowed herself to think about the life she had begun to taste the past few months: hours spent in dizzying conversation, talk that propelled her into ideas that stretched the horizon further than she had imagined possible. At the center of this new universe was Brandon Richards. B. R. Brash and reckless. And, to Rachel, mesmerizing and elusive.

Elusive? Yes. What did she really know about him? He talked non-stop, but never about himself, his family, or his home in the west. She didn't even know where in the west. She guessed California, though, when pressed for details, he always changed the subject or tossed off an answer that revealed nothing.

She wasn't even sure of his address or what classes he took. She knew he worked nights, cleaning offices at a professional building in town. During the day, he spent a lot of time in the coffee shop. Talking. Always talking. Words were playthings to B.R. No, not playthings. Building blocks. He created worlds from words. Rachel had never met anyone like him. The people in the life she was so eager to leave behind used words differently, sparingly. Her father, the scientist. Her mother, part of the staff of the district attorney's office. Her friends, obsessed with the Philadelphia sports scene. All of these people used words in an earthbound manner. Their words were tools, a means to an end, used to describe something concrete. B.R.'s words were different. They flew higher, promising something well beyond their dictionary definition. And yet, for all the magic and charisma surrounding him, Rachel sensed a longing. For what, she had no idea, and the need to know bewitched her, challenged her in a way nothing else ever had.

The afternoon before she left State College for Doylestown, she'd asked him when he was leaving to go home for the holidays. She thought she'd seen a fleeting glimpse of sadness in his eyes. Then he'd shrugged and said he wasn't going home, that he had a chance to earn a few extra bucks. Wasn't money what this whole holiday hoopla was about anyway? He flashed his dazzling smile and said he was going to outsmart the system and make money instead of spending it.

Rachel had toyed with the idea of asking him to take at least Christmas day off and spend it with her family in Doylestown. The thought of introducing him to her parents had stopped her. And Tony, of course. She hadn't yet officially broken up with Tony and B.R.'s presence would be an enormous complication. So she'd held back on the invitation. She needed to prepare her old world for this person who represented her new world.

Now, she wondered what would have happened if she had acted on that impulse. Would he have accepted? Probably not. But ... if he had? What would her parents have thought of him? How would they have acted? They'd be polite. She knew that. Would they have known that she was secretly in love with him? She was pretty sure her mom would guess. Would Tony have? Their friends? Would any of them have understood what she saw in B.R?

# # #

She drove along College Avenue and saw the parking place from which B.R. had so blithely *borrowed* the car. A wave of nausea rose, forcing her to slow to a crawl.

Horns blasted from every side.

She looked in her rearview mirror and saw a hairy fist raised, middle finger erect.

She waved an apology, resumed normal speed, and wove through the streets until she found a parking spot in a residential neighborhood a couple of blocks away. She left the car and walked back to the center of town, determined to find B.R. It was almost eleven on a Thursday morning. She assumed he'd worked last night, but he should be up by now. Probably in his favorite coffee shop.

She saw him through the window, hunched over a book, one hand on his head, clutching the wiry, coppered-colored curls, the other gripping a steaming cardboard cup. In this rare moment of stillness, he looked different. Ordinary. Doubt washed over her. How could he give her the help she'd come seeking? She almost turned away, but had no idea where to go.

She entered the shop and approached his table. He didn't look up until she said his name. "Hi, Brendan." She didn't know why she called him by name, not the initials that represented the brash, reckless persona he'd adopted as his own.

His body stiffened. He slid one finger down the page, presumably marking his place. For a split second, when his eyes met hers, Rachel saw something she had never seen before. It was gone before she could identify what it was. She sensed she'd taken him from a place and thoughts he wasn't used to sharing.

"Hey." He flashed the familiar B.R. grin. "Couldn't take the warm, fuzzy Christmas scene with the folks, huh?"

Rachel attempted to smile back. "That's not it." She hesitated. "I need to talk to you."

He waved toward the chair opposite him.

She shook her head. "Not here."

A quizzically lifted eyebrow asked for an explanation.

"Something's happened." She choked on the last word and had to stop for a breath. When she could speak again, she said, "I don't know who else to talk to." When he didn't respond, she took his hand. "Let's go somewhere quiet."

For a moment, he remained rooted in the chair, staring at her. "Okay," he finally said. He closed the book, rose and grabbed his scarred leather jacket from the chair back. He paused at the door to drape a long, white scarf artfully around his neck.

Rachel watched, knowing it was a look he'd copied from an old movie, an affectation that in the past had made her smile. Today, it seemed sad.

They both shivered when they stepped outside. It was colder than it had been the past few days and the sky was an unbroken slate gray. B.R. had no gloves. He slipped his hands in his pockets, holding the book against his side with one arm, and looked at Rachel. "Well?"

She blurted it out in a whisper: "I killed someone."

He looked at her, his brow furrowed, but there was no doubt he knew what she'd said.

"I didn't mean to. It ... happened." She could tell he didn't believe her. Not at first. Then he did.

"You didn't mean to? So ... you had an accident?"

"Yes, that's what it was. An accident. Well, not exactly. I ..." She stopped, unable to go on. The moment she'd driven away, leaving Tony lying by the side of the road flashed before her, choking off her words.

Twenty-Nine

Peace stood at the window, shoulder to shoulder with Flannery, Snap-snap and Poppy. They watched a white van, decorated with the logo of a local TV station, ease into a tight parking spot two doors down.

A blond woman, petite and perfectly coifed, stepped out. A man holding a bulky camera exited the van from the driver's side. The girl they'd come to think of as the leader of the picketers approached the woman, with the other girls following in her wake.

Flannery said, "She's showing him her phone."

Butterflies danced in Peace's midsection.

"The video," Snap-snap said in a voice barely above a whisper.

Poppy let out a long, audible breath.

The reporter spoke to the leader a few minutes, then signaled to the cameraman, who responded by pointing the lens toward the reporter and the cluster of girls.

They watched the leader make a sweeping gesture toward the house. It didn't take much imagination to guess what she was saying. Minutes later, the reporter spoke to the man with the camera. He nodded. They crossed the street and stopped a few feet from the steps leading to Peace's front porch. The reporter brushed her hair off her face, adjusted the collar of her coat, and stood facing the camera for a moment before she half-turned and pointed to the house.

Viewing her in profile, Peace could see only that her head was nodding and her lips were moving. After a few seconds of that, she completed the turn and started up the porch steps. Peace was prepared for the knock that followed but, still, it made her jump. She put her hand on her stomach to calm the butterflies and looked at the others.

Snap-snap put one arm around Flannery's waist and pulled her close.

Poppy looked ready to pounce.

Peace opened the door. "Hello."

The reporter pushed the microphone toward her. "Channel−"

Before she could finish identifying herself, Poppy was there. He stepped in front of Peace. "I suppose you're here about the accident." His voice was grave, but managed to convey authority.

"Yes."

"We're very sorry about what happened, but my granddaughter is also a victim." When the reporter held the microphone closer to his face, Ben added, "This is a tragedy for everyone concerned. We have nothing more to say." He closed the door firmly in the reporter's face, went to the window, and pulled the drapes closed.

Another knock, louder this time.

Poppy stood between Peace and the door, shaking his head.

The four of them remained utterly still until they heard the engine start and a vehicle pull away. Even then, no one spoke for a moment. The silence of the room amplified the sounds on the street. Once the engine faded, the voices of the teenaged girls, high-pitched with excitement, traveled across the street and penetrated the walls. Then the voices stopped, replaced by other sounds.

Peace went to the window and lifted the side of one drape slightly away from the frame. Through this narrow slit, she watched the girls pick up their backpacks and shove in the signs they'd been carrying, pushing the stick down so that the messages rose above the book shapes that bulged against the sides. They helped each other shrug the packs over their shoulders and trooped off with the signs protruding crookedly over their heads. They moved quickly, laughing and chattering, seemingly elated over their morning's adventure.

She glanced at the clock and was surprised to see that it was only seven fifteen. The kids are leaving now," she said. "Looks like they're going to school."

Karalee looked at Ben. "See, they're not a bunch of derelicts. They're not truants. They set this up early so they could get to school on time."

"Is that supposed to make me like them?"

"Maybe not," she said. "But it's something to think about. Don't underestimate them. They're a force to be reckoned with."

"They're kids!"

"Yes, they are, but they thought ahead and arranged for the press to meet them here before they went to school. That takes planning. Imagine how they're going look on camera. A bunch of fresh-faced schoolgirls fighting for justice."

"Justice? In America, that's supposed to mean innocent until proven guilty. Those little she-devils are trying and convicting Flannery without knowing what happened. You call that justice?"

"It doesn't matter what I call it. I'm talking about how it will look in short clips on TV. And I'm sure by the time this airs, they'll have copies of those videos showing you trying to grab the sign and then ..." She paused, her voice slowing, enunciating each syllable. "Throwing water on children."

Flannery, who had been quiet until now, burst into tears. "I didn't do anything wrong! Why doesn't anyone believe me?"

Peace added her voice to Ben's and Karalee's, all three of them assuring Flannery that they believed her.

"No, you don't!" She flounced across the room and plopped into a chair. "At least not completely. No matter what you say, a part of you wonders if I did this terrible thing. I see it in your eyes."

No one had an answer for that.

Karalee broke the silence. "Ben, it's time for us to go home." Her words were spoken softly, but they carried more force than Peace had ever heard from her, hinting at a steel core within the demure southern lady. There was no doubt in Peace's mind that by *home,* her grandmother meant Virginia.

Ben pulled his phone from his pocket without acknowledging his wife's statement, though it was clear from the narrowing of his eyes that he'd heard her.

Karalee stepped closer, making it impossible for him to ignore her, and added, "I mean it. Not just for ourselves. It's what's best for Flannery."

"No." Ben's square chin jutted out and his teeth were clenched. "We're going to see this through. We can't afford to look like we're running away." After a quick look toward Flannery, he concentrated on his phone.

Karalee asked, "Who?"

"I'm calling Leyland."

"You think we need an attorney?"

"We should at least run this by him. See what he says."

"I agree, but I still think we should get out of here. If we disappear, they'll ..."–she paused to nod toward the window– "... forget about us."

"No, they won't. Those little girls have bees in their bonnets. They won't let it go, especially now that they've been on television."

"Maybe not, but they can't follow us all the way to Richmond. The police will continue their investigation and, eventually, they'll figure it out." When Ben didn't answer, she asked, "Can the police make us stay?"

He shrugged. "I don't think so. I'll ask Leyland." He pushed a button on the phone and walked into the kitchen.

Karalee went to Flannery and gathered her in a tight hug. "It's going to work out, honey. Don't worry."

Peace, sitting on the sofa with her fingers buried in Henry's soft fur, hoped her grandmother was right. She listened to Poppy's side of the phone conversation. After he explained the situation, there was a long period of listening before he said "thanks" and joined them in the living room.

"Well?" Karalee said. "Can the police make us stay?"

"No. They can't hold Flannery unless they bring charges and they obviously don't have evidence to do that. We're better off staying here and toughing it out."

Peace broke in. "Maybe you should tell your side of the story."

Flannery scoffed. "That's what I've been trying to do, but no one will listen."

"I mean to the TV people. They tried to get a statement, but ..." Peace paused to look at Ben. "You sent them away." She smiled when she said this, hoping he wouldn't be offended by the implied criticism. When he didn't seem to be, she added, "Maybe you should talk to them."

He gave a short laugh. "That's pretty close to what my lawyer just advised."

Peace thought she detected something new in his eyes, something she hadn't seen before. Love, yes. She'd seen love and a willingness to welcome her into his world, but it had been an undemanding love—much like the affection she showered on Henry. This time she saw respect. Pride swelled through her, the feeling that she'd crossed a new threshold.

Thirty

B.R. stared at Rachel. "Are you saying what I think you are?"

She looked back, too miserable to even nod.

They were standing in the middle of the sidewalk, with people eddying around them.

B.R. grabbed Rachel's wrist and pulled her over next to the building.

She waited for him to say something, trying to read his expression, unwilling to give up the idea that he could somehow make it right.

Finally, he asked, "Why are you telling me this?"

"I need advice."

"Why me?"

"There's no one else." Tears ran down her cheeks, stinging when the cold air hit them.

"What about your family?"

"I can't tell them. It would break their heart."

B.R. looked around, like he was searching for an escape route. After what seemed forever, he looked back at Rachel. "Let's get out of here."

She nodded. "We can go to my room. My roommate's gone home."

"No. Some place more private. Did you drive?"

She nodded.

"Where's the car?"

"I parked a couple of blocks from campus." She pointed in the direction from which she'd come.

Still holding her wrist, he started walking that way. "Did anyone see you?"

"What difference does that make?"

"Look, Rach, I'm sorry. I don't want any part of this. Not if the police are after you."

"They're not. They don't know I'm involved. Nobody does." She took a couple of skipping steps to keep up with him.

"So why are you running away? Why're you here?"

They were within sight of the car now. When they reached it, she put her hand on the door and said, "Let's sit in there. It'll be warmer."

B.R. looked around before he got in and, once inside, he leaned forward, holding his hand so that it hid most of his face from passersby. "Why me?"

Rachel explained about the breakup, about *borrowing* the car, how important it had been to talk to Tony and make him understand.

"Yeah, yeah, yeah, I got that." He held up one hand, "But what does it have to do with me?"

"I took the car because of you. I did what you taught me to do."

"I never ran over anybody."

"I didn't run over him. He threw himself on the hood and, when I started the car, he fell off." The image of the dead deer flashed before her. "I think he broke his neck. That's not my fault, is it?"

"I can't believe you stole a car."

"You do it all the time."

"No, I don't do it all the time. I took a car one night and I knew the owner. I knew he was going to a party and he'd be gone for a couple of hours. You took a stranger's car. There's a difference. You had no idea when they'd be back."

Rachel stared at him in disbelief. "You let me think ..."

"I can't help what you thought."

His words echoed in the car. They rang in her ears. Nothing was as she had thought. The brave new world she thought she'd discovered spun beyond her reach. She rested her head on the steering wheel. "I can't think any more." After a few minutes, she lifted her head and looked at him. "I need someone who isn't involved to tell me what to do."

He was quiet for a few minutes, studying her, drumming his fingertips on his knees. "You're sure nobody suspects you?"

"Yes." She clasped the steering wheel and let it go.

"So? Why don't you just ride it out?"

"Because there's someone they do suspect and I'm the only who knows she's innocent."

"If she's innocent, she'll be okay."

"But if she's not? Okay, I mean. Innocent people get convicted all the time. And even if she doesn't, it'll be hanging over her head. It could ruin her life.

"That's her problem. You got your own life to worry about."

"That's all you have to say about it?" She looked sideways, seeking the leprechaun, and saw the face of Mephistopheles.

"What else is there?" he asked. When she didn't answer, he added, "You want my advice? Go home. Keep your mouth shut." He opened the door, but before he got out, he said. "I'm not going to tell anyone what you told me. And there's no reason for you to tell anyone we talked about it."

She sat alone in the car after he left, her head against the seat back, her eyes closed. Her last hope dashed. Her idol shattered. She opened her eyes when someone tapped on the window. She had no idea how long she'd been sitting there.

A man with a neatly-trimmed beard mouthed through the glass, "Everything okay?"

She nodded and forced a smile.

He looked skeptical, but he crossed the street and went into a house with an ivy-covered chimney. The light that spilled out when he opened the door was golden, reminding Rachel of home.

She looked around. Streetlights cast a blurry glow against an almost-dark sky. Cars pulled into driveways. People emerged from them carrying briefcases. Some looked at her curiously but, except for the bearded man, no one approached. She was alone, an alien in a neighborhood that looked eerily like the one she called home.

She shivered, her first realization that she was cold. And hungry. She hadn't eaten since an early breakfast with her parents. It seemed long ago, another world, a place of warmth and safety. B.R. was right. She should go home. How could she? Even there, she was an alien. Where else could she go?

Her phone rang. She picked it up and looked at the screen. *Mom.* She turned it off and tossed it aside. *I'll call her later.* She started the car and drove aimlessly around town, looking for a place to eat. Every restaurant she passed, she rejected, afraid she'd run into someone she knew.

She headed out of town, hesitated when she approached the turn onto 322, but not knowing where else to go, she remained on the road leading home. There was another moment of hesitation when she came to 80, but she made the turn, still heading toward home. The road ran through wild country, with only an occasional farmhouse light making a puny attempt to keep the darkness at bay. Her headlights fell on winter-bare trees, their limbs reaching up as though in supplication. Another dead deer lay at the roadside, its open, glassy eyes reflecting the light. She shuddered, thinking again of Tony. An exit sign caught her eye. Loch Haven. Drawn by the idea of a haven, she turned, heading north. More forested land bordered the highway. Ahead, she saw a neon sign over a sprawling building proclaiming *Biggest & Best Burgers in the County*. She pulled into the parking lot, hoping food would fill the hollowness inside.

The interior was semi-dark and filled with murmuring voices that stilled for a moment when Rachel entered, then ignored her and resumed their conversations. Rachel caught the eye of a woman taking orders at a nearby table; the woman nodded and waved, indicating that she could seat herself. In the back, running the width of the room, there was a bar with a deer head mounted over it. Rachel chose a chair with its back to the dead animal's glassy stare. The burger she ordered may not have been the biggest in the county, but it had to be close. She managed to get through half of it and, not sure what was next, asked to have the other half wrapped.

Back in the car, she turned on the phone and listened to her mother's message: "Rachel, we're worried. Call. Let us know you're okay." She turned the phone off, intending to gather her thoughts and come up with a plan before she returned the call. No plan came. She'd have to wing it. She turned the phone back on and discovered a text from B.R.: *I was a creep. Don't know if I can help. Will try."*

Her hand shook as she punched in his number.

"Hi, Rachel. You okay?"

"No." She choked on the word, an admission she hadn't meant to make.

A long pause, then, "Listen, sorry about this afternoon. Still want my advice?"

"Yes." The word came out as a sigh. Relief, tinged with hope. "Thanks."

"Where are you now?"

"In the parking lot of a restaurant on the road to Loch Haven. Where are you?"

"Working. But it's not too bad tonight. I can take a break ... maybe half an hour ... then come back and get everything done before seven. That's when I'm supposed to be out of here."

"You're sure you don't mind?"

"Yeah. I don't have wheels though. You'll have to pick me up."

"Sure. Where?"

"You know where I work?"

"Yes."

"Pull up in front. I'll do the front offices first. Blink your lights a couple of times. I'll be watching for you."

She checked messages again. Another voice message from her mother: "Rachel! Where are you? If we don't hear soon, we're calling the State Police."

State Police! As much as she wanted to get to B.R., the last thing she needed was to have a bunch of Staties looking for her. She pushed in the house phone number.

Her mother answered immediately. "Rachel! Thank God. Are you okay?"

"Of course." She forced a laugh. "Sorry I didn't call. I got to talking with some friends and forgot." She remembered all the calls she'd ignored. "I turned off my phone and just saw your messages."

"Just so you're safe. Daddy and I were worried sick. Thought you'd been in an accident."

"I am. Safe, I mean, not in an accident. I thought I'd stay here for a couple of days. Give Amanda a chance to cool down."

Her mother gave a short bark of a laugh. "I don't think that's going to happen anytime soon. She was all over the news at noon, then again this evening. Frankly, I think she's having the time of her life."

"Really?"

"Yes. Then, on the evening news, that girl and her family were on too. Said they wanted to set things straight. It's a big story here."

"What'd she have to say? That girl."

"About what you'd expect. Insisted the car was stolen. That she had nothing to do with Tony's death."

"Do you believe her?"

"I'm not sure. She didn't come across very well. Sounds and looks like a spoiled brat. Very pretty. The kind of girl who takes it for granted everybody loves her. An older man, her grandfather, I think it was, had his arm around her shoulders the whole time she was talking. Other ..." Her mother's voice drifted.

Rachel heard her father say something in the background, then her mother again: "Your father and I both think you're better off staying there. If you're here, Amanda will find a way to drag you in."

Relief washed over her. "That's what I was thinking, but I didn't know how you'd feel about it."

"As much as I hate to say it, it's probably best." Another pause. "Where will you stay?"

Rachel said the first thing that popped into her head: "I ran into Bethany today. When I told her what happened, she invited me to spend a couple of nights with her. She lives in Williamsport. About an hour from here. You met her once when you were here."

"I remember. Nice girl." Another pause. Rachel heard her mother updating her father; then: "It's only eight days 'til Christmas. We want you home then. Amanda or no Amanda."

"Of course." Then, because she needed to get to B.R. as soon as possible and knew her mother didn't want to let her go, Rachel said, "Look, I'm supposed to meet some friends. I'll call you in the morning."

"Don't forget this time."

"I won't. Love ya. Bye." Without waiting for a response, Rachel disconnected, started the car and headed back to State College.

She spent most of the drive thinking. Not so much about B.R. She was glad he'd called, but she wasn't counting on him to solve her problem. Their meeting this afternoon had awakened her from that dream. She realized he was not as much of a free spirit as she'd thought. Mostly, she thought about Amanda and the whole business with the media. She had no idea how to deal with that–and no doubt that sooner or later, she'd have to. Unless she could disappear, an idea that had planted itself in her head, an invasive refrain that refused to go away.

Thirty-One

Peace sat on the floor. Henry's big head was in her lap, his sad eyes offering to fix whatever was upsetting his mistress. Her grandparents, Ben and Karalee, occupied the sofa with Flannery between them. The evening news was over and the television had been turned off, leaving an ominous quiet in the room. Peace fidgeted. What should she say? What *could* she say? A harsh jangle broke the silence.

Flannery said, "Probably Aunt Holly. I'm sure she saw it too."

Peace gave Henry a gentle shove and rose to get the phone. It wasn't Holly; it was Kirk.

"Wow," he said. "I just watched the news."

"What did you think?"

"Umm ... well ..."

"Want to come over?"

"Sure."

Two minutes later, the doorbell rang.

Peace opened the door and, against her will, stole a look across the street. The picket line processed solemnly, casting shifting images as it moved back and forth under the streetlights. The time was six thirty, well after dark in December in Pennsylvania. There'd been a respite during most of the day, presumably while the girls were in school, but activity resumed about five o'clock. At first, they were raucous, reinforcing the message of their signs with shouts, but about half an hour into the demonstration, a police car stopped and motioned for the girls to approach. After the car left, the line resumed its motion, but there was no shouting. When the girls spotted the open door, they broke their silence, chanting: "Confess!" There was a break and a single, clear voice called out: "Admit what you did."

Kirk slipped through the door.

Peace tried not to resent it when Flannery greeted him with a hug that seemed excessive in view of the short time she'd known him.

Kirk didn't seem to mind. He returned the hug, then held her at arms's length. He tilted his head toward the street. "How long has that been going on?"

Flannery said, "They were here before dawn."

"All day?"

Peace said, "They left when the TV people did, apparently went to school, and came back about an hour ago."

He looked at Flannery and said, "They're just kids. I wouldn't worry about them too much."

Flannery didn't look convinced.

He said, "You looked really good on TV."

"Thanks," she said. "But let's be honest. Next to those kids, I looked like the Wicked Witch of the West."

Ben stood up, ready to take charge. "It wasn't that bad. At least you have manners. Those girls are like vultures. Preying on someone else's misfortune. Enjoying the spotlight."

Privately, Peace thought the girls had come across pretty well. They'd been passionate, yes, but when they told their story—that of a young hero cut down in his prime—you'd have to have ice water in your veins not to sympathize. As expected, someone had given the station the two cell phone videos—one of Ben reaching for the sign and one of him throwing water on the kids. Both were shown in the broadcast. Particularly striking was Ben, standing on the porch, towering over the girls, his mouth open, his eyes narrow slits, making the girls look even younger, more innocent. As for Flannery, this time her perfect hair and stylish clothes worked against her. She looked like the spoiled, pampered darling of a wealthy family.

Spoiled and pampered? That's pretty much what Peace believed her to be. But was she guilty of murder? Of this, Peace was less sure. Logic seemed to point to her, but there was something else, something Peace couldn't put her finger on, that whispered there might be another answer.

"Peace?" Kirk's voice snapped her out of her reverie. When she looked at him, he said, "Your family's trying to decide about dinner. What do you think?"

What *did* she think? If they went out, the girls would probably follow them to the restaurant, maybe even picket outside. She tried to recall what she had in her pantry. Not much. Cereal. Tuna. Canned soup. It was Thursday. The family had been here since Saturday and there had been no time to think about preparing meals for a crowd. Besides, she wasn't exactly a gourmet cook. "We could order pizza," was the best she could come up with.

The suggestion was greeted by an emphatic "no" from Ben. "I refuse to let those girls dictate to me. I planned to take my family out to dinner tonight and that's what I'm going to do." He looked first at Peace, then Kirk. "One of you must have a suggestion." A sheepish grin crept over his face as he added, "Maybe not right here in town."

Kirk said, "How about Piper Tavern. That's fairly close, but they can't follow you there unless they have cars."

Ben looked at Kirk, still dressed in his painting clothes. "It's good? Not some ragtag place?"

"Ben!" Karalee said, then turned to Kirk. "Don't mind him. He's only half civilized when he's hungry."

Kirk laughed. "Definitely not ragtag. It's an old Bucks County tavern. My parents usually go there on their anniversary. They like it because there're no TV screens. Plus, of course, great food."

Ben put his hand on Kirk's shoulder. "My wife's right. Don't mind me. I just want a nice place to take the family. You're invited too, of course."

"Uh, well, I ..."

Flannery looked up at him through those long, dark lashes. "Please come."

"I need to grab a shower and change." He looked back at Ben. "If you don't mind waiting."

"Of course not."

Peace watched and listened, not sure if she wanted Kirk to come or not. His presence had always been a safe place for her, a feeling that she was just fine as she was. No need to reach for a more sophisticated persona. Or so it had been. Now, seeing his response to Flannery's fluttering lashes, she began to question things she'd thought were carved in stone. Most of all, she was beginning to realize that being part of an extended family, a condition she'd dreamed about for most of her life, was a mixed blessing. She'd never before appreciated the comfortable, straightforward life Caroline had made for her. She'd listened to school friends complain about their families, only half believing the stories they told. She heard about rivalries between siblings and cousins, but couldn't imagine feeling that way. She'd been sure if she were lucky enough to have a cousin, she would treasure her. A sister would have been pure Heaven. As for a brother, since the day she moved into this apartment and met Kirk, he'd filled that role to perfection. Now, she was taken unawares by what she had to admit was jealousy when she saw him with Flannery.

# # #

Peace noticed Ben taking in details as they walked through the bar area on their way to the dining room. She saw him nudge Karalee and point to a sign that urged visitors to *Let us linger here in the foolishness of things.*

The hostess led them to a round table, perfect for the six of them: Peace, Kirk, Flannery, Ben, Karalee, and Holly. She seated them with the usual smile, looking at each of them without really seeing any of them. It wasn't until a waitress came to take their drink order that Peace knew for sure their notoriety reached beyond Doylestown. The woman's eyes widened when she saw Flannery. She opened her mouth as if to speak, then closed it and glanced around the table at the rest of them. When she got to Ben, there was another flicker of recognition. Ben had stood by Flannery's side when she made her statement for the evening news. By the time the salads were served, it was clear the waitress wasn't the only one who recognized them. Other people darted surreptitious glances their way and leaned forward to speak in whispered tones. It wasn't hard to imagine what they were talking about.

Karalee set the tone for the family, keeping up a stream of light banter. Ben went along, holding up his end of the repartee, but it was clear to Peace that he was having a hard time not confronting the other restaurant patrons.

They were almost finished with the meal when an elderly gentlemen came to their table. He focused on Flannery. "Are you the young woman who ran over one of our boys?"

She looked for a moment like she would burst into tears, but rallied and looked him in the eye. "I know that's what people are saying, but it's not true. Did you see me on television?"

"Yes."

"Well, then you heard what happened. It was exactly like I said in my statement." Her hands, resting on the tabletop, clenched into tight fists, scrunching the cloth and threatening to topple her water glass.

The man studied her for another minute, then turned and left without apology.

Even without looking around, Peace knew that everyone in the dining room was staring at them.

Holly, who was sitting next to Flannery, reached for her hand and squeezed it. "It'll be okay, honey," she said. "The truth will come out eventually."

Flannery responded to her aunt with a brave smile, but her lower lip was trembling.

Ben said, "I think it's time we gave the truth a little help. As far as I can tell, the police in this town aren't doing much. I'm ready to take matters in my own hands."

Karalee said, "Haven't you done enough?"

He lifted his chin, thrusting it forward. "I intend to find out who did this."

Thirty-Two

Rachel hit the switch, flashing her headlights against the building, holding her breath and praying silently. *Please come.* When B.R. appeared, she released the breath and sent up another quick prayer. *Thank you.* She hadn't admitted to herself how unsure she'd been.

"I appreciate your coming," she said when he opened the car door.

"No problem." A sheepish look then, "Look, I don't have much time. We'll talk here. Pull around back. No one will disturb us there."

She did as he said and, after she'd turned off the engine, thanked him again. The smell emanating from the overflowing dumpster, not more than a yard from where she'd parked, penetrated the car, so strong she almost gagged. She tried not to think about what might produce such an odor. Yellow light from overhead fixtures illuminated graffiti drawn in neon colors on the building they faced. She looked away, embarrassed by the lewd images and lurid suggestions. Her gaze fell on B.R.'s profile, outlined against the window. Just an average guy. How could she have thought he would save her?

He started talking without turning to face her. His voice was a husky whisper. "I don't know what you should do, but I'll tell you some things about myself. Stuff nobody else knows. Nobody around here anyway." A long pause, then: "My brother's a drug dealer." He turned and looked at her through half-closed eyes. "Don't think he's a bad guy. He's not. He's the best person I know. He took care of me. Raised me. He's five years older than I am." He paused, staring out the window for what seemed a long time before he resumed. "Doesn't seem like that much now, but when you're a kid, five years is a lot. Our parents were ..." He caught his lower lip between his teeth and stopped again. Whatever he was going to say about his parents remained unfinished. After a minute, he continued. "Colin, that's my brother, didn't want me to deal. He wanted me to stay in school. Told me he'd beat the crap out of me if I didn't. I knew he didn't mean it. Not about beating me up, I mean. He never hit me. But he wanted me to finish high school so I stayed. I always tried to do what he said." B.R. hesitated, his lips twisting into a grimace.

Rachel could tell he was fighting for control. She wanted to touch him, but was afraid to, so she waited, hardly daring to breathe. Her phone rang. She glanced at it as she turned it off.

"Your parents?"

"Yeah."

"They know where you are?"

"Sort of. They knew I was coming up here. Matter of fact, they were all for it. I talked to my mom a little bit ago. She was upset because I didn't call to tell them I got here safely."

"You always do that?"

She nodded.

"You're lucky," he said. "About your parents, I mean. My brother used to keep track of me. I hated it. Now I miss it."

"Used to?"

"Um hmm."

"What happened?" When he didn't answer, she asked in a whisper, "Did he die?"

"He's in jail." He hunched his shoulders and flashed a semblance of the old brash and reckless grin. "Shocked?"

"No." She was telling the truth. She wasn't shocked. A week ago, she would have been, but the world had taken on a different tilt in that short time.

"Like I said, I tried to stay in school. It was tough. Not classes. I never had a problem there, but the rest of it ..." He stopped, bit his lip, looking straight ahead as though remembering. "I didn't fit anywhere. The smart kids thought I was a loser. The losers didn't like me 'cause I was smart. So I snuck some weed from Colin's stache one morning. Took it to school with me." He gave her a sideways look. "Everybody knew about my brother. Knew I had a supply. Somebody was always after me to get something for them. So I did. Thought it would help me make friends." Silence. "I got caught. It wasn't much and it was the first time, so they called my mom instead of the cops. Told her to come get me. She never showed. I think she meant to, but ..." He paused, shrugged his shoulders. "Doesn't matter." More silence. "They asked if there was anyone else I could call. I wouldn't give them Colin's name because he didn't need any more trouble. So, they called the cops. Colin found out about it. I don't know how. Anyway, he showed up at the station. He told them he'd put the stuff in my backpack to hide it and forgot to take it out. They let me go.

Mostly, I think, because they didn't know what else to do with me." He stared at his hands, painted a sickly yellow by the light.

Rachel asked, "How'd you end up here?"

The question seemed to revive him. He squared his shoulders and looked directly at her. "Colin. He took all the cash he had and drove me to the bus station. Bought a ticket to Pittsburg and gave me the rest of the money."

"Pittsburg? All the way from California?"

He shook his head. "California's not the only place west of here. I grew up in Oregon. Bend." He went on: "Colin wanted to get me as far away as possible. Pittsburg was what he could afford and still have money to give me. Told me to get a job, find a school to go to and stay out of trouble." B.R. stopped again, put his hand in front of his eyes.

Rachel dug a tissue out of her purse and handed it to him. "You miss him a lot, don't you?"

He nodded.

Knowing it was up to her to keep the exchange going, Rachel asked, "What did you do when you got to Pittsburg?"

"Kept clean. Got a job. Scrubbing floors in the library nights. Got a library card." He looked at her. "You got one?"

Rachel nodded.

"Figured you would. Anyway, started reading all kinds of stuff. During the day, I hung out in the library. Sometimes I talked to this old guy who was always in the magazine room. Got my GED." He looked at Rachel. "You know what that is?"

"Of course."

"Okay. Wasn't sure you would. You probably never needed to know stuff like that."

"I'm not as sheltered as you think I am."

He half-smiled at her, like he knew her truth better than she did. "Anyway, after I got my GED, I came here, enrolled part-time." He shrugged. "You know the rest." After a minute, he added, "What do I think you should do? I don't know. I'm telling you this so you know if you decide to run, it's possible. But it's not easy being on your own. Not for me. Probably be worse for you 'cause you're not used to taking care of yourself. Besides, I imagine it's harder for a girl."

"Are you in touch with your brother?" She had to ask.

"Yeah. I found out he was in jail when I called to let him know I got my GED. When he didn't answer his cell, I called the house and got my mom. She told me he got caught once too often. He's not a juvie any more, so ..." He looked at her and shrugged. "Anyway, my mom seemed glad to hear from me. Gave me an address for Colin. Told me to write to him. Said it would keep his spirits up. Give her credit for that."

"Do you? Write to him?"

He nodded. "Once a week. He writes back too. Says he's proud of me. That's what keeps me going. Keeps me in school. When he gets out, I want to have a good job so I can help him for a change."

"You going back to Oregon?"

"No. I'm going to bring Colin here. He can start over. Like I did." He was quiet for a minute, then looked at his watch. "I have to go. I have three more offices to clean. I can't lose this job. You understand why now, don't you?"

"Definitely."

"And why I can't help you? I don't want to be mixed up in anything against the law."

She nodded and, after a moment, asked, "Why'd you risk stealing a car?"

He threw back his head and looked at the car ceiling. "Bad night. Seeing all you little innocents, I went a little crazy. Wanted to impress you. Didn't dream you'd ever try it yourself." He ran his hands through his hair. "If anybody finds out about that ..." He looked at her.

"I won't tell anyone. No matter what."

He opened the door, turned to Rachel again. "Listen. Good luck." He pointed to the phone on the dash. "If you decide to run, get rid of that. It's the first thing they'll use to trace you." He blew a kiss in her direction and left.

FRIDAY

Thirty-Three

Ben enjoyed watching his wife apply her makeup. There was something about being privy to this very personal side of her that stirred feelings of tender gratitude. He studied her face, the delicate features, high cheekbones, small, straight nose, and large dark eyes, comparing it to that of the twenty-two-year-old he'd married the week after they'd both graduated from the University of Virginia. The years had been kind to Karalee, softening her features without blurring them, accentuating the kindness in her eyes. That quality—kindness—was what had attracted him to her even more than her beauty.

This morning, however, it wasn't soft kindness he saw when he looked at her. This morning, the set of her chin held his attention. Like most couples who've been together a long time, each was expert at interpreting the subtle signals sent by a head tilted just so, eyes ever so slightly narrowed, or, in this case, a chin thrust forward. Not that they didn't talk to each other. They did, but over the years a shorthand had developed that said more than words exchanged.

So ... Ben knew Karalee was not happy with him. True to his nature, he didn't try to distract her with small talk or pretty compliments, but stepped forward to meet the challenge head on. "Go ahead. Say it. Tell me what I did."

She carefully replaced the cap on her mascara before she answered. "Nothing yet, but I really worry about this idea of yours to solve the crime for the police."

He sat down on the bed. "What's the alternative? Let the investigation drag on? Ruin our visit? We came up here to get to know our new granddaughter. Now, this ..." He ran his hand through the thick, only slightly-graying curls that framed his square face.

"I know." Karalee's disapproval wilted. She came to sit beside him, was quiet for a moment before she said, "I wish we hadn't brought Flannery. I was afraid she'd end up stealing all the attention." She paused and a little shiver went through her. "Nothing like this, of course."

They both sighed and lapsed into silence.

Ben spoke first. "What could we do? She wanted to come. How could we say no?"

Karalee slipped an arm around his waist. "You've never been able to tell her no. Maybe that's part of the problem." She felt his body shift and added, "I know. I'm guilty too. We all are. She's so lovely, bright as a sunbeam. It's impossible not to spoil her."

He rose, and turned to face her. "Her being spoiled has nothing to do with this. Whoever took that car didn't know her. They just saw an opportunity and took advantage of it."

Karalee leaned forward a little. "Has it ever occurred to you that we don't really want to know the truth?"

"What's that supposed to mean?"

"I think you know." When he didn't answer, she added, "Surely it's crossed your mind that Flannery isn't telling the truth."

Still no response.

Karalee relented, but only slightly. "I'm not saying I believe she really did hit that young man, but ... well ... I have moments of doubt. Not that I'll ever admit them to anyone but you."

"I should hope not!"

"Ben, be honest. Hasn't it occurred to you that ... you know?"

"That she's lying? That she ran over someone and left him to die?"

Karalee nodded numbly. "I know she wouldn't do it on purpose, but once the accident happened, she might panic and drive away, then try to cover it up. You know, tell herself there was nothing she could do to help him, so why hurt herself?"

Ben turned away, went to the window, and stared out into a December sky the color of pewter. Finally, he turned. "I can't even think about that. If she is guilty, then not owning up is almost worse than the act itself." He stopped, struggling to find the right words, and finally went on, "If she did hit him ... and I don't believe she did ... that was an accident, but lying and refusing to accept responsibility, that's a deliberate choice. She's better than that."

"I hope so, but ..."

"You have moments of doubt?"

"And you?"

He nodded silently, his eyes filled with pain.

The quiet in the room spoke more than their words had. Karalee broke it, rising from her position on the bed and taking her husband's hand. "Okay," she said with a bright smile. "Enough of that. Time to put our best faces forward and go meet our granddaughters."

He smiled back at her. How could he not? "Remind me again where we're going today."

"Peace is taking us to the Pearl S. Buck House."

# # #

"It's on the right just after the stone bridge," Peace said, then, "Here."

Ben nodded and turned into the gently curving lane.

"Look," Karalee said when they came to a small parking area and a sign pointing to a garden area on the other side of the drive. She half-turned to Peace in the back seat. "Should we stop at her gravesite?"

"We can do that on our way out. The tour's at eleven. It's almost that now."

Ben hesitated when they came to a fork in the driveway. "Which way?"

"Left," Peace said. "The Welcome Center. Her Pulitzer and Nobel prizes are on display there." She glanced over at her cousin and added, "There's a gift shop there too."

Flannery, who had been unusually quiet all morning, responded with a smile that was obviously forced.

# # #

Ben and Karalee, true southerners that they were, loved old houses, especially if they had a history. And this house was filled with history—from the art deco Steinway piano, which the docent informed them had been played by Oscar Hammerstein, to the desk and typewriter on which Pearl Buck had written *The Good Earth.*

"In three months," the docent said, as proudly as if the accomplishment had been her own. She pointed out the Korean soapstone chess set with the note perched in front of it, signed by Ms. Buck proclaiming that on such and such a date Janice, one of her seven adopted children, had beaten her. "Pearl Buck never let the children beat her. She believed that everyone must do their best all the time. That's why Janice insisted that her mother sign that note."

So the morning went, with story after fascinating story distracting Ben and Karalee from their doubts about the integrity of their beloved granddaughter. The accounts of the children the writer had adopted prompted them to exchange stolen glances at each other, then at their other, new-to-them, granddaughter. Each knew the other was wondering how this young woman, abandoned as an infant herself, felt hearing about these children, unwanted, considered an inconvenience by their birth families. Did she feel the stigma of being a mere accident? Would she ever feel truly a part of the family that had allowed her to be given away?

As for Peace, there was no outward sign that she considered herself less because she had once been abandoned, but her grandmother couldn't help wondering what scars she carried in her heart.

Thirty-Four

"Call her," Paul said.

Lisa shook her head. "Not yet. Those girls probably spent half the night talking. They'll sleep in this morning." She paused and added, "Bethany seemed like a sensible girl. I hope she'll be able to make Rachel see that none of this is her fault."

Rachel's father looked doubtful. "She wouldn't listen to us."

"True, but coming from someone her own age, it'll have more weight."

They both stared into space. Words were not necessary. Each knew what the other was thinking.

Paul broke the silence by reaching across the table for his wife's hand. "Call," he said. "If you wake her up, so be it. If you don't, you'll have a rotten day." He gave her hand a gentle squeeze and assumed a teasing note. "Look at it like this. You owe it to your colleagues. You won't be able to concentrate on anything until you've talked to her."

Lisa gave him a grateful nod and picked up the phone. After a minute, she spoke, using the precise tone people adopt when they have to leave a message. "Rachel, honey, it's me. Mom. Just want to make sure everything's okay. Call when you get a chance." Her shoulders slumped when she lay the phone down, but she forced another smile.

Paul smiled back. "I'm sure she's fine. Kids have no idea how parents worry."

"I'm not worried. Just missing her."

That she was lying was so obvious he didn't bother to dispute the statement. He looked pointedly at the clock and retrieved his briefcase from a chair. "Call when you hear from her."

"Sure."

A light kiss on her forehead and he was gone.

A good ten minutes later than she usually left for work, Lisa gave up, put her on coat and grabbed her purse. Like an unwatched pot, the phone rang when her hand was on the doorknob.

Thank you!

The light went out of her eyes when she saw who was calling. She considered not picking up, but her conscience wouldn't allow that. "Bella," she said, "How are you holding up? Any news?"

There was a tumble of rushing words, punctuated by sniffling pauses.

Lisa shrugged out of her coat and sat down. This call deserved her full attention. The office would have to wait. She forced even thoughts of her daughter out of her mind as she listened. "I know," she said. "We still can't believe it either." Then Bella made a request that sent her mind racing. She hesitated briefly, then answered as gently as she could. "Rachel's up in State College. I'm sure she'd go with you if she were here, but she ... uh ... had to take care of something. I'll have her call you. If there's anything Paul and I can do ..."

After she hung up, she hit the digit for her husband's private number. He answered immediately. "Have you heard from Rachel?"

"No. The phone rang just as I was going out the door, but it wasn't her. I thought it would be, but ..." A heavy sigh. "It was Bella. The Rosinos want her to go to mass with them on Sunday."

"They're never going to let go of her, are they?" After a moment, he added, "Not that I blame them. If we lost Rachel ..." His voice trailed. "Does Bella have Rachel's cell number?"

"Of course."

"You better call her. Warn her that she'll be hearing from Bella."

"Right." After saying good-bye and promising she'd keep him posted, Lisa tried Rachel's number again. When there was no answer, she left a message: "I'm leaving for work now. Call my cell." She reached for her coat, changed her mind, and went up to her daughter's room to see if she could find a number for Bethany's family. A jumble of papers covered the surface of the desk. Near the top of the stack, Lisa found a list of numbers. She located one she hoped was right and called.

A male voice answered.

Assuming it was Bethany's father, Lisa tried to remember the family's last name, gave up, and said, "Hello. This is Lisa Woodard, Rachel's mother. Is my daughter still there?"

"Excuse me?" He sounded confused.

"Rachel, the girl who spent the night with Bethany. I need to speak to her."

Silence, then: "I'll get Bethany."

Lisa heard the phone being laid down, a voice calling, "Bethany."

A few disembodied words, then a girlish voice: "Mrs. Woodard?"

"Is this Bethany?"

"Yes."

"Is Rachel still there?"

There was a long silence, then, "I haven't seen Rachel for a couple of weeks."

"Really?" Lisa's heart started to pound. "I thought she was spending the night with you. I must have misunderstood. Do you know who she might be with?"

"No, I'm sorry." A long pause. "To tell the truth, we kind of drifted apart lately. I don't know any of the people she's hanging with now."

Lisa said good-bye and hung up. She stared at the phone. *What next?* She called the office, told them she was sorry she was late, and that she'd be in after lunch.

"Don't worry about it. Take the whole day. As much time as you need. You have a lot going on now. We all understand that."

"Thanks." After a few seconds, she added, "I think I will take a few days. I have some personal time coming and I'd like to be on hand for Rachel."

"How is she?"

"So so. I wish they'd find out who did this. Then she can at least begin to get back to normal."

"The end may be in sight. The witness is coming in this afternoon and we're having her meet with the sketch artist."

"Let me know how it goes, okay?"

"Sure."

Without laying the phone down, Lisa pushed in her daughter's number. No answer. No surprise. She left another message: "Rachel, call. Immediately. I just talked to Bethany." A pause to let that sink in. "I want to know where you are. And why you lied to me."

She made more coffee and tried to concentrate on the crossword puzzle while she waited. It wasn't too long, maybe twenty minutes, before Rachel responded.

"Mom, I'm really, really sorry."

"Never mind that. Are you okay?"

"Yeah."

"Where are you?"

"In a little town near school, Loch Haven."

"Are you with friends?"

"No ... uh, I ..."

"Where did you spend the night last night? Was it with a boy? Is that why you broke up with Tony? Is that why you thought you had to lie?"

"No! That's not it. I just need to think."

The desperation in her daughter's voice blunted Lisa's anger, but intensified her concern. "Where did you sleep?"

Silence.

"Rachel?"

"My car."

"The car! Do you know how dangerous that is?"

"It's not as bad as you think, Mom. There's a school here. I'm on their campus. The parking lot by their rec center."

"Why didn't you go to a motel?"

"I don't know. I ... couldn't think where to go."

"Do you have money? Your credit card?"

"Yeah."

"Go to a motel. Call me when you're checked in. Your father and I will there as soon as we can."

"Mom, no!"

Lisa tried to guess what was going on in her daughter's mind. Unsuccessful, she told herself, *She's a good kid. Smart. She won't do anything stupid.* Aloud, she said, "Promise me you won't spend another night in your car. It's not safe. Go to a motel. Better yet, come home. Immediately. Or we're coming up."

"Twenty-four hours. Okay? Can you give me that?"

"What's going on, Rachel?"

"Nothing. I just need some time. Something major has happened in my life. I need time to process it."

"What you need is to be with someone who loves you."

"I'm eighteen, Mom! Not a little girl any more. You and Daddy need to realize that and give me some space."

That brought Lisa up short, reminded her of her own youth. "Okay, but keep in touch." She started to say goodby, then remembered the reason for her call. "Listen, there's something I need to tell you. Bella is trying to get in touch with you. She and Angelo want you to go to mass with them this Sunday."

"Church with Tony's parents is the last thing I need now."

"I don't disagree, but I'm sure you'll be hearing from Bella. You need to think about what you're going to say."

"All right."

"And find a motel. A decent one. Call me when you do. Let me know where you are."

"Mom! Could you stop a minute? Just back off!"

Thirty-Five

It was quiet in the car when they left Pearl Buck's home. Ben and Karalee were in the front, with Ben driving and Karalee resting her head against the seatback. Flannery was gazing out the window. She looked a million miles away.

Peace found the lack of conversation unsettling. Three months ago, when she'd learned the family would be visiting, she started thinking of ways to entertain them. She suspected they pitied her and couldn't bear that thought. She wanted them to know she was more than the abandoned infant they'd heard about. She was determined to show them how good her life was, how interesting the area where she'd grown up. Green Hills Farm, where Pearl Buck had lived most of her life after leaving China, was one of the first places that came to mind. Could anyone fail to be impressed by the stories told there? She looked at the other persons in the car.

So much for Peace's carefully-laid plans. Of course, when she'd made them, the situation had been different. She thought she'd be dealing with a clean slate. She hadn't anticipated a cloud of this magnitude hanging over them. How could she? Even so, she had hoped the house tour would be a distraction. She should have known better. How could anything distract them from the threat of a murder charge?

Ben interrupted her thoughts. "What are we doing about lunch today?"

Karalee sat up straight and looked at Peace, one eyebrow arched, a question in her eyes.

Peace thought a minute. "Let's go back to my place. I'll make lunch. You haven't had a real Philly cheesesteak yet." She saw her grandmother open her mouth, presumably to protest, and added, "You've been treating me the whole time you've been here. It's my turn."

Karalee reached over the seat to touch Peace's arm.

That touch told Peace that her grandmother understood and respected her need to not just be a taker.

Ben, after a quick glance at his wife, said, "Sounds good to me. Steak and cheese is the way to this man's heart, no matter what city it's named for."

# # #

"I won't be long," Peace said when Ben pulled into the supermarket parking lot. "I just need to pick up the steak and some Provolone. Everything else I have on hand." She insisted on the others waiting in the car. This was to be her treat and she didn't want an argument at the checkout counter about who was going to pay.

At home, she busied herself slicing the steak as thin as possible and set it aside while she sliced onions, peppers and mushrooms into three small, separate pans. She went all out, making a bigger production of it than she usually would, unwilling to let the day be a complete bust.

Snap-snap and Poppy hovered, watching, offering encouragement, commenting on the wonderful smells, and generally making proud grandparent noises that delighted Peace.

Flannery remained aloof, either from jealousy or because of the cloud hovering over her. Peace couldn't tell which and, though she hated admitting it even to herself, didn't really care. She was sick of thinking about Flannery and her problems.

When the sautéed vegetables were almost done, she quickly browned the steak, breaking it into smaller pieces with the spatula, then placing the cheese on top and, when it had melted and merged with the meat, she scooped the combination into soft Italian rolls.

"Okay, here's your basic cheesesteak," she said when she placed a sandwich before each of them. She put some hot sauce and the sauteed onions, peppers and mushrooms on hotpads in the center of the table. "Now's the best part. You get to add whatever you like. Make it personal."

The cheesesteaks got rave reviews. Such raves, in fact, that Peace wondered if it was a bit too much. She pushed these doubts aside and decided to accept the compliments at face value.

After the heavy lunch, Karalee announced that she could use a nap. She looked at Ben, who was pacing and obviously too restless for a sedentary afternoon. "I'll go back to the B and B. You can stay here with the girls."

Ben nodded and mumbled, "Um."

That settled, Karalee put on her coat and, after a quick kiss on Ben's cheek, left the three of them alone.

He went to the window and watched her drive away. When the car disappeared, he resumed his circuit of the room, which seemed to become smaller moment by moment.

Peace dreaded spending the afternoon cooped up with a restless grandfather and a gloomy cousin. She glanced from one to the other, knowing it was up to her to think of something. She approached Ben and put a hand on his arm. "How about a walk? You said you were interested in checking out the local architecture."

"Sure," he said, then: "We should get away before school's out. I have a feeling those little girls,"–he tilted his head toward the window–"haven't given up with their picketing."

Flannery shuddered and shrank further into the corner of the sofa. "I'll stay here if you don't mind. Frankly, I've had enough of this quaint little town."

Peace bit off the first response that came to mind. After all that had happened, who could blame Flannery for not appreciating the town's charm?

Ben looked torn for a moment before he turned to Peace. "Guess we're on our own. Mind conducting a private tour?"

"Not at all."

"Holly told me there's a Civil War Museum here."

She nodded.

"Ever been there?"

"Yes. It's pretty good. They have a lot of stuff. Not just old guns. Other things too, but it's only open on Saturdays."

"So much for that. What do you suggest for today?"

"There's a lot of variety in the residential areas. And you might like to see the new Justice Center."

# # #

They walked along Ashland Street, past fine old buildings, stately and solid, as though they'd been built to last forever. Ben stopped in front of most of them, commenting on details.

"It's fascinating to look at these through your eyes," Peace said. "I walk past them almost every day, but I guess I take them for granted."

"They're worth studying," Ben told her. "Be sure to look up." He pointed toward the rooftops. "There's a lot going on above our usual sightline. Eaves and cupolas. Rainspouts, gables, beautiful stonework. Whimsical details." He paused, smiling. "That gargoyle, for instance."

Peace followed the direction of his hand. "Looks like he's laughing at us."

Ben nodded. "The architect who put him there had a sense of humor. Always a good thing."

They continued their ambling stroll, by turns chatting and lapsing into companionable silence, getting to know each other. When they came to Broad Street, Peace said. "The Civil War Museum's just up the hill. Too bad it's not open today."

"That's okay," Ben said. "Tomorrow will be better anyway. Your grandmother can come with us."

"Is she interested in the Civil War?"

He laughed. "All southerners are interested in the Civil War. It's a hangnail we can't leave alone. Besides, she loves poking around any place where they have old things." He looked at Peace with a rueful smile. "Another southern trait, I'm afraid. See what you missed by not growing up in the bosom of the Francis family?" He put his hand on her shoulder. "You can't know how glad we are to have you now. And, truth be told, I welcome the different background you bring. Adds a touch of class."

"I'm glad too. I think our differences make us both better. My mom always says diversity is both the biggest problem and biggest asset of this country."

There was a moment that threatened to become heavy. Ben saved it, saying, "Well, let's focus on the asset part of that. Where next?"

"We can walk uptown. To the Justice Center."

"Sounds good."

Peace watched Ben's face as he studied the building's facade. She couldn't tell if he admired it or not and was about to ask him when she saw the familiar figure of Chief Grimaldi exiting the building.

Peace waved when he glanced their way.

He nodded, but kept moving, heading toward the street.

Ben noticed Grimaldi as he was about to cross the street. Leaving Peace behind, he hurried after him.

She followed, catching up in time to hear Ben say: "Any news on who stole my granddaughter's car?"

"Afraid not," Grimaldi said.

"Any leads you're following?" When Grimaldi didn't answer, he tried another tack. "I understand my girls paid you a visit and Flannery offered to be part of a line-up."

The only response from Grimaldi was an intense frown while he chewed on his lower lip.

Undeterred, Ben went on, "How about a polygraph? Would that convince you she's telling the truth?"

"What makes you think I don't believe her?"

Ben returned the chief's harsh look. "Whether you believe her or not, there's an element in this town that doesn't. I assume you're aware that a group of young people have been harassing us."

Grimaldi's expression didn't change.

Ben kept poking. "You must know about their picket line. The insults they've shouted. Did you see them on TV? That one-sided newscast?"

Grimaldi shrugged, but said nothing.

Peace could sense her grandfather was about to lose his temper and it occurred to her the chief was deliberately trying to provoke him.

After a short but intense staring contest, Grimaldi said, "I saw the newscast. It didn't seem all that one-sided to me. Your granddaughter had a chance to tell her side."

"Yes ... well..." Ben's voice drifted. He was beginning to lose his bluster. He finished with a mild, "If there's anything we can do to end this ..."

Grimaldi stopped chewing his lip long enough to say, "There may be something."

Ben latched onto the statement like he'd been thrown a lifeline. "Just tell us what. We want this to end."

"No more than I do."

When Ben looked about to speak again, Grimaldi held up his hand traffic-cop style. "Remember I said 'maybe'. I'll let you know if anything comes up." Before Ben could say more, the chief was halfway across the street.

Thirty-Six

Rachel watched the screen on her phone go black. What if the last words she ever said to her mother were "back off"? She shook her head. *It won't come to that.*

She started the car and drove randomly until a sign perched high above the roadway caught her eye.

She pulled into the motel parking lot, approached the desk and handed over her credit card. It crossed her mind that might not be a good idea. She pushed that thought away, trying to dismiss the idea lurking there.

In the room, she hung up her coat, shed her wrinkled clothes, and headed for the shower. After a night in the car, the warm water streaming over her shoulders felt Heaven-sent, a balm to both body and spirit. She flexed her shoulders and breathed deeply, managing to push her current dilemma to the back of her mind. Even the scent of the generic soap provided by the motel seemed luxurious. Afterwards, she took her time toweling off, savoring the comfort of the ordinary ritual. The hair drier had a strange hum, but it did the job.

Refreshed, ready to move forward, she sank into a chair, ready for serious thought.

A plan. I need a plan.

Nothing came. Too frazzled to sit, she got up, paced, and finally settled on the bed. A nap might help. Sleep wouldn't come. She sat up, tucked her feet under her, Buddha-style and tried to empty her mind. It didn't work. Instead, a series of tableaus marched through her head, none of them good. Which was the least bad?

She knew what she *should* do. Go back to Doylestown, march into the D.A.'s office, and confess. Throw herself on the mercy of the court. The problem with that ... Actually there were multiple problems, but the first that came to mind was that her mother worked in that office. She shuddered at the thought of walking past her mother ...

She wouldn't do it that way. She'd go home, tell her parents, and ask her mother who was the best person to confess to. Maybe they'd go together. A new thought hit.

What if they think Mom knew all along?

It would be better to just go. Confess. *Then* tell her parents. They'd be shocked, but they'd get over it. Except they wouldn't. Their world would fall apart. She couldn't do that to them. Or to the Rosinos. Confessing wouldn't bring Tony back. Surely it was kinder to let them believe his death had been random, that no one had borne their son malice. Which, of course, was true. No malice had been involved. So Rachel told herself. The more she thought, the more tangled the web became.

If only she could disappear. Never have to face anyone who'd known Tony. She let the idea floating in her thoughts surface. Could she do it? Should she?

Or should she keep to her current course and hope no one figured it out? And why would they? No one had a reason to suspect her. Unless ...

She clicked on the TV. The midday news was on. Would there be anything about a murder in Doylestown? She watched to the end. There was a sweet story about a dog and his owner being reunited. Everything else was grim, but at least it didn't involve her personally. No mention of Doylestown. She switched off the TV, determined to focus on a plan. Something workable. Realistic. One that would hurt the fewest people.

Her phone sounded. Bella's name showed on the screen. Rachel stared at the phone, scarcely breathing, remembering her mother's words, "Bella and Angelo want you to go to mass with them this Sunday". Only when the phone stilled with no message being left, did she begin to breathe normally. If Bella and Angelo wanted her to go to church with them, they didn't suspect that she was involved in their son's death. Maybe B.R was right. Maybe she could ride it out. She wondered about the witness. She couldn't recall anyone driving by so it must have been quick. They hadn't stopped. Could they have seen enough to be helpful? *Mom might know. She didn't go in today, but her office seems to be keeping her in the loop.*

She picked up the phone and pushed in her mother's number.

Lisa answered right away. "Hi, honey. Where are you?"

"A motel in Loch Haven." *No reason not to tell her.*

"Is it in a safe neighborhood?"

"Very."

"Good."

Rachel sensed her mother's hesitation and remembered her harsh "back off" the last time they spoke. "I'm sorry I snapped at you before, but I really need some time."

"I know. I appreciate your letting us know where you are. I almost called you earlier, but I didn't know if you'd answer."

"I would have," Rachel said, not sure if it was true.

"Anyway, since you're on the phone now, I'll bring you up to date. My office called. The witness was in, but she wasn't much help. All she could remember was seeing the back of a young man who was leaning into a car and the profile of someone in the car. She's sure the person in the car was female, but doesn't remember details."

"That's a shame," Rachel said, hoping her relief didn't register over the phone.

"There is hope, though," her mother went on. "Someone suggested a forensic hypnotist. It's possible, under hypnosis, she'll remember enough for the artist to create a useful sketch."

"What're the chances?"

"Apparently pretty good. They've done this in other jurisdictions with success."

Silence. Rachel knew she was expected to say something. She asked, "When?"

"Monday. The witness is coming in again and she'll meet with the hypnotist and an artist." A sigh, then: "Maybe the end is in sight."

"Let's hope so." Rachel managed, just, to get the words out and say goodbye.

She placed the phone on the bedside table and stared at the ceiling, her hand on her chest. Her heart was pounding, her mind racing.

She thought more about disappearing. *Is it possible?* She tried to work out the logistics. Where would she go? How would she live? She got up, took her purse from the drawer where she'd placed it before she lay down, emptied her wallet on the bed, and counted her cash - $76.48. A crumpled MAC receipt showed a balance of $311.53 in her account. More than she usually had, but still not much. It would go fast and, if she didn't want to be traced, she couldn't use her credit card. Still, almost $400 would get her somewhere and she could get a job. What kind of job? Something under the radar. That paid cash. What could she do? Her only experience was babysitting and working in summer camps. No chance for employment there. No one would hire a stranger without references for childcare these days. She'd helped out at Tony's family's restaurant a few times. Possibility there. The area was dotted with small towns. Most had diners. She'd get a job as a waitress.

Voices in the hall, chattering away in another language, its cadence lilting and graceful, provided counterpoint to her disjointed thoughts.

She half-listened, all the while wondering: *Can I do it?* She wasn't sure that was what she wanted, but couldn't leave the idea alone. It was so tempting to flee, to never face the disappointment in her parents' eyes. It had always been like that. No punishment they could mete was as bad as the feeling she'd let them down. Consequently, she'd perpetually been the good little girl. A dutiful daughter. Until she stole a car and ... The image of Tony, his head at an unnatural angle, flashed before her. She put her hands to her head. *Don't think about it. You need a plan. Concentrate.*

If she *did* disappear ...

Sure, she told herself, they'd be sorry and would wonder where she was and if she was okay, but would that be as bad as having their daughter in prison? She imagined being in prison, them visiting her there. A wave of nausea swept over her. *No! I won't let that happen.* If she disappeared, they'd never know for sure why. They'd probably guess. But would guessing be as bad as knowing? Wouldn't it be kinder to give them at least a slim hope that their trust in her had been justified?

Could she do it? She looked again at the money scattered on the bed. It wasn't much. But she knew there were people, whole families, in fact, who managed to start a new life on less. She tuned in to the voices in the hall–unfamiliar phrases, mixed with broken English, spoken by women pushing the carts outside her door. They didn't sound unhappy. She looked again at the money on the bed. *They probably started with less.*

If only she knew where to begin. B.R. would know. He'd had less when he'd arrived in Pittsburg. She wondered what he was doing now, debated whether to call him, decided it was unfair to involve him, and resisted the urge to pick up her phone.

The resolve didn't last long. She left a message, asking him to meet her, assuring him it was the last time she'd bother him.

He called back and agreed.

Same time. Same place.

# # #

"The first thing you have to do is lose your phone." B.R. paused to give Rachel a long look. "I mean really lose it. Take the batteries out. Smash the phone. Throw it in the river. If you're serious about this, that phone is your worst enemy. It's the first thing they'll use to trace you."

SATURDAY

Thirty-Seven

Peace rushed to open the door for her grandparents.

Karalee scooted through, pulling Ben with her. Half-way in, he turned to salute the picketers with a jaunty wave.

The seven stony-faced teenaged girls stood straighter and held their signs higher. Large black letters spelled out MURDERER and COWARD.

Karalee pulled him the rest of the way in and closed the door, scolding, "Don't antagonize them. You'll only make it worse."

He shrugged off her hand, moved to the window and waved again. "Just being friendly."

"I doubt they see it that way." She jerked the drapes closed.

He managed to get off one more salute before the wall of cloth separated him from the girls, then turned to face his family with a defiant grin. "A little levity never hurt anybody."

Flannery said, "Oh, Poppy. Anything you, or any of us, do, they'll take as an insult."

"She's right," Karalee said. "It's best to ignore them."

His grin disappeared. "Somebody needs to teach them a lesson."

Karalee surveyed him with a rueful smile. "Try to look at it from their point of view. How would you feel if one of your golf buddies was killed by a hit-and-run and you thought you knew who did it?" She gave his chest a forceful poke with one finger. "And saw them getting away with it?"

He met her eyes for a moment, then looked away without answering.

Peace stood to one side, watching and listening. An only child, raised by a single mother, she was fascinated by the dynamics within her newly-discovered family.

Ben turned to her. "So ..." he said. "What do you think? Should we ignore them?"

"I doubt it'll make much difference what we do." Peace spoke quietly. "When people have an agenda, it rarely does." Noting the look exchanged by Ben and Karalee, she said, "I know all about agendas. Don't forget, my mother's a peace activist. I grew up going to marches and rallies." She directed her gaze toward Ben. "You're probably right, though, about a little levity being a good thing. Better than yelling at them. Mom always says 'The louder you shout, the less likely you are to be heard.'"

"How about ignoring them?" Karalee persisted.

Peace smiled. "I wouldn't know about that. Mom's not good at ignoring things."

Karalee didn't comment on this. Instead, she looked at Ben. "Has it occurred to you that your wave felt like a shout to them? Like you were mocking them? Belittling their grief?"

He looked surprised and opened his mouth as if to answer, but Flannery cut him off. "Do we have to keep talking about it? Isn't it bad enough to know they're out there?" She waved toward the window. "With their creepy signs. Waiting for us to show our faces?"

Poppy and Snap-snap exchanged another look.

Snap-snap said, "She's right. There are lots of other, more interesting, things to talk about."

"Such as?" Ben asked, and went to the side of the window, where he pulled the drape aside just enough to peer through the slit between cloth and window frame. After a minute, he turned away, tensed his shoulders and stretched his arms over his head. "If we stay in this house ..." He looked over his shoulder. "With them out there, we'll go crazy. It's Saturday. The Civil War Museum'll be open. How about we check it out?"

Flannery darted a nervous glance toward the window.

Karalee looked at Flannery, then at Ben. "Maybe another time. Today, I'd rather stay in here where it's warm and cozy."

Flannery settled into the sofa. "Me too."

Ben turned to Peace. "How about you? Are you game? Or would you rather be safe and warm?"

Peace hesitated, but only for a moment. "I'd love to go."

"Hallelujah!" Ben raised both arms toward the ceiling.

Karalee looked at Peace. "Don't let him bully you."

Ben said, "I'm not the bully here." He jerked his thumb toward the window. "I'm choosing not to be intimated by bullies."

Karalee said softly, "They're children."

"Doesn't mean they're not bullies."

Peace went to get her coat, unwilling to become embroiled in another of the endless discussions her new family loved. When she returned, Karalee and Flannery were in the kitchen, smearing peanut butter on toast, ignoring Ben. He was standing in the center of the room, whistling tunelessly and radiating suppressed energy.

When they stepped out onto the porch, loud chants greeted them: "MUR-DER-ER. MUR-DER-ER. COV-ER UP. COV-ER UP."

Ben reached for Peace's hand and gave it an encouraging squeeze. After a brief look into each other's eyes, they turned their faces away from the picketers and set off.

They heard footsteps behind them and knew at least two of their tormentors were following. Another hand squeeze. They kept moving at a steady pace, resisting the urge to run.

The light turned yellow just as they reached the corner. Ben tightened his hold on Peace's hand. They exchanged a quick nod and dashed into the street.

A horn blasted and a man leaned out of his window, shouting when they darted in front of his car, but they managed to reach the other side of the street intact and with a steady stream of traffic between them and the young picketers.

Ben turned for one last wave. His grin spread ear to ear.

Their pursuers shot baleful looks, but did not attempt to cross the street. Nor did they return the wave.

Noting their reaction, Peace admired Poppy's spirit, but thought Snap-snap was right. Ignoring them would have been the wiser course.

# # #

They continued to the museum at a brisk pace, hurried along by the wind stinging the backs of their necks. They reached the building at the same time as three middle-aged men, all of whom were wearing high, old-fashioned boots that Peace thought must be throwbacks to the Civil War era. One of the men went ahead of them. He opened the door and waved Peace and Ben in, his manners as old-school as his clothing.

They stepped into a small vestibule. On the left, behind a glass partition, was a room furnished with comfortable-looking chairs arranged in a ragged circle. The men who had come in with Peace and Ben paused to give them a friendly smile, then went into the room on the left, joining an assemblage that looked prepared to spend the day. Peace noticed that two of the men had on stiff, heavy gloves that almost reached their elbows. Again, vintage clothing, if her guess was accurate.

One of the seated men rose and came out into the vestibule to greet Peace and Ben.

After shaking his hand, Ben nodded to the people on the other side of the partition. "Looks like we're interrupting something? Would it be better if we came back another time?"

"No, no," the man assured them. "Just our usual Saturday morning confab. I'll be happy to show you around and walk you through the exhibits."

Ben pulled out his wallet, extracted a twenty and put it in the jar sitting on a writing desk by the door.

Their guide nodded his thanks and asked, "You from around here?"

In his easy southern drawl, Ben explained that he was from Virginia, but that his granddaughter was local. "She recommended this place to me," he said, then added, "But I'd heard about it before. I understand there's a connection to our museum in Richmond."

Peace, a quiet observer during the exchange, thought she noticed a change in the guide's demeanor when he heard her grandfather speak. She saw him take a quick but thorough look at Ben's face, then glance at her. *He recognizes us. Probably from the newspaper or the TV news. Maybe both.* She couldn't shake the feeling he was studying them while trying to appear not to. She had a hard time concentrating on the artifacts or listening to the guide's words and was taken unaware when he held out a long, serious-looking weapon to her.

"Want to hold it?" he asked.

Not knowing how to refuse, she said, "Sure," and stretched both hands to receive the gun. She almost dropped it. "I didn't know it would be so heavy."

The man nodded. "Imagine carrying it all day, sometimes running to dodge bullets."

"And scared out of your wits," Ben broke in. "Most of those men weren't professional soldiers. Some weren't even men, just kids, caught up in a struggle they only half understood."

Peace said, "Isn't that the way all wars are fought?"

Both men smiled, but neither argued.

Peace still had the feeling their guide recognized them and wondered if this is what her life would be from now on. *It's not about you*, she scolded herself and made an effort to concentrate on the displays. She succeeded for the most part and was surprised that the exhibits featured items from both the North and the South. Particularly interesting to her were personal articles not related to men trying to kill one another, but small things that showed them as human beings missing homes they weren't sure they would ever see again. One corner was filled with items that demonstrated Native American participation in the conflict.

When they left, the man extended his hand. "Hope you'll visit us again some time."

"Thanks," Ben said. "If you're ever in Virginia ..." His smile finished the invitation.

Outside, Peace asked, "How does this compare to the Civil War museums you have in Richmond?"

"It's always interesting to see events told from a different perspective."

"Is it very different?"

He gave her a long look before he answered. "Different, yes, but not as much as you might think. Southerners are not all racists."

"I didn't mean that!"

"No?" After what seemed an eternity to Peace, his stern look morphed into a smile. "Maybe we can talk about it over a cup of coffee. Or tea if you prefer. Know a nice warm place where we could do that?"

"The Zen Den is just up the street."

"That way?" He tilted his head to the side.

"Yes."

# # #

Ben studied the list printed on the blackboard for a moment, shook his head, and looked at the young man waiting behind the counter. "I'll never get the hang of all these special brews. I want a cup of coffee. Plain. Strong. Black."

The young man filled a white crockery mug, handed it to Ben, and turned toward Peace. "How about you?"

"Hot chocolate."

They spotted an empty couch in a corner and carried their drinks over there.

Peace sipped her chocolate, buying time, unsure what to say after her grandfather had interpreted her innocent statement to mean that she considered him a racist. She waited for him to say something, aware of him studying her over the rim of his cup, but he didn't speak. She figured it was up to her to break the silence that had grown between them. "I'm sorry if it sounded like I think you're a racist just because you're from the South."

He put his cup on the table in front of them. "I admit I'm a little sensitive on the subject. Most southerners are. We're used to being judged by the actions of a few diehards who can't acknowledge that their ancestors were part of a terrible evil."

"Were your ... my ... ancestors part of it?" She swallowed before she went on to ask what she really wanted to know. "Did they own slaves?"

He nodded. "A few. And I like to think they treated them well. Not that I believe that makes it right. It's pure arrogance to believe that one human being has a right to own another. I know that." He picked up his cup and took a slow sip, all the while surveying her with sad eyes. "But that's the way it was. And we didn't invent the system." Another sip. Another look, this one angry. "Where do you think the wealth of those self-righteous New Englanders came from?" When she didn't answer, he leaned forward. "Slave trade." He whispered the words, giving them the ugly connotation they deserved. "Something they choose to forget."

Peace smiled feebly, not knowing how to respond.

Ben sat back and took a deep breath. "Sorry. I tend to get touchy sometimes. I don't like being considered the bad guy in everything that's wrong with our country."

"Nobody thinks that."

He tilted his head and looked at her.

"I don't," she persisted. "I know you didn't have anything to do with it."

He hunched his shoulders. "No, I didn't, but my ancestors did and I don't like it when people dump on them." He stopped and looked off into the distance for a few seconds. "In some ways, it's worse having your family criticized than being criticized yourself." He looked back at Peace. "Can you understand that?"

"I ... don't know." It was a truthful answer. She didn't know how she felt about her ancestors. Growing up, she'd been filled with curiosity and a longing so deep it was almost painful, to know something about her biological family. Wondering what kind of people they were. Wondering, most of all, why they didn't want her. Her adoptive mother had always told her they must have had a reason to leave her in that carriage shed and reminded her of how she'd been dressed: in a fine linen Christening dress, with a delicately-embroidered pillow placed next to her. "Just like the baby Moses," Caroline had said. "And I was the lucky one who found you." She'd taken Peace's then-small hand in hers and guided her fingers over the the pillow's tiny stitches. "These are family heirlooms," she'd said. "And somebody wanted you to have them." Peace hadn't known at first what an heirloom was and still didn't completely understand why the items had been passed along to her. She now knew that they'd been handed down through Snap-snap's family and that it had been her decision to pass them along to the infant her daughter was about to give away. As much as she appreciated Snap-snap's words and her gift, she couldn't help wondering what had really prompted it. *Love? Or guilt?*

Ben seemed to realize the confusion his question had raised. "Enough of the heavy stuff," he said. "Let's go home and see what Snap-snap and Flannery are up to."

They walked back to Peace's apartment, side by side, mostly quiet, each trying to guess the other's thoughts, both hesitant to ask.

Peace thought about what Poppy had said and wondered if that ancestor/family protective instinct worked both ways. Backwards and forwards? If he were so quick to defend the generations behind him, would he also do whatever it took to protect those that followed? If Flannery had committed the crime of which so many suspected her, would he do everything in his power to protect her?

Would he help her get away with murder?

Thirty-Eight

Rachel gripped the icy steel of the bridge railing and watched the small rectangular shape descend in a slow spiral, followed by a hovering shadow. A bird. Large-winged and black. Blacker even than the abyss below. The creature swooped. Grabbed the phone in its talons. Rose and flew straight toward her face.

She tried to look away, but could not. Another swoop brought the creature closer. She ripped her hands free and made a frantic grab for the phone. The air lifted her up, then her let go, abandoning her to the mercy of currents that sent her spinning. Face up, staring into a sky black with clouds. Face down, suspended above a swirling cone of inky darkness.

She tried to call for help. Could only howl.

Sounds broke through her desperate cries. Loud knocks. A voice: "Hello?"

She opened her eyes. A red light seemed to signal from far away. She blinked, then opened her eyes and made out a round object surrounded by a sea of dingy gray.

More knocks. Louder than before.

She sat up, now fully awake, but still not sure where she was. She looked around: a bare, white wall; a low dresser; a blank TV screen. *A motel room.* She looked up toward the pulsing light. *Smoke alarm.*

The voice again: "Everything okay in there?"

A different voice, deeper this time, belonging to a man: "Do you need help?"

"I'm fine." She hardly recognized the croaking sound as coming from her.

Loud whispers outside the door.

"I'm fine," she repeated. "I had a nightmare, that's all."

More whispers.

The man's voice again: "We're coming in."

She pulled the sheet up to her chin.

The door opened.

A woman appeared—short, roundish, with alert, dark eyes that darted to all corners of the room. The woman looked over her shoulder, nodded, and a man appeared. He held out both hands, as though to show that they were empty, smiled at Rachel and said, "I'm the manager." He checked the corners of the room with a sweeping glance and nodded to the woman. She returned his nod and ducked into the bathroom.

Rachel heard the shower curtain being pulled aside.

The woman reappeared and spoke in a low tone. "Everything looks okay."

"Everything *is* okay," Rachel said. "I told you. I had a nightmare."

The man smiled at her, obviously embarrassed. "I had to check," he said. "I hope you understand."

Rachel forced a smile. "I do. I should probably thank you for waking me."

He shrugged and left.

The woman stayed behind. "Can I get you anything?"

"No," Rachel said. "I'll be fine." She nodded toward the small table with a coffeemaker and some cardboard cups. "I assume there're tea bags there."

"Yes."

"Is it too late for breakfast?"

A tic of hesitation, then: "I can find something for you."

"That's okay. I'm not really hungry." Rachel glanced at the clock. Ten nineteen. She looked back at the woman. "Thanks for checking on me."

The woman smiled and left.

Alone, Rachel sat a few more minutes, then swung her legs over the side of the bed and headed for the bathroom.

She took a long time brushing her teeth, resolutely not looking at the phone lying on the counter. She knew her parents must be frantic to hear from her. She also knew the wisdom of what B.R. had said. The phone was the surest way to trace her whereabouts. She should get rid of it. She tried not to think about the nightmare from which she'd just awoken as she rinsed her toothbrush and placed it on the counter. Her fingertips hovered over the phone, but she didn't pick it up. Killing time, she fiddled with the little bottles on the counter. Her fingers reached for the phone again. She shook her head and left the bathroom, closing the door behind her.

She clicked on the TV, found an all-news station. Nothing of interest there. She went back to the bathroom and picked up her phone. She turned it on and thumbed through the messages. There were four from her mother. She scanned those quickly. Nothing new. A name came up that made her catch her breath: Amanda Wright. She read: *U missed it. We made the news. Ck youtube.*

Rachel clicked on the link that followed the message. She watched, fascinated and repelled. Not only did the news clip show Amanda and the picketers, it included footage of the accused girl, identified as Flannery Donohue, standing next to her grandfather. She looked and sounded guilty as sin. *Who said pictures don't lie?* Rachel turned off the phone and stared into space. She turned it back on, watched the video again, this time more carefully, especially the girl.

She pushed in B.R.'s number and was surprised when he answered.

"Hi, me again."

"Yeah." His answer was terse, almost obscured by background noise.

"Uh ... where are you?"

"Beanery."

"Alone?"

"Um hmm."

"I know I said I wouldn't call again, but I want to show you something." The words came out in a rush. Rachel knew she sounded desperate and forced herself to slow down. "Can you meet me?"

"Uh ... sure."

"Where can I pick you up?"

There was a long pause. "Same as last night. Behind the building where I work. Meet me there."

"Are you on your way to work?"

"No ... um ... I ..."

It took her a minute to understand his hesitation. *He doesn't want to be seen with me.* She gave herself a mental kick. "I'll be there," she said. "It'll take me about an hour. Is that okay?"

"Yeah. See ya." Rachel heard a voice say B.R.'s name, followed by a disconnect. She felt a quick stab of guilt for drawing him into her mess, but didn't call back to cancel.

# # #

She studied his face as he watched the video, then watched it again. And again.

Finally, he handed the phone back to her. "You don't have to run. You can pull it off." He gave her a long, searching look. "If you want to. Do you?"

She let out a long breath. "Well, I don't want to go to prison."

"So? What's holding you back?"

"That other girl. I don't want her to go to prison either."

"They can't convict her without evidence. According to what you've told me, they won't find any."

"But it'll be a cloud over her head."

"Not your problem. She looks rich. Somebody'll take care of her." He looked away, stared out the window for a few seconds. "Want to know what I'd do?"

"Yes."

He nodded to the phone. "Call your folks. Tell them you're on your way home. Go back and tough it out. Be the grief-stricken girlfriend."

"Come with me." The words came out in a breathless rush. Rachel could hardly believe she'd spoken them. She didn't expect him to say yes, but was glad she'd found the nerve to ask.

Silence.

She added, "To give me courage."

More silence.

She stared at him, trying to guess what he was thinking. She felt like there was a hole in her heart.

Finally, he spoke. "You don't get courage from someone else."

"Just help me over the first hump. Then I'll be okay."

Dead silence.

Rachel said, "I know you're worried about being seen with me if I'm involved in anything illegal, but if you're right, no one has to know that. I think, with your help, I can pull if off. And when your brother comes, maybe I can help you in some way."

He turned his head and looked out the window, his eyes half-closed, as though he were concentrating on something not visible to Rachel. After a few minutes, he shrugged and turned to face her. "What the hell. Why not?"

"Really?"

"Yeah. Have to make a phone call first. Get someone to cover for me here." He waved toward the building where he cleaned.

"Think you'll be able to?"

He keyed in a number on his phone. "Guy owes me a favor."

Rachel held her breath while she listened. It was all taken care of in a few sentences. Afterwards, he flashed a thumbs-up and his heart-stopping grin.

There was no holding the tears back.

He leaned over and brushed them away. "Look, I said before I didn't want to get involved, but you've been nicer to me than anyone except my brother." His voice was tender. For a moment, she thought he was going to kiss her. Instead, he looked away and sat up very straight. His hands were cupped over his knees, his knuckles white.

Rachel wanted to reach out and touch his face, to run her finger along his profile, tracing the line of his long, straight brow, down the curve of his small nose, over his lips, and let her finger come to rest in the deep cleft of his chin. The air surrounding them in the car seemed alive, filled with unexplored possibility.

"Just hold up your head," he said, breaking a silence that felt hours long. "Don't let anyone know you're afraid. That's half the battle."

"I don't know if I can."

"I'll teach you. I'm a pro." Another grin, this time accompanied by a wink.

Rachel held up her phone. "Here goes."

He held two thumbs up.

She speed-dialed home. When her mother answered, she said, "Hi. I'm on my way home. Well, almost. I'll be leaving in a little bit." She hesitated for a split second, then said it fast. "I'm bringing someone with me." She immediately turned the phone off and took a deep breath.

Thirty-Nine

The protestors were still parading back and forth when Peace and Poppy returned home.

This time Poppy ignored them. He looked at Peace and said, "Have to give them an A for persistence if nothing else." He glanced at his watch. "Almost four thirty. What time did they show up this morning?"

"I don't know exactly. It was barely light out."

He whistled through his teeth. "On a Saturday! Impressive for a bunch of kids."

Peace knew the admission was grudgingly made.

When they reached the porch, she stopped for a moment and studied the picketers. Except for the girl who seemed to be in charge, it was a different group. Larger than it had been earlier. It was hard to be sure of the exact number because of their constant motion, but she guessed about a dozen young people were parading back and forth. The formerly all-female troop now included four males. Sturdy-looking boys, whose broad shoulders seemed at odds with their young faces. Peace guessed they were the dead boy's football teammates. They looked slightly older than their leader, but seemed to be following her directions without question. Each carried a sign. No shouts this time. They marched quietly, a silence that added dignity, even eloquence, to their message.

Peace's eyes met those of the young leader, the one among them whose presence had been constant. She nodded and attempted a smile, wondering if it would be possible to talk over their differences.

The girl glared at her. No answering nod. Certainly no hint of a smile. Just steely-eyed determination.

Suspecting anything she said would make matters worse, Peace followed Poppy into the house.

Henry greeted her at the door, wagging his tail. She knelt and buried her face in his fur, grateful for his uncomplicated devotion.

Karalee and Flannery were seated on the sofa, their heads close together, looking at the phone in Flannery's hand.

Ben asked, "What's going on?" He crooked his neck, trying to see what they were looking at. "Anything I should know about?"

Flannery answered without looking up. "We're checking out things to do in Philadelphia. There's a lot to choose from."

He shook his head. "I've been out all day. I'm ready for a nap."

Karalee scowled at him. "We need a change of scenery."

He scowled back. "You should've gone with us to the museum. You'd have liked it."

"I was thinking of something further away." She tilted her head toward the door, without actually looking at it. "Away from all this."

He put his hand on her shoulder. "You can't hide from what's happened."

Flannery said, "We're not hiding. Just staying out of their way."

"There's a difference?"

Flannery looked up at him. "I remember once you told me the only way to win some fights is not to get into them."

Unable to resist his granddaughter, Ben leaned down to kiss the top of her head. "And I didn't think you ever listened to me."

She held up a paper on which she'd listed half a dozen possibilities.

He took it from her, studied it for a moment and finally asked, "Do you have a preference?" Before either Flannery or Karalee could answer, he looked at Peace and added, "Silly question. These two always have a plan." He handed the list to Peace, who was sitting on the floor with Henry's head in her lap. "What would you like to do? I don't usually get to vote. Maybe you'll have better luck."

"I can't go. I'm supposed to meet with Kirk about the music for the museum's Christmas program."

Karalee said, "We're not going anywhere without you. You're the reason we're here in the first place. We'll wait 'til you're finished."

Peace shook her head. "I don't know how long it'll take. I'd prefer you just go ahead."

Karalee looked ready to protest.

Flannery broke in, "If no one else has a preference, I say let's head into Philadelphia, find a place to eat, then follow our nose."

The sky was beginning to darken when they left. When Flannery stepped onto the porch, the protesters broke their silence. MUR-DER-ER MUR-DER-ER.

Watching from the doorway, Peace couldn't see the faces of her cousin or her grandparents, but she saw Poppy and Snap-snap move closer to Flannery, shielding her as they rushed down the steps and into the car.

The leader and one of the boys moved into the street, holding their signs high as the car pulled away.

Much as she hated to admit it to herself, Peace was relieved to see them go. She started to close the door, intending to head for the kitchen and a cup of tea when she noticed the picketers were clustered together, listening to their leader. After a few words from her, punctuated by much arm waving, they began gathering up their stuff. More relief. Henry seemed to share her feeling. He jumped into his chair by the window, circled a couple of times, and lay down with his nose between his paws. Within seconds, his snores added to the aura of wellbeing.

Peace settled into a corner of the couch, sipping her tea, looking forward to the evening with Kirk, hoping to return to the uncomplicated relationship they'd always shared. That's what she told herself, but when the doorbell rang, her heart jumped. She paused at the mirror on her way to the door and took a minute to brush her hair off her forehead and tuck an errant curl behind her ear, frowning, telling herself, *He's seen you looking worse.*

Henry was already at the door, his head tilted as though asking, "Why the fuss? It's Kirk."

Kirk breezed in with his usual nonchalance. For him, nothing seemed changed. Peace twisted a lock of hair between her fingers, aware that, for her, everything had—an awareness she acknowledged with mixed feelings. On the one hand, she savored the tingling sensation she now felt in his presence. On the other, she missed the easy camaraderie that had once been there.

He looked around and said, "Family's not here?"

By "family", Peace assumed he really meant "Flannery". "No," she said. "They went down to Philly. Flannery needed to get away." When he didn't respond, she said, "So ... I guess it's just you and me. We can get this wrapped up."

He pulled a folded scrap of paper from his jeans pocket and handed it to Peace. "Here's what I had in mind. The usual Christmas carols. That's what people want this time of year. No need to get fancy."

While Peace was scanning the list, he surprised her by asking, "What do you think happened?"

There was no doubt what he meant by the vague question. "I don't know," she said. "I was skeptical at first, but I'm more and more inclined to believe the car was stolen." She paused to gather her thoughts. "It's funny, I'm beginning to believe Flannery, but I think Snap-snap and Poppy have their doubts."

"Really?"

"Yes. At first I thought they believed her totally, but as I've gotten to know them, I can see chinks in their armor."

"For instance?"

Peace was thrilled that Kirk's trust in Flannery was less than she had thought, but couldn't forget that he had accused her of being judgmental, so she spoke carefully. "Today at the museum, Poppy started defending ..." She hesitated, thinking back. "No, defending isn't the right word. It was more like explaining the position of southerners on the issue of race."

"What's that have to do with this?"

She stopped him by holding up her hand. "Hear me out. He wasn't saying it was okay. Nothing like that. Just that the present generation feels the need to justify their ancestors. The way he said it made me wonder if he would defend anyone in his family, no matter what." She wondered if Kirk understood what she was trying to say.

His expression showed that he did. After a minute, he said, "I've been trying to reconstruct the whole thing in my head. You know ... the logistics of what might have happened."

"What did you come up with?"

"Nothing that makes sense." He took a minute to stroke Henry's ears. "Her story about the car being stolen sounds fake."

Peace couldn't suppress the grin that spread over her face. She said, "I seem to recall you telling me I should give her the benefit of the doubt."

Kirk looked directly at Peace. "That was more about you than her."

"Me?"

"Yeah. I'm used to you being on the side of the underdog. It set me back when you were ready to condemn your own cousin."

"I didn't condemn her. Her story just seemed a little farfetched. Plus, I admit my first impression was that she's a spoiled brat who's never been made to own up to her mistakes." She held her breath, waiting to see how he would react to her calling Flannery a spoiled brat.

He didn't seem to notice. He asked, "What changed your mind?"

She smiled at him. "Mostly you. When you said it was not about me."

"I thought that made you mad."

"It did at first. But when I thought about it, I knew you were right. All anyone seemed to think about was poor little Flannery. I guess I resented her getting all the attention. I'd been looking forward to meeting my family and I really thought they were looking forward to meeting me. After that letter, it seemed–"

"Letter?"

"Right after Fran ... Holly ... told me she was my birth mother, I got a letter from Snap-snap. Kind of a welcome to the family." She stopped to swallow the lump in her throat. "You've always had grandparents, so you can't imagine how I felt. It was ..."

"You never told me about a letter."

"I didn't tell anyone. Not even Mom." She hesitated, recalling the day the letter had come, the feelings it had unloosed. She'd read it over and over, her first instinct being to hold it close, to guard it as a precious secret. Now, she felt the need to share it, to have someone tell her how special it was. "Want to see it?"

"Sure." He tilted his head and added, "If you want to show it to me."

She rose and went to the drawer where she kept the letter. She let her hand linger on Kirk's when she handed it to him.

Scarcely breathing, she watched him open the envelope and remove the pale blue pages. A small paper with curling edges fell out, fluttered downward, and came to rest at his feet.

He looked startled and stepped back.

She retrieved the photograph and examined its yellowed surface. "It's okay. No harm done." She motioned for him to read the letter. She'd read it so often she knew it by heart—both the words and the delicate handwriting in which they were written. Certain phrases danced in her head: *you have your grandfather's eyes; I hope to one day dote over you; let me meet you some day.*

He read silently. When he came to the end, he spoke the signoff aloud: "Your affectionate and most impatient grandmother." After a moment, he gave the letter back to Peace.

She ran her fingers along the paper's worn corners, her emotions a jumble of pride and embarrassment. "You can tell it's been read a lot."

"I can see why."

She handed him the photograph. "This is the picture she mentioned in the letter."

He examined the picture and returned it to her. "Nice."

That's all he said, but it was enough. She felt closer to Kirk at this moment than she ever had and wanted to tell him so.

Before she found the right words, he changed the subject. "Back to Flannery. Just for the sake of argument, let's assume the car wasn't stolen. How'd she end up on Saw Mill Road?"

"I don't know. All I can think is she got turned around and went the wrong way when she left the shopping center. That's just about where she'd realize her mistake and turn off."

"Makes as much sense as anything. And if that happened ..." He paused, holding up one finger. "Just speculating now ... let's say she hit the guy on the bicycle, panicked and drove away. How'd she know how to get to the B and B?"

"She had a map that Holly drew for her."

"Okay. So ... she headed for the B and B to tell your grandparents, saw Fannie Chapman's parking lot when she was almost there, decided to abandon the car and make up the story about it being stolen."

Peace said, "It could have happened that way. But, say she's telling the truth. She came out of the store and couldn't find the car. She wouldn't want to admit she'd been careless and left the keys in it ... if that's what happened. So she decided to walk to the B and B, knowing Poppy'd stick up for her." A long pause while Peace considered this scenario. "It's a pretty long haul from the shopping center to the B and B." She looked at Kirk. "About how far would you say it is?"

"Let's find out." His lanky body seemed to unfold as he rose from the couch. "Any plans for dinner?"

"No."

"Want to grab a bite uptown? Afterwards, we'll check the mileage."

"Sure."

Kirk shrugged into his jacket while Peace went to get her coat. For a change, she let him hold it while she put it on, even let him lift her long hair free of the collar as the coat settled onto her shoulders. She felt a tingle as his fingers brushed the back of her neck. Had the touch been accidental? Longer than absolutely necessary?

# # #

"A mile and a half. That's a pretty long walk." Kirk said what Peace was thinking.

"Long, but doable. I'll ask her about it."

"How are you going to do that? It'll sound like you're accusing her of lying."

" It won't be easy."

Forty

Rachel pulled the car into the garage, turned off the engine, and sat for a moment, preparing herself for the introduction she was about to make. She recalled her fantasy of introducing B.R. to her parents, of their being as captivated by his charm as she was. Those dreams now seemed part of a distant past, belonging to her innocent *before* life. What she faced today was far different. Never could she have imagined the disastrous detour her life would take. *If only* ...

B.R.'s seatbelt clicked open, returning her to the here and now. She looked at him, wondering if he was nervous. If he was, it didn't show. You'd never guess he was going into the home of strangers. Did he worry about how they would receive him? Did it bother him that he was going to help their daughter perpetrate a fraud? Cover up what most would consider a murder?

He flashed his impish smile and a thumbs-up sign. "Showtime."

That's how it felt to Rachel. Could she pull it off? She forced a smile when she opened the door leading from the garage into the kitchen.

There they were. Her parents. Waiting. Their faces, so different in features, but with identical expressions which she read as equal parts relief that she was home and curiosity about the guest she'd brought. She saw their eyes, first her father's, then her mother's, leave her face and shift to the figure standing behind her. She read their surprise as they took his measure and had no doubt they were comparing him to Tony.

In the few seconds that elapsed before either of them spoke, Rachel imagined the conversation that had taken place while they were waiting for her to arrive. She heard it as clearly as if she'd been present:

LISA: *She's bringing a friend.*
PAUL: *A friend? What does that mean? Male or female?*
LISA: *I don't know. She didn't say.*
PAUL: *You didn't ask?*
LISA: *No. I wondered, of course, but ...*

The scene continued to play in Rachel's head, there being no doubt of its accuracy, even as she turned to B.R. and said, "This is Brendan Richards. He's become a good friend." Aware of the speculation on her parents' faces, she was careful to emphasize *friend*.

Her father extended his hand. "Hello, Brendan. Nice to meet you."

B.R. stepped forward and grasped the outstretched hand. "Hi. Thanks for letting me come." His characteristic grin lit his face as he added, "Short notice and all."

Rachel's mother added her welcome, sounding just a tad too sincere. "We're always glad to have Rachel's friends."

Rachel felt compelled to explain. "B.R.'s from Oregon. He doesn't have any family here and it was too far for him to go out there for the holiday. Besides, he has a full-time job."

Both parents spoke at once. "Well, we're glad to have you."

"Thanks," B.R. said. "I appreciate that."

A uncomfortable quiet settled over the kitchen.

B. R. broke it. "I can't stay long. Just until tomorrow. Have to get back to work." He went on to describe how he cleaned offices to support himself while he went to school.

Rachel watched the expressions on her parents' faces change from guarded to respectful.

B.R. looked around and commented on what a lovely home they had and said again how much he appreciated their allowing him to share part of their holiday. He made a joke about the expense of flying across the country during the holidays.

Paul laughed and said, "Well, we're glad to have you. There's plenty of room in this inn."

Rachel and B.R. were still wearing their coats and holding their bags. The four of them stood in the kitchen, looking at each other with artificial smiles, trying to appear at ease.

Lisa suddenly seemed to remember her role as hostess. She looked at her husband. "Paul, why don't you hang up Brendan's coat." She turned to Rachel. "You can show him the guest room in a minute, but first we have to talk." She looked toward the clock.

Rachel could see that her mother was nervous and didn't understand why. She checked the time. *Not quite six.* She looked back at her mother, saw her square her shoulders and heard her say: "Bella and

Angelo are coming for dinner. They'll be here in an hour." She reached for Rachel's hands as she spoke.

Rachel pulled away. "No!" She couldn't breathe. Her knees seemed filled with jelly. "Tell them not to come!"

"I can't do that." Lisa's voice was firm. "Bella's been calling constantly, wanting to know how you are. Even with all they're going through, they're worried about you. I finally invited them over."

"Why didn't you tell me they were coming?"

"You didn't give me time." She paused to let her words sink in, then went on, "They're bringing a cake and a couple of casseroles from all the stuff people have been bringing to them. I'm just making a salad." Lisa's nervousness disappeared when she began speaking about the mundane subject of food. She smiled sadly. "Imagine. Taking food to Bella Rosino. If that's not the ultimate ice to Eskimos." She looked off into the distance. "Still, it's what you do."

"Mom, I can't."

"Yes, you can. And you will. It won't be easy, but we have to think of them. They've been hit by the worst thing that can happen to a parent. It'll be awkward, but we'll manage. We have to."

Rachel looked at B.R.

He said, "Want me to disappear?"

Rachel reached for B.R.'s arm. "Don't go."

Paul looked at the young man "Do you know who we're talking about?"

B.R. nodded. "The parents of the guy who ... got killed in the accident."

Lisa said, "Yes. They're overwhelmed. Well, you can imagine."

"I shouldn't have come." He focused on Lisa. "What do you want me to do?"

Paul answered for her. "You're a friend of our daughter, a guest in our home. No need to explain."

Lisa looked doubtful, but said nothing.

Rachel wanted to hide in her room. Go back to State College. Crawl under a rock. Anywhere she wouldn't have to face Tony's parents.

B.R. must have read her thoughts. He put his hand on her arm. "It'll be okay. I'll tell them how much you talked about their son and how devastated you are by what happened."

# # #

Rachel sat on the bed, holding the small velvet box at arm's length. There was no way around it. She had to wear the ring. She knew if she didn't, Bella would ask why. What about B.R.? Did she have time to explain to him? Headlights flashed on her bedroom window. The Rosinos were pulling into the driveway. Maybe he wouldn't notice. No time to think about that now. She steeled herself, removed the ring from the box and slipped it on her finger.

By the time Rachel reached the bottom step, her father was in the driveway, opening the car door for Bella, helping her and Angelo bring in the food.

Bella, as soon as her hands were empty, rushed over to Rachel and threw her arms around her. "I didn't know you'd be here. Your mother didn't tell me."

Lisa said, "We talked so briefly, I ...." Her voice trailed into nothingness.

Angelo stepped forward. "It's good that you're home. This is where you should be."

"Yes," Bella said. "At a time like this, we belong together." She released Rachel from her suffocating embrace and caressed her cheek. "You need to be surrounded by people who love you."

Rachel's face felt hot. She tried unsuccessfully to smile.

It was enough for Bella. She ran one finger along Rachel's cheekbone and said, "Such a brave, brave girl." Her hand sought Rachel's. She found the ring and caressed it with her fingertips. "Little daughter."

"Yes," Angelo said.

Somehow, his one-word response seemed to Rachel the saddest thing she'd ever heard. She looked over Bella's shoulder at him. "I'm glad you're here. It's good to see you." What else could she say?

Paul spoke for the first time, holding out both hands. "I'll take your coats. Then maybe a glass of wine?"

Lisa said, "Yes, something to warm you up. First, though ..." She paused and looked from the Rosinos to B.R. "You haven't met our other guest. This is Brendan ... I'm sorry. I don't remember your last name."

"Richards." He came closer and held out a hand to Angelo. "Rachel told me about your son. I'm sorry for your loss." He spoke formally, a little stiffly. Somehow, the awkwardness gave credibility to the words.

Rachel held her breath. She watched Bella and Angelo look B.R. over and quickly dismiss him. She needn't have worried what they would think. They hardly noticed him. Clearly, it never occurred to them that this young man could be a rival to their beloved Tony.

Dinner went off without a hitch. Rachel was more listener than participant in the conversation, but no one seemed to expect more of her. She sat across the table from B.R., next to Angelo, who was almost as silent as she was.

True to his promise, B.R. told the Rosinos how much Rachel had talked about their son and how sorry he was that he'd never had a chance to meet him.

Rachel listened and watched, marveling at his composure, the ease with which he carried out the deception, and thinking this was how she'd have to live the rest of her life, wondering if she could do it.

Forty-One

Henry's ears perked forward, his usual signal to Peace that someone was on the front porch.

She patted his head. "It's okay, boy. Relax. Just the family returning from Philly." She marked her place in the book she'd been trying to read, and put on a welcoming smile.

Flannery came in by herself, took off her coat, and tossed it on Henry's favorite chair, drawing a disgruntled look from him. Too polite to bark at the offense, he stationed himself at Peace's knee. She repressed a smile and glanced toward the door. "Poppy and Snap-snap aren't coming in?"

"No. They said to tell you they're tired. They'll call in the morning." She looked around. "Kirk's gone already?"

"Um hmm. He left a while ago."

"Everything all set for your program?" Flannery asked, but didn't seem particularly interested in the answer. She prowled the room, stopping in front of the frame containing the Christening dress.

Peace waited for her to say something, to remind her again that, because of her, none of the other grandchildren had worn it, but Flannery just stood there, staring at the dress, her expression inscrutable.

Peace asked, "Did you have a good time?"

"As good as can be expected." She moved away from the dress and sat down on the other end of the couch. "How about you? Did you and Kirk get the program all settled?"

"Yes," Peace said, then took a deep breath, figuring this was as good a time as any to ask the question that needed to be asked. She spoke as casually as she could. "Afterwards, we went uptown for sandwiches. Then, just out of curiosity, we checked the mileage from the shopping center to the B and B."

Flannery's back stiffened.

Peace noted the change, but forced herself to go on. "It's a mile and a half. Further than I realized. Did you know how far it was when you started out?"

Flannery jumped up and crossed the room, then spun to face Peace. "What are you saying?"

Sensing a threat to his mistress, Henry lifted his head and the fur on his neck rose.

Peace kept her voice level. "No hidden meaning. Just curious."

"Sure." Flannery stepped closer. "You think I don't know why you're asking?"

Henry stood, effectively positioning himself between the two women. Peace put her hand on his head and spoke a few soothing words. Knowing how upset Flannery was, she was tempted to drop the matter, but this was a discussion they had to have. She forged ahead and asked again, "Did you realize how far it was?"

"How could I?" Flannery remained in the center of the room, glaring at Peace. When Peace didn't respond, she said, "I had the map Aunt Holly drew. I could tell it wasn't real close, but I didn't know what else to do, so I started walking." A shudder passed through her. "I had to do something."

"You had your phone. Why didn't you call?"

"What good would that have done? Poppy and Snap-snap didn't have a car." Another hard look. "Remember? They didn't pick up the rental until the next day."

"Your aunt Holly had a car. Why didn't you call her?"

"I wanted Poppy and Snap-snap. I knew everybody would be mad at me and I needed somebody on my side."

"You didn't think your aunt would be?"

"My *aunt* is your *mother!*"

That statement, spoken with such venom, sent Peace's thoughts spiraling in a new direction. She realized that Flannery was as confused by the new family dynamic as she was—and was as threatened by it—something she hadn't considered before. She waited a minute before she spoke. "We need to talk. Frankly. It's time to stop dancing around this."

"This? What?"

"This ... everything." Peace waved her hand through the air, and, after a minute, rose and went into the kitchen. After she filled the kettle, she turned to Flannery. "You said before tea doesn't solve problems. That's true, but sometimes talking it out does. At least it's a place to start. So ..." She paused, nodded toward a chair, and when Flannery was seated, held up two boxes, one labeled *Earl Grey* and the other *Soothing Camomile*. "What'll it be?"

Flannery stared at her for a moment. "I'll take the soothing one."

"Me too," Peace said. She put the selected tea bags in cups and pulled out the chair across from Flannery. "I'll start. First of all, I don't consider your aunt Holly my mother. She gave me away the day she gave birth to me." She lifted her chin defiantly and added, "I'm not saying that because of any hard feelings. I know she had her reasons, but, as far as I'm concerned, my mother is Caroline Morrow. Period."

Flannery looked ready to interrupt.

Peace held up her hand. "You don't have to defend Holly. She explained the situation to me. She was nineteen. Unmarried. She thought she was giving me to someone who would give me a better life than she could, but something happened. Either my father lied to her or things didn't work out like he expected. I'll probably never know the whole truth. It's okay. I can live with that." She stopped for a moment, searching for the right words. It was important that Flannery understand. "Actually, it did work out. Just not quite like they planned. I have a good life ... and the best mother anyone can imagine. I mean that. The. Best. I feel like a higher force reached out and put me exactly where I was meant to be. I don't know if you believe in such things, but that's how it feels to me." She stopped for a moment and leaned closer to Flannery, emphasizing each word. "I'm not some waif you have to feel sorry for."

Flannery stared at Peace, clearly stunned by her words. "You don't want us in your life, do you?"

"That's not what I meant. I'm glad I'm having a chance to meet you. I just–"

Cheerful notes from the phone in Flannery's pocket interrupted the somber conversation. She stood to dig it out. A quick glance at the phone, then a longer one. She looked at Peace, her eyes saucer-wide, and said, "Bucks County D. A." She pushed a button. "Hello." Then: "Yes, I guess so." Followed by a period of intense listening, with an unreadable expression.

Peace listened and watched Flannery, wondering what could have prompted a call on a Saturday night from the office of the District Attorney. She thought back to the day before, when she and Poppy had run into the police chief at the Justice Center. What was it he'd said? There might be something they could do to end this? *Something like that.*

The kettle whistled.

Peace got up and poured water over the tea bags, trying to recall Grimaldi's exact words and, at the same time, not miss what Flannery was saying.

"Whew," Flannery said when she placed the phone on the table. "I didn't expect that."

Hardly daring to breathe, Peace asked, "Good or bad?"

"In a minute," Flannery said. "First, I need a piece of paper."

"Sure." Peace fumbled in the junk drawer until she located a pen and a small notebook, which she handed to Flannery.

Flannery scribbled a couple of lines on a page, ripped it out and tucked it into a pocket. That done, she answered Peace's question. "It's good." A long pause. "At least I think so."

Peace was about to jump out of her skin. "What did he want?"

Flannery sipped her tea and stared into space, as though gathering her thoughts. "It was kind of strange. The guy ..." She removed the paper from her pocket and looked at her notes. "Charles McNeal's his name ... said he was from the District Attorney's office and asked me ... very politely ..." She stopped, stared into space again, her eyes narrowed, her lips pursed, then went on, "It was almost like he was asking me to do him a favor or something."

It was all Peace could do not to grab her cousin by the shoulders and shake the information out of her. She asked again, "What did he want?"

Instead of a direct answer, Flannery said, "Have you ever heard of a forensic hypnotist?"

"No."

"Well, apparently there is such a thing. He's going to be in the courthouse Monday and the guy who just called asked if I'd like to come and meet him. Let him hypnotize me to see if I can remember anything else about the day the car was stolen. Said it was entirely voluntary, but that it might be helpful in reconstructing what happened."

Peace said, "That sounds good."

"Yeah, it does," Flannery said. "Almost too good. I hope it's not a trap."

SUNDAY

Forty-Two

Rachel examined her reflection: the navy dress with tiny polka dots, not too short, sedate but not funeral attire. That, she knew, would come later. Her parents had filled her in on the heated discussion about whether or not to have a memorial service now, and a quiet ceremony later when Tony's body was released. Believing the Woodards were connected to them as family, Bella and Angelo Rosino had included Lisa and Paul in the discussion. She knew how uncomfortable the ensuing argument had made her parents feel.

Her mother's account of it played before her as clearly as a scene in a movie: Bella's sturdy, compact figure firmly planted before her husband, hands on her ample hips; her adamant declaration: "I won't have a ceremony without my son." Her chin thrusting forward as she added: "I want him there. Don't tell me it's just his body. That body came from mine."

Angelo argued with her, saying a ceremony might help the young people get on with their lives.

Bella refused to budge. "Why should they get on with their lives? My Tony has no life."

He tried to coax her, saying that a memorial service would bring at least partial closure and settle things down, especially for Tony's friends.

"It's not settled until the monster is in jail," Bella had countered.

Tears in his eyes, Angelo spoke of the circus atmosphere, pleading: "Is this how you want our son remembered?"

"I want justice!" she screamed back at him.

"You want revenge."

"Yes!"

That anguished cry had settled it. There would be no ceremony until Tony's body was released and could be properly put to rest.

Rachel shut her eyes, trying to block the imagined scene. After a moment, she opened them and stared into the mirror at her modest little dress, debating whether or not jewelry would be appropriate. She avoided looking at the small square box on the dresser and picked up the pearls she'd received as a graduation gift from her grandparents. She held them against her throat, shook her head and dropped them onto the dresser top. They fell in a snaking curve whose end pointed to the box. There was no escaping it. She had to wear the ring. Bella was sure to notice if she did *not*. As would Amanda. Amanda didn't miss anything.

Rachel didn't know if B.R. had noticed the ring last night. He hadn't mentioned it. And she hadn't brought it up. By the time the Rosinos left, she was wrung out, too spent to explain. As soon as they were gone, she'd helped her mother settle B.R. in the guest room and gone straight to her room. Relieved to be alone, she'd removed the ring, replaced it in the box and switched off the lamp.

Unable to avoid it any longer, she lifted the box, opened it and, suppressing a shudder, eased the ring onto her finger.

"Rachel," her mother called from the foot of the stairs. "They're here."

"Coming."

Tony's parents were waiting in the foyer. They greeted her with a smile that did nothing to hide the sadness in their eyes. Too old-fashioned to adopt the casual attire now acceptable even at Sunday mass, they were formally dressed. Angelo was wearing a dark suit, crisp white shirt and a striped tie. Bella had on the navy wool coat she reserved for Sunday with a coordinating hat pinned to her gray curls.

After a hurried good-bye to her parents, who were skipping church this morning, she turned to B.R. "I'll see you when I get back."

"Sure," he said. In a lower tone, he added, "Remember, I have to leave right after lunch."

Rachel nodded.

The Rosinos watched without comment, then escorted Rachel to their car.

# # #

The mass seemed interminable, the press of humanity in the overheated church suffocating. The scent emitted by the pine boughs decorating the church, usually refreshing, this morning felt cloying to Rachel. Wedged between Bella and Angelo, aware of their shoulders brushing against hers, she felt trapped. She glanced at Angelo, seated on her left, head bowed, eyes closed, his lips moving silently as the beads of a rosary slipped through his fingers. On her right, Bella sat, head high, stony-faced, glaring at the front of the church as though challenging God to avenge the terrible wrong she had suffered.

Unable to face the pain she had caused, Rachel switched to thoughts of her own life, the choice she'd made. *I can do this.* She lifted her chin and looked toward the front of the church. She took a deep breath when she heard the priest intone the solemn words: "Go in peace, glorifying the Lord by your life."

She felt Bella's hand reaching for hers as they exited the pew. Tethered to the other woman by firm fingers, she made her way toward the light coming in the open door at the back. She gulped the cold fresh air when they stepped outside, telling herself the worst was over. Now, if she could just escape the loving tentacles of Bella and get home. It would not be easy. She, Bella, and Angelo were immediately surrounded by well-wishers offering condolences. The service just over had been the usual Sunday mass, but the attention they received made it feel like a memorial service.

Bella absorbed, sponge-like, the sympathy that was poured over her. She melted into every hug and radiated a sad glow as person after person extolled Tony's virtues and reiterated what a loss the community had suffered. Angelo, on the other hand, held himself stiffly erect, visibly flinching at each mention of his son's name. Rachel was dry-eyed, too numb to know her own feelings, though part of her brain was aware enough to wonder how other people perceived her. She braced herself when she saw Darren and Amanda approach.

Bella held out her arms to Darren, tears flowing. "My second son." Then, to Amanda. "My little warrior." She wiped tears from her cheeks with the back of her hand and lifted her chin. Focusing on Amanda, she said, "We will find justice." Her words rang out. A declaration of war.

Darren was openly weeping.

Amanda's eyes were red-rimmed, but no tears were visible.

Other young people, the gang who'd been friends of Tony's all though school, stood nearby. Most were blinking back tears. The shifting postures of this age group gave testimony to their grief and the awkwardness they felt trying to express it. After their initial, halting words to Tony's parents, they turned to Rachel.

She felt the shift as a physical blow. No fist in the face could have inflicted greater pain. She twisted the ring on her finger, trying to focus on the words coming toward her like missiles—all hitting the mark, if not the mark to which they had been directed.

Amanda pushed herself to the front of the group. "When'd you get back?" Without waiting for an answer, she said, "We've been carrying on without you. Did you see the youtube video?" When Rachel didn't answer, she added, "I sent you the link."

Rachel managed to stammer, "I did." She was searching for more to say when she felt Angelo's hand on her elbow.

His lips were a tight, downturned line. His eyes were dry, but held a sadness that brought tears to

Rachel's. She saw that, with his other hand, he was tugging at his wife's arm. Bella, after a searching look at her husband's face, pulled away from a stout woman whose arm was draped over her shoulder and let Angelo guide her toward the parking lot.

As they were getting into the car, Rachel heard a familiar voice call from across the street. "I'll stop by later." She hoped Amanda was directing her statement to the Rosinos, but was pretty sure that was not the case.

# # #

Rachel and B.R. perched on stools at the kitchen counter, the remains of lunch before them. Her parents were in the living room, their voices meshing in the comfortable rhythm that was uniquely their own. In the kitchen, it was quiet.

Rachel poked at her half-eaten sandwich with one finger, and finally pushed it aside. She put her hand in her pocket, letting her fingers graze the ring she'd slipped off as soon as Bella and Angelo drove away.

She glanced at B.R. and saw that he was studying her, tapping his fingers on the countertop.

After a moment, he asked, "So, you were engaged?" He smiled and added, "The ring. You only wear it when his parents are around."

"It's like I told you. We broke up, but ..." Her voice trailed as she relived the night she'd told Tony she wanted to date others. After a moment, she said, "His mother pushed the ring on me. She said he was going to give it to me for Christmas. I guess he hadn't told her about the breakup. He probably thought he could talk me out of it." The memory of that terrible morning when Bella had thrust the ring into her hands was too painful to even think about so she changed the subject. "You really have to go?"

"I can't lose this job," he said. "I was lucky to get someone to cover for even one night. Usually, there's somebody glad to make a couple bucks. It's different this time of year. Everybody wants to be with their family" He hunched his shoulders. "I'd stay if I could."

She nodded, feeling guilty for suggesting that he stay another day. It was too much to ask. She knew that, but the prospect of facing the world alone terrified her. She suppressed the thought that she would spend the rest of her life afraid someone would learn her secret, squared her shoulders, and lifted her chin. "Of course," she said. "I appreciate your coming. It helped me over the first hurdle. I'll be fine now."

"You don't believe that," he said. "But it's true. You will be. Just remember ... when you don't know what to say, don't say anything. Keeping your mouth shut won't get you in trouble."

Rachel wasn't so sure about that. She wondered what would have happened if she hadn't kept her mouth shut the day of the accident. If she'd called 911 right away, the whole thing would probably have been treated as an accident. She'd be in trouble, but nothing like she faced now. She was about to say something to that effect when Lisa appeared.

"Company." She tilted her head toward the front hall. "Amanda and Darren are outside." She'd hardly finished speaking when the doorbell rang.

Rachel heard her father say, "Come on in. Rachel's in the kitchen."

The brother and sister trooped in, Amanda first, with Darren close behind.

Rachel knew the exact moment Amanda became aware of B.R. She stopped so abruptly her brother ran into her and almost sent them both sprawling to the floor.

B.R. sprang up and grabbed Amanda's arm, saving them.

She shook off his hand without bothering to thank him. Instead, she turned to Rachel. "Who's this?"

"A friend from school." Rachel managed to keep her tone neutral.

B.R. said, "Brendan Richards. My family's all on the west coast and Rachel was nice enough to invite me to spend a day with hers."

Amanda looked him over and finally said, "I didn't see you at mass. Did you go with Mr. and Mrs. Woodard to their church?"

Rachel said, "Mom and Dad played hooky from church this morning and B.R. stayed with them."

Darren, obviously curious, but also embarrassed, said, "Not that's it's any of our business." He looked at B.R. "You'll have to excuse my little sister. We haven't managed to civilize her yet."

"No harm." B.R. smiled, not his usual high-wattage grin, but a wary upturning of the corners of his mouth that didn't reach his eyes. After a minute, he turned to Rachel. "I better get going. Your offer to take me to the bus stop still good?"

"Of course," Rachel said.

To Darren and Amanda, she said, "He rode home with me yesterday, so he doesn't have a car. I have to take him to King of Prussia to catch the bus. He has to get back to his job tonight." She paused, then added, "So, if you'll excuse us ..." She focused on Darren, deliberately not looking Amanda in the eye.

# # #

When Rachel returned home, her parents were waiting, wearing their *what's going on?* expressions.

Rachel tried to slip by without dealing with them. "I'm really beat," she said. "That whole church thing was a beast. I'm going to bed."

"Now? In the middle of the afternoon? No dinner?" her mother asked.

"I'll get some cereal later."

"You don't have anything to tell us about this B.R. person?"

"I told you. He's a friend."

"Um." Lisa obviously was not convinced.

Paul spoke up. "Your mother has news."

Lisa said, "Good news, I think. Remember, I told you they were thinking of bringing in a forensics hypnotist?"

"Yeah."

"Well, Sally called while you were gone and the hypnotist will be in the office tomorrow."

Rachel felt her knees go weak and sat down on the steps. "When did this happen?"

"It was set up last night."

"Saturday? I didn't think your guys worked weekends."

"I told you they're making Tony's death a priority. Charlie McNeal ... you know he's in charge of the case, right? I think I told you that."

"Yeah."

"Charlie called the hypnotist. He's really busy, but he's a personal friend of Charlie's and when Charlie told him he hoped to wrap this up before the holiday for Tony's parents, he agreed to squeeze it in tomorrow. So they made the arrangements. It's pure luck that it's working out."

"What's he going to do?"

"There was a witness ... remember that?"

Rachel nodded.

"He's going to see if she can remember more about the person in the car. Maybe enough for the sketch artist to come up with something useful."

Rachel placed her hands on her shaking knees.

"There's more," her mother went on. "The girl who said her car was stolen has agreed to be hypnotized too."

"What good will that do?"

"I don't know. Maybe none. Charlie figures it's worth a try." She paused for a moment and looked hard at Rachel. "Remember, this is all confidential." Another pause. "They're scheduling the girl right after the witness. They plan to have her wait in a room where the witness will see her, hoping it will jog the witness's memory. They won't tell the witness who's in the room. Just make it seem casual. As was suggested by the hypnotist."

"They're that sure the girl's guilty?"

Lisa nodded. "Pretty sure, but there's no concrete evidence."

Rachel hated to ask, but it was so obvious to her, she wondered what the investigator was thinking. "Doesn't the fact that she's willing to be hypnotized prove she's not hiding anything?"

Her mother shrugged. "You'd think so, but Charlie is convinced she's guilty and she's arrogant enough to think she can bluff her way through."

MONDAY

Forty-Three

Ben checked for danger on the street. "Coast is clear." He opened the door a little wider and motioned the rest of the family through.

They didn't realize until they were on the sidewalk the coast wasn't as clear as Ben thought. The young picketers were nowhere in sight, but a lone figure emerged from a parked car when they stepped off the porch. A compact, matronly figure. The brisk wind ruffled her hair into a feathery nimbus that almost matched the gray coat she wore. After a hard look at the family, she turned and wrestled a cumbersome sign from the car. She planted her feet and held it up for them to see.

CONFESS!!!
TAKE RESPONSIBILITY FOR YOUR
MURDEROUS ACTION

The sign was crudely made from posterboard with letters trailing downward. The last word was squeezed together, hardly fitting onto the surface. The woman herself stood straight, solid as a thorn bush, and thrust out her chin, giving weight to her message, despite the flimsy appearance of its medium. The wind caught at the sign's edges, threatening to rip it from the wooden slat to which it was fastened. She looked up and shifted it slightly so that the words faced the accused family. Then, without a word, she did a half turn and began to march. So many steps to the left, a militarily precise turn, then right, always managing to keep the face of the sign pointed toward her target audience. Her short legs and quick steps brought to mind the strutting of an outraged pigeon. Under different circumstances, it would have been laughable, but the woman's sorrowful expression turned comedy to tragedy.

Peace glanced at her grandfather. His eyes were focused straight ahead. The veins in his neck stood out. She held her breath, afraid he might turn and say something. From the corner of her eye, she saw Snap-snap put her hand on his arm and shake her head ever so slightly.

He glanced down at his arm, at the fingers of his wife resting there, and nodded, first at her, then to the rest of the family. Without the necessity of words, they formed into their own military formation: Holly and Peace were in the first rank, with Flannery in the center, and Poppy and Snap-snap serving as rear guard. Thus, they made their orderly march to the Justice Center.

After they passed through the metal detector, they were directed to a room where they were told to make themselves comfortable, that someone would be with them soon.

The women sat down, but Poppy stalked the space, looking at his watch every few seconds, radiating enough energy to power a small country.

Snap-snap watched him for a few minutes before she exploded. "For Heaven's sake, Ben! Light somewhere. You're making everyone nervous."

He smiled weakly and moved to a chair. The stationary position did nothing to dissipate his energy, merely concentrated it to the lower half of his body. His knees moved up and down like pistons. The heels of his shoes struck the floor on each downstroke, reverberating through the space and echoing off the bare walls.

Flannery gazed into the distance, seemingly separate from the rest of the group.

Peace had no idea how long they remained like that. Waiting. More waiting. It seemed like hours. Finally, she heard voices in the hall. A moment later, a group of three—two men and one woman, appeared at the entrance to the room. They paused momentarily before entering.

Peace assumed they'd come for Flannery, to brief her for the hypnosis session. She glanced toward the rest of the family. If their expressions were any indication, they shared her assumption. It turned out to be false. None of the people who had come into the room approached. Instead, they seated themselves on the opposite side. The woman acknowledged their presence with a nod. The men didn't look at the family, though their body language told Peace they were aware of them. One of them, an unusually tall man, slender to the point of gauntness, with salt and pepper hair and a sparse brush of a mustache offered the chair directly across from Flannery to the woman, and after she was seated, he and the other man arranged themselves around her.

After a short internal, during which the three spoke in low tones, the tall man stood and offered his hand to the woman. "Thanks for coming in. We appreciate it."

"Sorry I wasn't more help."

"You've helped more than you realize. Every detail counts. If you think of anything else, please let us know."

"Of course." She slipped on her coat, gathered her purse, scarf and gloves, and left.

The two men exchanged coded glances. After a moment, the tall one approached Flannery. "Ms. Donohue?"

Flannery stood and extended her hand.

"Charles McNeal." He shook the proffered hand and added, "Thanks for coming in. Sorry for the delay. If you'll be patient for−"

Poppy stepped forward. "I'm Ben Francis, Flannery's grandfather. I'd like to be with her during the hypnotism."

McNeal shook his head. "Sorry. That's not possible."

Ben stood taller. "I insist that a family member be present."

"You'll be allowed to watch through a window, but it's important that there be no distractions. The only person allowed in the room will be Mr. Anderson, the hypnotist."

"But ..."

"It's not negotiable." The tall man stood straighter, accentuating his height advantage over Ben. Having done that, he turned to Flannery. "If you don't wish to do this, that's up to you. We made the suggestion in the hope that you might remember something that would assist in our investigation.

You are under no obligation." The words were spoken in a crisp, no-nonsense manner. When Flannery didn't respond, he said, "If you decide not to continue, there will be no prejudice against you. I don't want you to feel any pressure." Those were his words, but his manner said something very different.

Ben looked ready to object again, but Flannery stopped him. "Poppy, I can handle it." She shifted her attention to McNeal. "I honestly don't see how it can help, but I'm willing to try. Anything to get this over with."

# # #

At home, over lunch, Flannery recapped her recollection of the session. "At least now I know what happened to the keys. Someone bumped into me just after I got out of the car." She looked at her grandmother. "You know how sometimes I slip my keys in my pocket so I don't have to dig for them in my purse? You do it too."

Snap-snap nodded.

Flannery went on, "Anyway, the keys didn't make it to the pocket. They fell out of my hand when I got bumped. I heard them jangle as they hit the pavement. Someone must have seen that and, they waited until I was out of sight, then picked up the keys and stole the car."

"If you dropped them, why didn't you pick them up?" Ben asked.

"I didn't realize it at the time. I remembered when I was hypnotized. Mr. Anderson said I might continue to recall things. If that happens, I'm supposed to call him."

Peace chimed in. "What about this person who bumped into you? Do you think it was deliberate? Like maybe he wanted to distract you so he could get hold of your keys?"

"It wasn't a he. It was a she. A young woman. Maybe younger than me. And, no, I don't think it was deliberate. She seemed distracted. Actually, more than distracted. Upset. She was mumbling to herself. We were walking in opposite directions and we collided. She apologized and I kept going. I think she saw the keys fall. I heard someone call after me. It must have been her."

"You didn't stop?"

"I wasn't aware of it at the time. I guess I was thinking of something else. Today's the first time it registered."

Peace's mind was working a mile a minute. She said, "If she saw the keys fall and called after you, why didn't she chase you when you didn't stop?"

Flannery shrugged and raised both eyebrows.

Peace couldn't let it go. "You said you didn't think it was deliberate, but if she's a professional thief, she'd know how to look innocent."

Flannery looked skeptical. "She was young. Just a kid."

"Describe her."

Flannery threw up her hands. "I did all this for the hypnotist and for the investigators afterwards." She glared at Peace. "Then again for a sketch artist."

Peace asked, "Did you see the sketch?"

"Yes."

"Was it a good likeness?"

"I guess."

"What'd she look like?"

Flannery put her hands over her ears. "Stop. Please. Just. Stop."

Unwilling to push Flannery further, Peace let it drop. *Later*, she promised herself.

Poppy, who'd been uncharacteristically quiet listening to his two granddaughters, persisted. "Go ahead. Tell us what she looked like."

"What good will that do?"

"What harm can it do?"

Flannery sighed and closed her eyes, almost as if she were recreating the hypnotic state. She stood quietly for a moment, her hands clasped at her waist.

Peace held her breath, waiting.

Finally, Flannery began to speak. "She was about my size. Her height anyway. It was hard to tell if she was fat or thin because she had on a puffy coat. She was wearing a scarf. Bright yellow."

Peace felt a niggle she couldn't explain. She pushed it aside, listening as Flannery continued to speak.

"... and a hat. Pulled forward, almost halfway down her forehead. It hid her hair so I'm not sure what color it was, but I'd say dark. Her eyebrows were dark, almost black. Her eyes were brown. And sad." A long pause before Flannery, eyes still closed, went on. "Really sad." Another pause, longer still. Flannery opened her eyes and finished: "Something was bothering her."

"Doesn't sound like much to go on," Poppy said.

Snap-snap wanted to know more about the sketch. "Did you remember enough for the artist to work with?"

Flannery nodded.

"How does that work?"

"They showed me different mouths, different noses, different chins, and we kept trying various combinations until he came up with a pretty good likeness. Problem is, she had an ordinary face. And the wind kept blowing the scarf in her face."

The niggle in Peace's brain pulsed. She tried to think, but there was too much going on. Everyone was talking at once. She grabbed Henry's leash and her coat. "Henry!" She jiggled the leash in front of where he lay dozing on the floor.

He opened his eyes.

Peace jiggled the leash again. "Walkie?"

The big dog lumbered to his feet.

"Want some company?" Poppy asked.

Peace didn't look at him, just shook her head, and snapped the leash to Henry's collar. She knew she was being rude. Too bad. She'd deal with that later. Right now, she needed to be alone to sort out an idea that was buzzing in her head. She hustled out the door, down the steps and off the porch, aware that the family was watching, maybe wondering if they'd offended her. She pushed that thought aside. Right now, she needed time to examine an idea that seemed too crazy to be true.

Forty-Four

Mondays were always catch-up time in the D. A.'s office. It was nearly one thirty when Lisa Woodard came in. Needing a minute to shift from concerned mother to dedicated civil servant, she paused to look around when she entered the room. The intense expressions on the faces of her co-workers were at odds with the holiday doodads that graced their desks. Most had just returned from lunch and were hard at work sorting through the chaos that followed weekends and rose to a climax when the holidays approached.

She made her way to her personal work space, put her purse in the bottom drawer, and stood for a moment, staring at the stacks of files resting there, labeled in her own neat handwriting: "Do now!", "Need more info", and "Soon". She hadn't realized until she walked through the door how unprepared she was to face the day. How conflicted. On the one hand, she wanted to be here to find out how the investigation was progressing. On the other, she wanted, no needed, to be at home with her daughter. Well, so be it. She was here, with much to do after her time off.

Before leaving the house, she'd asked Rachel if she minded being alone, hoping she'd say *yes*, hoping even more that spending the day together would result in confidences about their recent house guest. It was hard to tell if Brendan Richards was a romantic interest or *a friend* as Rachel insisted. And that was unusual. Typically, she could read her daughter pretty well. This time something was off. It had been ever since she'd come back from State College. Part of it, she told herself, was to be expected, a consequence of the distress they all felt at Tony's death, a storm of emotions that had turned everyone's world upside down. And filled Rachel with undeserved guilt. Lisa wished she could make her understand that it wasn't her fault. It was unfortunate that the breakup and the accident had occurred so close together, but just a coincidence. A cruel twist of fate. Even if that hadn't happened, Rachel was in the midst of a major new experience—going away to college, being exposed to people with different ideas and life styles. How could she expect things to be the same?

Lisa glanced at the two photos on her desk: Rachel in a cap and gown, looking serious and so grown-up it had shocked her parents when they'd first seen it; the other, an informal shot of Rachel and Tony, sitting on the deck, eating ice cream, laughing—a greeting card image of young love. She picked up the second photo and studied it, especially Tony's face, still finding it impossible to believe he was dead. Such a strong life force. Gone. How could that be? Tears stung her eyes. She brushed them away and focused on the image of Rachel—young, radiant, innocent. Eager for each day to begin.

Lisa continued to stare at the picture, trying to remember exactly when it had been taken. Two years ago? It was summer. Must have been two and a half. She thought about her relationship with her only child, the long talks they'd shared, from accounts of holding hands in the movies to that all-important first kiss. Were those confidences gone forever? Had she lost her daughter? Would she ever get her back?

A tap on the shoulder startled Lisa. She looked up to see Sally, her closest friend in the office, holding out a piece of paper.

"Here," she said. "You haven't seen this yet, have you?" She handed Lisa a piece of paper. "It's the sketch of a person of interest."

Lisa looked at the sketch. Her breath caught in her throat. She looked closer, then at Sally, waiting ...

No reaction.

She doesn't see it. Lisa leaned forward and laid her hand over the picture, hoping the movement seemed casual. Natural. She asked, "Is this from the description by the witness?"

"No. They tried, but she didn't see enough to make it worthwhile. Just got a glimpse as she was driving past and, besides, Tony blocked her view of the person in the car."

"So ... this is?"

"From the description given by the girl who said the car was stolen."

"She thinks this is who stole it?"

Sally tilted her head, birdlike. "I forget you just got in. The hypnotist was here this morning. Hypnotized both the witness and the girl. Then they each met with the sketch artist." She pointed to the paper partially hidden by Lisa's hand. "So that's hot off the presses or, to be more precise, fresh from the artist's pencil."

Lisa attempted a smile, not trusting herself to speak.

Sally hoisted herself up on the corner of Lisa's desk, obviously ready to tell all. Her short legs dangled above the floor. One stocky-heeled pump slid half-way off her foot and swung from her toes. "They had the witness meet with the hypnotist first, then the girl ..."

"The girl?" The words came out as a croak. Lisa took a deep breath. "Sorry," she said, "Frog in my throat." Another breath. "You mean the one who said her car was stolen?"

Sally nodded. "The plan was to put her in a room and take the witness in to see if she recognized her. I thought I told you that was the plan."

"You probably did. My brain's like mush these days. Was it like a lineup?"

"No, no." Sally flashed an impish grin. "They didn't say anything or do anything to plant an idea, nothing that would taint the evidence. Charlie's too smart for that. They just went into the same room and made sure the witness had a chance to see the girl. They were so sure she'd recognize her ..." She paused dramatically, grasped the edge of the desk, and leaned forward before she went on. "Didn't work. They positioned the witness so that she was directly facing the girl. No reaction at all. Zero. Zip. Zilch."

"So ... they think the girl's telling the truth?"

"Not necessarily."

"But if the witness didn't recognize her ..."

Sally waved off the objection. "She didn't get a good look the day of the accident. She was driving on Saw Mill Road and saw a car stopped on the shoulder. Her view of the driver was blocked by a male leaning against the car. She couldn't even identify Tony for sure, but we're sure it was him because the time fits. She couldn't give the sketch artist anything about the driver except that it was a female."

Lisa tapped her fingers resting on the sketch. "Then where'd this come from?"

"The suspect, the one who said her car was stolen. Under hypnosis, she remembered someone bumping into her in the parking lot and causing her to drop her keys." Sally pointed to the sketch. "This is the person she says bumped into her. It's pretty generic. The girl said the other person had on a scarf that kept blowing in her face, so she didn't remember much about her features. They're speculating that the person saw an opportunity, picked up the keys and took the car. If the car was really stolen. Charlie has serious doubts about that."

"What's the status now?"

Sally shrugged. "Not sure. They expected the witness to identify the girl as the one she'd seen in the stopped car talking to Tony. She didn't, so ..." Another shrug.

"Any other leads?"

"They're not giving up on this suspect. Her story is believable. Kind of. But it's too pat."

"Did they ask her if she ran Tony down?"

"Of course. She denied it."

"Under hypnosis?"

Sally nodded.

"I thought you couldn't lie under hypnosis."

"Charlie asked the guy about that. He said you can lie just as easily as when you're awake, maybe easier."

"Really?"

"You have access to other resources in your brain. You may be more creative."

"Sally," a voice called out from across the room.

Sally looked in that direction. "Gotta go." She hopped off the desk and trotted away, leaving the sketch behind.

Lisa picked it up. Not trusting her first impression, she looked away, then back again. Shook her head. She continued to study it, finally coming to the conclusion that it couldn't be her daughter. *Young people look so much alike. Sally didn't see a resemblance.*

She lay the sketch aside and picked up her phone. She'd promised Rachel she'd call if there was news. While she listened to the phone ringing, she studied the composite, looking from it to the two photos on her desk. The unhappy face in the drawing bore only a slight resemblance to the laughing child with the ice cream or the proud young woman in the cap and gown. She turned the sketch facedown on the desk, unwilling to look at it again. *It can't be.*

"Hi, Mom." Rachel's voice. "Any news?"

"Not really."

"So they're no closer than they were a week ago?"

"It seems that way, but I've been around long enough to know a breakthrough can come at any time. They're gathering pieces, laying them out. Eventually, a pattern will emerge." Lisa thought about mentioning the sketch, but didn't. Instead, she said, "This will end sometime. Everything does."

Forty-Five

Peace looked across the street to the train station, but kept walking until she came to the spot where she'd had to dodge the young couple on the sidewalk that Saturday afternoon. After a moment, without thinking about where she was going or why, she headed toward the labyrinth. When she reached the corner where it was laid out, she sat on the bench and studied the swirling curves, wondering if there was a prescribed etiquette for the walk she was about to take. She glanced down at Henry. Would anyone's sensibilities be offended if she took him on the path? Surely not. More to the point, would she be able to give it her undivided attention if he were by her side? *No.*

She reached down to pat the velvety black head. "You're going to wait here, pal. Okay?"

He looked up at her, trusting and agreeable as always.

She slipped the loop at the end of his leash from her hand and put it under one of the legs of the bench. Even as she did it, she knew the light bench would be small deterrent. A squirrel might scamper by. No matter. Henry's nostrils would twitch and his gaze would follow it longingly, but he would wait. About that, Peace had no doubt. She put her hand under his chin and looked him in the eye. "Stay."

He immediately assumed a sitting position.

Peace gave his head another pat. "Good boy."

She approached the labyrinth hesitantly, with no clear idea what she expected from it. All she knew was that walking the intricate path was reputed to quiet the mind and open the heart, something she sorely needed. It would even, so they said, help you find your way. Something else she needed.

She took the first step onto the path, consciously focusing on the sequence of events that had begun a little over a week ago when she'd seen a group of young people getting off a train. She recalled a young man's dark hair falling into his face as he bent down to kiss the girl by his side, the girl turning so that the kiss landed on the top of her head. The faces of the young couple. His was so obviously one of love. Hers?

Peace pondered this as the path circled, leading toward the center, then outward again, but eventually looping back in an inward spiral. Could she have been wrong about the girl? Was her turning away significant? Or had she merely been trying to escape the cold wind? Peace wondered if she could have transferred her own conflicted feeling about the imminent meeting with her new family to the incident. She stopped for a moment, giving serious consideration to the possibility. If not for the young man's death, would the memory have stuck with her? Had his death given a simple head turn an importance it did not deserve? The thought lingered, turning in Peace's mind, as circuitous as the path she was traveling.

She tried to dismiss it. Could not. Because the young man did, in fact, die. The very next day. *And my car was the instrument of his death.* A coincidence? Her mother said there may be such a thing as coincidence, but they were few and far between. Most of the time it was the universe at work. Did that mean she, Peace Morrow, was meant to be there? To see the young couple in an unguarded moment? A necessary witness? She thought again of the girl's face. Not the face of love. But if not love, what?

Peace remembered Flannery's statement about the girl who had collided with her in the parking lot. *Something was bothering her.* Peace forced herself to recall the face of the girl at the train station. Could it be the same girl? "It was her. I'm sure it was." She said it aloud, though there was no one to hear her. She recalled the scene: the head turning, the chin thrusting to the side, and thought about Flannery's description of the girl: ordinary features, almost obscured by a scarf blowing in her face. Bright yellow. The girl at the station was wearing a scarf. Also yellow.

It seemed too bizarre to be true and yet ...

Another memory: she and Flannery returning home to find three women sitting on the porch steps, that awful moment when they'd all started screaming. Except they hadn't *all* been screaming. Not at first. The one she now knew was Rachel Woodard had hung back. Why had she been so quiet at first? Was it shock? A delayed reaction to seeing Flannery, the supposed killer of her fiancé? Peace didn't think so. She tried to put her finger on a reason for her doubt. She remembered thinking at first that the girl didn't want to be there. She'd seemed more embarrassed than distraught. She'd become frantic only when she realized Peace was looking at her. That's when the hysteria began. Peace couldn't rid herself of the notion that it had been more for the benefit of her audience than the result of a deeply-felt grief.

She came to the center of the labyrinth, stood for a moment, willing her mind to clear, to stop analyzing and let the pieces settle where they would. She didn't know how long she remained like that, but eventually she began to lose her doubt and to trust her instinct.

She turned and walked back out, moving faster than she had on the way in, but still following the path.

Henry stood as Peace approached and waited quietly while she removed the loop from the bench leg. She took a minute to tell him what a good boy he was and gave him one of the treats she always had in her pocket, then sat down on the bench and pulled out her phone to check for messages. None. A good thing. The family was getting along just fine without her. She started to put the phone back in her pocket, but instead pushed an app and typed in the name Woodard. An address in the north part of town appeared.

# # #

She made her way through town at a leisurely pace, examining every aspect of her growing suspicion. Her gut screamed she was right. Her head told her it didn't make sense. If the girl who'd bumped into Flannery in the parking lot had been one of the women who'd accosted them, why hadn't Flannery recognized her when she saw the sketch made from a description given by her?

She thought back to that day. A series of images flashed in her head: three women sitting on her porch steps; two of them rising to shout accusations; the older woman spitting on the ground at Flannery's feet; Flannery fleeing into the house. The one she now knew was Rachel Woodard hadn't begun screaming until after Flannery had gone inside. Could it be that Flannery hadn't actually seen her face?

Peace stopped for a moment when they reached the corner of the street that had come up as an address for the Woodard family. She still had no plan in mind. What would she say?

Henry turned to look at her, tugging gently at the leash.

She set her shoulders and turned onto the street.

Plan or not, she had to do something.

Forty-Six

This will end sometime. Everything does.

Rachel replaced the phone, with her mother's words echoing in her head. Were they true? Would it end? She dared to wonder how. There could be no happy ending. That much she knew. Tony was dead. An irrevocable fact. And she had caused his death. Another fact. Also irrevocable. Not on purpose, of course, but still ... Most people wouldn't hesitate to call her a murderer and a thief. They would say she deserved whatever happened to her. She had no doubt of that. She was well-liked, but Tony was beloved.

Yesterday, standing beside Bella outside the church, she'd listened to all those people offering condolences. So many had come forward, so many different words, all saying the same thing.

Tragedy had struck their town.
Tony's passing left a hole in the community.
He was a fine young man, with a bright future.

A shudder rocked Rachel's frame. She grabbed hold of the counter's edge to steady herself. This was the first time she'd actually thought about Tony's now nonexistent future. She'd been too busy thinking about her own. Her thoughts shifted to Tony and the future he should have had.

All he'd ever wanted was to continue in the business started by his parents and to live his life in the picture-perfect small town where he'd grown up. The All-American dream. Not Rachel's dream, but one which most would admire. At the football banquet last fall, when he'd been given every honor the school could bestow, he'd talked about coaching little kids some day, paying forward the joy the sport had given to him. And that's probably what he would have done. He'd have poured his energy and natural leadership skills back into the community that had made him a hero. It wasn't hard to imagine Tony ten years and more down the road, a role model to a future generation. He was a good person and should have had a long, productive life. A bright future that would never happen.

Her future? Did she have one? If the truth came out, her life was over as surely as Tony's. *Literally?* Not really. Being the child of an employee of the District Attorney's office, she was more familiar with legal procedure than most. She knew the death penalty was legal in Pennsylvania, reinstated in 1976, but a year or so ago the Governor had announced a moratorium on the death penalty. So, no, she wouldn't be executed, but if she were found out and convicted ...

What degree of murder they would file against her? She considered the facts of the case as they would be presented in court. If she had come forward immediately, the charges would be far different than if she were found out now. Chances are she'd have been charged with manslaughter—not exactly a pleasant prospect, but far less serious than first degree murder. First degree murder? Terrifying as it was, she forced herself to look at the worst case scenario. Murder in the first degree was punishable by a mandatory life sentence without parole. Would they really charge her with that? The definition of that charge was the intentional killing of another human being. *It wasn't intentional!* Rachel knew that, but could she convince anyone else?

When it came out that she had stolen a car, deliberately sought out Tony, and used the car as a weapon to take his life, who would not conclude that it had been intentional? How could she counter it? What extenuating circumstances could she claim to lessen the charge? Would anyone believe that the incident had begun as a mission of kindness? She'd gone looking for Tony to make him feel better. To make him understand that she didn't want to break up because of anything he'd done. She just needed to find her own path and she had truly believed that this was as much for his benefit as hers. Some day he'd find someone better suited, someone who shared his dream. If she said those things in court, would anyone believe her?

The image of the ring rose before her. She wondered what jurors would think of that. Would the fact that she'd been wearing it work for or against her? Would people assume she'd worn it to hide her guilt? What would they think when they learned she'd tried to refuse it? That Bella had, in fact, forced it on her? Would Bella recall that or had her grief blotted out Rachel's turning down the ring? If Bella did remember, what meaning would she give to the refusal?

These questions chased each other through the labyrinthine whorls of Rachel's brain as she paced from room to room. *It's not going to happen. There won't be a trial. B.R. thinks I can keep my secret. He believes in me.* With that thought, she lifted her chin, determined to banish the possibility of murder charges. She would concentrate on concealing her part in Tony's death. Could she do it? *It's been ten days now and no one suspects me.* That gave her hope. She knew every day that passed was in her favor. She resolved to stop thinking about things she couldn't change and, instead, to think about her own future.

I'll go back to State College and concentrate on classes. Maybe next year I'll transfer to another school, somewhere across the country, where I won't always be running into people who knew Tony. When I graduate, I'll find a job as far from here as possible. Maybe in another country.

She brightened. Planning her brave new life pushed the specter of Tony to the back of her mind.

Where would I like to go? Maybe ... A picture of the Eiffel Tower rose before her. *Why not?*

A sound, sharp and intrusive, broke her reverie.

The doorbell. She froze. Could she ignore it? She turned and saw a dark shape through the window at the top of the door. A light tapping sound followed. Whoever was there wasn't going to give up.

She put her bright dream on hold and headed for the door.

Forty-Seven

Peace shoved her hands in her pockets and stamped her feet against the cold. She leaned forward and peered through the glass. After the brilliance of the winter day, the interior was dim. She squinted and was able to make out a wraith-like figure approaching.

It's her.

She took a step back, fighting the urge to flee, and reminded herself why she'd come. She *had* to talk to Rachel Woodard. She took one hand from her pocket and rested it on Henry's head, seeking courage.

The big dog looked up at her, trust shining in his eyes.

I can do this.

The door opened. The girl seemed to notice Henry first. When she looked up and saw Peace, her eyes widened, but she said nothing.

She was smaller than Peace had expected and looked younger. Of average height, but slightly built, she was wearing faded jeans and a white tee shirt that swayed loosely around her narrow frame. Bare feet added to the air of vulnerability.

Peace stared at her, doubt-filled, unable for a moment to speak.

Could this child-like person be capable of what she suspected?

The girl stared back.

Peace forced herself to break the silence. "Rachel Woodard?"

A nod.

She extended her hand. "Peace Morrow."

The girl ignored the hand.

Peace forged ahead. "We need to talk."

"Have we met?" She looked Peace in the eye and smiled as though confident, but her voice quavered.

"I think you know who I am." Peace forced her lips into a smile.

"Oh?"

Peace repeated her name and added, "It was my car that ran over your friend." She paused, waiting for a response. When there was none, she added, "What I have to say is important."

The muscles in the Rachel's throat constricted. She gripped the doorknob as though for support. "This is a difficult time for me. I don't feel much like talking."

Peace took a step forward. "I understand that, but I have this idea and ..." She hesitated. *Just say it.* She lifted her chin. "I'd rather talk to you than the police."

An audible intake of breath, then, "Police?"

"May I come in?"

Still no movement from Rachel.

Peace abandoned the pretense of a smile and spoke firmly. "This isn't going away."

Rachel's face was a mask. Her hand was shaking on the doorknob. After what seemed an eternity, she opened the door wider and stepped aside.

Peace looked down at Henry. "Okay if he comes too? He's very well-behaved."

A nod.

Peace took a deep breath as she crossed the threshold. *No turning back now.*

The house was uncomfortably warm after the brisk air outside. Peace unbuttoned her coat and looked around.

To the left was a sunlit, airy room. A many-pillowed sofa was placed at a right angle to a brick fireplace. Two high-backed wingchairs flanked a spindly-legged table on which rested a glass dove that looked ready to take flight. A tall bookcase rose behind one of the chairs. The overall effect was one of comfort. Ease. At odds with the hard questions Peace had come to ask. She loosened her scarf and looked at Rachel. "Okay if I sit down?"

Rachel extended one hand toward the chair by the bookcase and, after Peace was seated, went to the sofa on the opposite side of the room.

Henry positioned himself between his mistress and the stranger.

A clock chimed in another room.

Peace tried to think of a tactful way to begin. Nothing came. She squared her shoulders and started talking. "You and your friends have been picketing—"

"I was out of town. I wasn't part of that." The words came out as a raspy whisper.

Peace looked at her for a long moment before she replied. "Not the actual picketing, perhaps, but you were there when the whole thing started. You and two other people." She paused, giving the girl an opportunity to tell her side.

Rachel sat rigidly still, perched on the edge of the sofa. Her arms were crossed in front of her, her hands clasping her elbows.

Though she was sure it wasn't necessary, Peace reminded her, "My cousin and I had been out. When we came home, you were waiting for us on the porch. You said terrible things." She stopped for a moment to let her words sink in. "You accused Flannery ... my cousin ... of murdering that boy." Another pause. "I'm pretty sure you know she didn't."

"How could I know that?" Rachel looked Peace in the eye, finally showing some spirit.

Peace leaned forward. "Did you steal my car?"

Rachel recoiled as though she'd been struck. "No!"

Her denial could not have been more adamant, but her eyes confirmed Peace's suspicion. "I think you did." She waited for another denial. When it didn't come, she said, "You need to go to the police. They may not suspect you now, but if they start investigating, something will turn up."

The muscles beside Rachel's mouth twitched, then froze. Her face became a mask.

Peace resisted the impulse to fill the silence that ensued.

Rachel lifted her chin and looked directly into Peace's eyes. "Sometimes things that *turn up* are interpreted differently than outsiders expect."

"What do you mean?"

A light shrug, then: "My family's respected in this town. Everyone knows us. You start making wild accusations, it'll backfire. No one will believe you." She eased back in the cushions. "Did you know my mom works in the D.A.'s office?" She paused and smiled almost sweetly.

Peace returned Rachel's gaze. "Your mother would hide evidence or twist it to point to someone else?"

"I didn't say that."

"Not in so many words." Peace saw that the girl's lips were trembling and asked again, "Did you steal my car?"

No answer.

"Why threaten me if you have nothing to hide?"

"I didn't threaten you."

"Why else tell me you mom works in the D.A.'s office?"

Silence.

Peace asked again, "Did you steal my car?"

Rachel's hands were shaking now. She clasped them together and put them between her knees. "Don't say steal."

Peace took no pleasure in the collapse she was witnessing, but she didn't relent. "Did you ... take it?"

Stillness.

"Did you run over your boyfriend?"

"It wasn't like that. I didn't mean to hurt him. We argued. He wouldn't listen. I tried to leave. He stood in front of the car. Right up against it." The words came slowly, disjointedly, two or three at a time, filled with desperation.

"So you ran over him."

"No! I'd never do that. I meant to put the car in reverse. I thought I had." She half rose, sat back down. "I can't explain it."

"Try."

Rachel looked blankly at Peace.

"To explain, I mean."

Rachel closed her eyes for a brief moment before she began. "I've gone over it a thousand times and I still don't know how it happened. I wasn't looking at the gear indicator. I was looking at Tony. He stood there, in front of the car, grinning at me. Like he was daring me." She tilted back her head and closed her eyes again. "I had to get away."

Peace thought back to the first time she'd seen the young couple, getting off the train. Tony, so obviously adoring, leaning forward with a kiss. Rachel, seeming to dodge his affection. She began to understand how it might have happened. She asked about the one thing she didn't understand. "Why did you take the car?"

Rachel groaned and buried her face in her hands.

Peace gave her a moment to gain control, then asked again, "Why did you take the car?"

"I don't know." It was the cry of a wounded animal. Rachel sagged to the side, her hands still covering her face. Her shoulders were heaving.

Peace remained silent.

After a moment, Rachel sat up. Her breath emerged in short, choking bursts. After a moment, she spoke. "I'd never done anything like that before. Never! So many things just came together. Everything at once." She looked Peace in the eye. "I'm not what you think I am. I'm not a thief. Or a murderer."

She shook her head in apparent disbelief. "I've always played by the rules. And, believe it or not, that's what I was trying to do. I told Tony the night before that I wanted to break up. He got mad." She stopped, seemed to be looking inward. "No, not mad. More like hurt. We'd been together a long time. Since we were in grade school. I didn't love him, but I did like him. I couldn't stand to see him so upset. I thought if I talked to him after he'd had time to cool off, I could make him understand."

She held out her hands as though her words were an offering. "Does that make sense to you?"

Peace nodded, though she wasn't sure it did.

"So you won't go to the police?"

Peace didn't answer.

"I don't deserve to go to jail."

"That's not for you to say. Or me."

Rachel rose and crossed the room. She stopped by the side of the chair and put her hand on Peace's arm. "Please. It isn't just me. Think of my parents. Tony's. They don't deserve this. Think of them."

Instead, Peace thought of Flannery, of Snap-snap and Poppy. She twisted sideways, freeing herself from the girl's touch. "I'm sorry."

Rachel shuddered, as though fighting something within. She opened her mouth as if to speak, but no sound emerged. She studied Peace for what seemed a long time, then put her hand on the frame of the bookcase.

A creaking noise.

The sound of objects knocking together.

Henry stood, the hair on his back bristling.

It took a few seconds for Peace to realize what was happening. She covered her head with her hands, dove forward and landed in a heap on the floor.

The bookcase toppled.

Books rained down.

Peace felt their impact on her legs and a sharp stabbing sensation in her face. She reached to touch it, felt a moistness, and withdrew her hand. Her fingertips were scarlet. *Blood.*

She felt Henry's big head against her side, pushing her toward the door.

She reached for him and saw a shard of glass protruding from her coat sleeve. *Thank God I didn't take it off!* She pulled out the glass, tossed it away, and put her hand on Henry's back. His body hummed with tension. His teeth were bared. This was a dog she didn't know. She followed his gaze.

Rachel.

The girl stood over her. Her face was blotchy red, her eyes dark and wild. One hand covered her mouth.

Understanding washed over Peace, flooding her with anger that threatened to explode from her chest. "You pulled that bookcase down. You tried to kill me!"

"I didn't mean it! Really, I didn't! I ... I ... I don't know ..." She sank to her knees, weeping.

The tenseness in Henry's body increased. He crouched, ready to spring.

"Henry! No!"

He shuddered, hesitated, and turned to look at Peace.

"It's okay," she told him, over and over again, stroking his side while keeping her eyes on Rachel.

The dog turned back toward Rachel. Gradually, he calmed. The hum in his body slowed. He turned and began to lick Peace's face.

She put her hand out to pat his head. It brushed against her cheek. More blood. She looked around. More broken glass. The graceful bird was shattered. One severed wing glittered in the light from the window. All of these sensations hit within seconds.

Rachel was on the floor a few feet away, curled into in a fetal position, crying softly.

Another wave of anger shook Peace. "Sit up!"

Rachel sat up immediately.

"Stop whimpering!"

A shudder shook her narrow frame.

The two women stared at each other.

Peace took a series of deep breaths, hard thoughts swirling in her head. This innocent-looking girl was, in reality, a monster who'd just tried to kill her. Almost as bad, she'd unleashed the killer instinct in Henry. Beautiful, gentle Henry. She had to pay for that. She reached for a book that had landed by her leg and raised her arm, aiming for Rachel's head.

Her mother's voice sounded in her head, clear and strong. *Violence begets violence.*

She surveyed the room again. The bookcase tilted forward, leaning unsteadily against the back of the chair in which Peace had been sitting, its contents strewn across the room. Books were everywhere, like scurrying mice whose motion had been stilled. Some were tented upside down. Others rested on their spines, their covers splayed, their pages crimped. Three of the delicate table's legs had snapped. The table lay on its top, the one remaining leg sticking up like an empty flagpole. The beautiful bird was broken beyond repair, no longer capable of flight. Proof of the result of violence Caroline Morrow advocated against.

Peace lowered her arm, but kept hold of the book, taking slow, deep breaths.

Rachel's voice came as if from far away. "How'd you figure it out?"

She forced herself to look at Rachel and told her about almost running into her and Tony as they were leaving the train station that day, how she had noticed the look on the boy's face and Rachel's dodging his kiss.

"For some reason, it stuck in my mind. When I saw the article in the paper and his picture, it came back to me." She stopped, trying to understand herself how she'd known. "That day when you were waiting on the steps. The way you acted. At first you held back. Then, all of the sudden, you went off. Something about it didn't seem right. Later, when I thought about it, it seemed like you were doing it to impress the others." She stopped. "And the scarf. My cousin was hypnotized and she remembered bumping into a girl with a yellow scarf in the parking lot the day the car was stolen. She remembered dropping her keys. You were wearing a yellow scarf that day at the train station." She shrugged. There was no need to say more.

"Are you going to call the police?"

"I don't have a choice." Peace braced herself for another assault, but saw only resignation in Rachel's eyes.

She seemed to be gathering herself. "Can I have some time?" she asked. "To tell my parents? And Tony's parents? This'll be a blow for all of them. I should be the one to tell them."

"When?"

"Soon."

"Twenty-four hours. No more than that. This has been hell for my cousin. My whole family."

Henry, still sitting by Peace, suddenly stood up and looked toward the back of the house.

A door creaked open.

Rachel froze. "My mom."

Another voice, unfamiliar to Peace, called from a different part of the house. "Rachel?"

"In the living room, Mom."

A middle-aged woman appeared in the doorway. She stopped abruptly and looked, a little dazed, from Rachel to Peace to the chaos that surrounded them. Her mouth opened, then closed. Her brow furrowed as though she wanted to ask a question, but couldn't decide how to frame it.

Peace nodded to the woman, pushed aside the books that were lying on her legs, and rose from the floor. She knew the woman was watching her, but she didn't speak. What could she say? She took hold of Henry's collar and guided him through the rubble, intent on keeping him away from the broken glass.

"Wait," she told him when they reached the foyer.

She looked back into the room and spied a small tablet and a pencil near the remains of the ruined table. She picked them up, jotted her phone number on the tablet, and thrust it toward Rachel. "Call me tomorrow."

Rachel accepted the paper without answering or looking at Peace.

Peace went to the door and let herself out.

Forty-Eight

Rachel listened to the door closing behind Peace and faced her mother, bracing for the questions she knew were coming.

Lisa looked at her daughter's face, then at the shambles of her once-cozy room. When she came to the bookcase, she shook her head. "It finally fell."

Rachel went to her mother and put both arms around her waist. "I'm so sorry."

"Thank God you're okay. This can all be replaced." She paused. "That girl? Is she okay?"

"I think so."

"Think so?"

"She's okay."

"Who is she?"

"Her name is Peace ... something or other."

Lisa looked puzzled for a moment. "The one whose picture was in the paper? The one whose car killed Tony?"

"Yes."

"I thought I recognized her. What did she want?"

"Can we talk about it later? When Dad gets home?"

"Rachel, this is ..." Lisa paused and hunched her shoulders.

Rachel couldn't tell what her mother was thinking. She said, "Later. Okay?" Without waiting for an answer, she bolted for the stairs.

In her room, she closed the door and lay on her bed, staring at the ceiling, terrified, yet oddly relieved. The day she'd been dreading was here. She listened for footsteps on the stairs, a knock on her door. Instead, she heard only the familiar sounds of her mother moving around in the rooms below. A little later, she heard a car in the drive, the garage door, her father calling out, and, finally, the blended voices of her parents. She listened to the last as to music, dreading what she knew she had to do.

The voices stopped.

Footsteps on the stairs.

A knock on her door.

Her parents.

"I did it," she said. No beating around the bush. None of the elaborate speeches she'd rehearsed.

She waited for one of them to ask: *Did what?*

Instead, they looked at her, waiting, trusting that whatever she'd done, it was something they could fix. They were her parents. There was no dragon too big for them to slay for her. They still believed that.

She looked from one face to the other, seeing that belief etched on their features and blurted out the hard part. "I stole that car and killed Tony." Her hands hung heavy at her sides. Empty. Needing something to grasp. Finding nothing. Waiting. *Say something!*

They didn't.

Rachel turned away. She'd been afraid of what they would say, but the silence was worse. Much worse. Nothing could be as bad as the crumpled looks on the faces of these two people—the rocks of her life. She turned back to look at them.

Her father recovered first. "Maybe you better tell us the rest."

The rest? What an odd way to put it. She knew, of course, what he meant. Still it did seem an odd statement. She felt detached, as though this were happening to someone else. The last two weeks of her life flashed before her as a movie.

"Rachel?"

Her father's voice called her to the here and now.

She swung her legs over the edge of the bed, gripped the bedspread, bracing herself. "I am so sorry." That seemed the most important thing to convey now. "I did a terrible thing. I let you down. Your lives ... all our lives—"

"Rachel," her mother said with surprising firmness. "Tell us what happened."

She sat straight and folded her hands in her lap, lacing and unlacing her fingers. "It started the night I told Tony I wanted to date others. He was so upset when he left. I didn't want to leave it like that. I thought I could make him understand. I took that girl's car—"

"When you left this house after I wouldn't let you have the car, did you go to the shopping center intending to steal one?"

"No! It wasn't like that."

"Then—"

Paul laid his hand on his wife's arm. "Lisa, let her talk."

He looked at Rachel. "Go on."

So she did. She told them about bumping into the stranger in the parking lot, picking up the dropped keys, thinking she could borrow the car and have it back before the owner missed it. A new thought occurred to her. She looked at her mother. "If you'd let me take the car, it would have been the same. About Tony, I mean. When I found him, we argued and ..." She went on to tell them about the argument, Tony's growing anger, his throwing the keys into the field, her frantic search. She started to shake, reliving her anger as she related the details. "When I tried to leave, he stood in front of the car, blocking my way. He was grinning at me! Like he'd won! I just ..."

She had to stop to catch her breath.

Her parents stood before her like great blocks of granite, silent and immobile.

She continued, "I don't really know how the rest happened. I tried to put the car in reverse and get away. But somehow it went forward. Next thing I knew Tony was on the hood. Then he slid off." She stood up, spun in a circle, ended up facing her parents. "I panicked."

Her father asked, "Did you think he was dead?"

"I don't know what I thought. I just wanted to get away. I pulled out into the road, heading for home. I was so upset I forgot I was in a stolen car until I was almost here. So I went back to the shopping center to return it. When I got there, I saw the girl wandering between the rows. I knew she was looking for her car. So I drove to the swim club and left it in the parking lot."

"Our office didn't find any fingerprints." Lisa's tone was flat, accusatory.

Rachel nodded numbly. "Seeing the girl looking for the car reminded me how much trouble I was in. I wiped the dashboard and the door ... everything ... down with my scarf."

"Where's the scarf?"

"In the back of my closet."

"You hid it?" Lisa leaned forward, her eyes narrowed. The shocked parent had morphed into an employee of the criminal justice system.

Rachel nodded.

"You realize that action takes everything to a different level? More serious."

"You mean ... premeditated?"

Before Lisa could answer, Paul broke in. "What do we next? How do we handle this?"

Rachel expelled a long breath. "I don't want to *handle* it. I'm ready to tell the truth." She looked from one face to the other. "It's you I feel bad for. I deserve whatever happens."

There was a long silence. Lisa recovered first. She looked at the clock. "It's not quite seven. I'll call Charlie now. No use waiting until tomorrow." Her voice broke, but she held her head high. "Get it over with." She reached in her pocket as if to retrieve her phone.

"Wait," Rachel said. "I have to tell Tony's mom and dad myself. I should do that before you call."

Lisa looked doubtful, but Paul said, "They deserve that."

He said, "It's Monday. The restaurant's closed. They're probably home now."

Rachel called the Rosinos and told them she needed to see them, that she had something to tell them.

#

Lisa and Paul drove Rachel to the Rosinos's home, but waited in the car. That was her idea, a compromise really. When she asked for the car, her father refused. "We'll go with you."

She shook her head. "I have to do this on my own."

"It's not going to be easy."

"I know."

Her mother said, "She's right, Paul." She looked at Rachel. "It's good that you're doing it on your own, but I don't want you driving home alone."

Rachel nodded, too full of churning emotions to argue.

#

She stood at the front door, staring at the bare surface—so different from Bella's usual extravagant holiday display. She reached for the doorbell, keeping one hand in her pocket, fingers curled around the velvet box.

Angelo answered the door. His face was arranged in a smile that couldn't erase the sadness in his eyes. He turned and called, "Rachel's here."

Bella immediately appeared and wrapped Rachel in one of her suffocating hugs. "My little daughter."

Rachel pulled away. "I have something to tell you."

Bella turned and headed for the kitchen. "We're having coffee. I'll make hot chocolate for you. Nice and rich. Extra dark. Marshmallows." She held up two fingers. "Just the way you like it."

Her kindness twisted Rachel's heart. She followed them into the kitchen, a cheerful, homey space, sparkling clean and filled with bric-a-brac. A high shelf that ran the perimeter of the room held Bella's collection of rooster pitchers, each one different, each dazzling in its colorful detail. As always, warm aromas filled the space. When Bella started to open the refrigerator, Rachel placed a hand on her arm. "You should sit down."

Bella started to protest, but, after looking at Rachel's face, she dropped into a chair. "It's about Tony?"

"Yes."

"That girl. She confessed?"

"No."

Angelo sat down too and reached for his wife's hand.

She told them, sparing no detail, continuing to talk even as tears seeped from Bella's eyes and ran down her cheeks, dividing into rivulets as they flowed down the wrinkled surface. Angelo remained stoic until the tale was finished. Then he rose and went to stand behind his wife. He laid his head on hers, pressed his cheek into her hair, and closed his eyes. His fingertips began kneading her shoulders.

They remained like that, neither speaking for what seemed to Rachel a long time.

Then, without warning and with an agility that rivaled that of her dead athlete son, Bella rose and lunged toward Rachel. She slapped her. A hard, resounding blow that rocked Rachel's head to the side.

Rachel accepted the pain, actually welcomed the distraction of a hurt that was physical, compared to the mental anguish she'd experienced over the past two weeks. She stood facing Bella, unsure what was coming next, but determined not to duck.

Angelo grabbed Bella before she could strike again. "You should go," he said without looking at Rachel. His voice held a quiet bitterness that cut more deeply than Bella's blow had.

She placed the small box containing the ring on the table and left them sitting in their kitchen.

Bella's keening wail followed her, a sound she knew she would never forget.

# # #

The night was cold. The sky was black. The few stars seemed far away. The car was a dim shape at the curb. As Rachel approached, she saw her father get out and open the door for her. The light stabbed her eyes. She got in the back and didn't wait for them to ask. "It was bad," she said. "As bad as I thought it would be." After a moment, she said to her mother, "Will it hurt to wait until tomorrow to tell the investigator? I'll go with you to the office and tell them myself. I think that will be best."

A strangled cry escaped Lisa's throat.

Rachel had never seen her mother cry before. Not like this. There'd been tears at her first formal dance, her graduation, the day they'd left her at college–all the important milestones in her life–proud, sentimental tears, but those had been tempered with laughter. This was different. These tears slipped noiselessly down her cheeks and fell, unchecked, onto the collar of her coat.

Rachel thought again of the other mother, the one she'd left crying in the sadly cheerful kitchen. And of the son who would never come home.

CHRISTMAS EVE

Forty-Nine

Peace sat in the crowded pew, one shoulder touching her mother, the other touching Kirk. She breathed deeply, savoring the nearness of the two people she loved most in the world.

Seldom had she been so sharply aware of her surroundings. The scents of pine and candle wax blended to create a unique and pleasant bouquet. She looked toward the front of the church, different from the Quaker Meetinghouse where she usually worshipped, but not as different as some churches she'd been in. These walls were white, as were the walls of a meetinghouse and, for the most part, were free of adornment. Poinsettias rested on window sills and a tiered arrangement on the altar formed the shape of a tree. The large cross suspended from the ceiling was something she knew one would find in most houses of Christian worship. Lights shining on the cross from two sides created shadow crosses on the brick wall behind it–a reminder, Peace knew, of the earthly end to the life whose beginning they were gathered to celebrate. In the Quaker tradition, the very lack of symbols epitomized the inward nature of worship. Was it really so different?

To her, the strongest sensation was sound: footsteps, the rustle of clothing, voices. Mostly the voices: friends greeting friends, wishing each other the spirit of the season. While she did not object to this, she did find it disconcerting. She was used to absolute quiet when she came into a meetinghouse, a quiet intended to foster stillness of mind and body, to open one's self to the Spirit in a Living Stillness.

She thought back to this time last year. She and her mother had attended a pot luck breakfast the Sunday before Christmas and, on the eve of the holiday, they'd spent a quiet evening at home together. She smiled, marveling at the changes that had occurred since then. She'd met the family she'd so longed to know—not just met them, but gone through a crisis with them, had seen them at their best and worst. They were a complicated bunch. Easy to love, impossible to understand. She remembered her mother's oft-repeated warning: *Be careful what you wish for* and smiled again.

Kirk nudged her and, when she turned to him, asked, "What's with the Mona Lisa look?"

She laughed aloud at that, then put her hand to her mouth and looked around, but no one seemed disturbed by the unseemly noise. In fact, it blended with the general clamor. She said, "I was just thinking how different this Christmas is from last."

He cocked an eyebrow, inviting her to say more.

"Last year it was just Mom and me." She glanced to her other side and was not surprised that her mother was looking at her, listening, obviously curious what she would say next. She reached for her mother's hand and squeezed it before she went on. "Now ..." She tilted her head toward the other end of the pew, where Poppy, Snap-snap, Flannery, and Holly had managed to crowd in. "I have a whole family."

Kirk leaned closer and whispered, "What do you think of them? Really?"

She grinned and whispered back, "A mixed blessing, but I'm glad I have them."

He reached for her hand and squeezed it.

She looked at him, really looked, and thought about more changes she hoped the coming year would bring. Her heart warmed. She was ready. She returned the pressure of Kirk's fingers and leaned against his shoulder.

The organ began to play. Voices became softer. Some worshippers stopped talking. Others spoke in lowered tones.

Peace looked around, speculating about the people gathered here, all the separate lives come together on this night, united in celebration of the idea of universal good will.

She reflected on the ordeal her family had recently come through and sent up a silent thank you. Her thoughts drifted to those other two families: one torn by loss, the other facing an uncertain future. She couldn't rid herself of the image of Rachel as she'd last seen her, ankle-deep in the wreckage of a once-cozy room: young, scared, her life irrevocably changed by one fatal moment, one bad judgment. What was this night like for her?

The papers had been full of the news. Headlines screamed *Rachel Woodard killed Tony Rosino*. Reporters painted with lurid strokes a picture of her stealing a car and running him down. Flannery was completely exonerated. Peace glanced again toward the end of the pew where her cousin sat. Was the family darling changed by the threat to her privileged position? Peace couldn't tell. She'd gloated a little at being proved innocent and had basked in the attention showered on her, but her gratitude to Peace had been genuine, her praise almost embarrassing in its profusion. Snap-snap and Poppy were equally effusive. They couldn't stop saying how wonderful Peace was and how lucky they were to have her in their lives. They clucked over the wound to her cheek and dubbed it her red badge of courage.

None of the news stories mentioned Rachel's attack on Peace. *Guess she didn't tell them quite everything.* She ran her finger around the outline of the bandage covering the stitches on her left cheek, glad of the doctor's assurance that any scar would be minimal. *My wound will heal. I don't think hers will.*

She felt a tickle on the back of her hand. Kirk's fingers. Moving. Tracing a shape. She marked its circular path. No. The fingertips strayed from the circle, dipped down, made a sharp point, slanted upward. *A heart?* She turned to him.

The answer was in his eyes. *Yes, a heart.*

Around her, the voices gradually softened to quiet murmurs and, finally, stilled altogether, letting the soaring tones of the organ fill the space. Familiar melodies that had become trite from repetition in shopping malls became beautiful again, proclaiming a message common to the religious traditions of both families.

Peace on Earth.

ACKNOWLEDGEMENTS

My heartfelt thanks to:

Anne Kahler, who was kind enough to read an early draft and help me see other possibilities. Talking about books over a cup of tea with Anne is a literary education and a real pleasure.

My critique partners, Nancy Labs and Linda King.

Linda Watt, who encouraged me when I was most insecure and Mary Renn, who allowed me to borrow the name Snap-snap. Where would any of us be without our families?

Polly Iyer, for creating a cover that I love. She listened to my vague ideas and came up with just the right image.

Doylestown, where the Peace Morrow stories take place. The stories are fiction, but the town is real—and totally charming.

JoAnn Maroney, who inspired Doylestown's labyrinth, and generously shared her story with me.

The Delaware Valley Chapter of Sisters in Crime. I continue to learn so much from all of you and treasure the friendships within our group.

And you, the reader. As P. L. Travers so wisely said: "A writer is, after all, only half his book. The other half is the reader and from the reader, the writer, learns."

ABOUT THE AUTHOR

If you'd like to know more about Sandra Carey Cody and learn about her other books, please visit her website or check out her blog.

www.sandracareycody.com
www.birthofanovel.wordpress.com

If you visit either of these sites, please consider sending an email or leaving a comment. She loves hearing from readers. All writers do. Readers are their lifeline.

If you enjoyed *An Uncertain Path*, you might be interested in *Finding Peace*, a short story that tells how Caroline Morrow discovered the infant who grew up to be Peace Morrow.

Love and Not Destroy is the first Peace Morrow novel and is a traditional mystery. In this book, Peace learns the identity of her birth parents and discovers who killed one of them.

Both of these titles are available as ebooks from Amazon. *Love and Not Destroy* is also available in print from the usual outlets.